After PROFFITT

A Novel

a sequel to THE TICKER

Robert M. Davis

After Proffitt

Cover designed and illustrated by Bob Archibald.

Published by:

 **Robertson Publishing**™
www.RobertsonPublishing.com

Printed in the USA and UK on acid-free paper.

1st Edition

Also by Robert M. Davis:
    The Ticker
    The Crackerjack
    Stuffed, Thanksgiving will never be the same

To purchase books go to:
    amazon.com
    barnesandnoble.com
    www.rp–author.com/robertdavis

DEDICATION

To Martha Clark Scala,
a multitalented writer, artist, poet, editor, and great friend.

CHAPTER ONE (SEPTEMBER 11, 2001 7:40 AM EST)

The traffic cop at Logan International Airport signaled first with a hand motion and then whistled for the cab to keep moving. Oliver Kane grabbed his briefcase from the back seat, threw open the front passenger door, and launched his loafers onto the pavement. The cop's shrill whistle notched to a higher pitch as Kane darted into a white-striped crosswalk zone abandoning his luggage in the cab's trunk.

Kane didn't bother to look back at the driver, Morgan Proffitt. It would only slow him down. His elbow bumped a cane-aided man out of his path. Apologizing to the old guy wasn't a consideration. Making his flight was all that mattered. Running in slick-soled shoes hindered his speed as he raced through the terminal entrance and headed for the departure gates. The 1970s rental car commercial with O. J. Simpson sprinting through an airport flashed in his mind. Grunts of air puffed from his mouth, drowning out an announcement through hidden speakers. He removed his ticket packet from his coat's inner pocket. How many seconds did he have before his plane departed to Los Angeles without him?

Gate 26 came into view. The area was vacant, except for an airline employee standing behind a counter pounding on a computer keyboard. Breathing hard, Kane skidded to a stop and waved his ticket in front of her face.

"It's vital I make it onto my plane." He paused to catch his breathe and wiggled a finger at a closed door to her left. "Is that the entrance for the flight headed to L.A.?"

"Yes, sir." Her eyes shifted from the screen to his face to give him her full attention. "However, the mobile ramp was removed several minutes ago once all the passengers were seated."

"Correction, not all of the passengers have been seated," he shouted, flapping his ticket at her again. "Tell them to bring the ramp back. I paid for a seat on that plane, and it's my right to be able to board before it takes off."

"Sir, I can certainly see you have a ticket for that flight. And I fully understand your frustration." Her expression didn't change. "I'm sorry, but your plane is preparing to taxi into the runway lineup as we speak."

"I have a simple solution for you, honey," he said. "Take that walkie-talkie sitting idly on the counter and order them to stop the plane and re-hook up the ramp so I can board."

"No can do, sir. Once again, I'm very sorry, but I don't have that authority."

"What did you not understand about my urgency to be on this flight?"

"To that point, sir, what did you not understand when I told you I don't have the authority to honor your request?" She turned and pointed behind her. "If you go to the window over-looking the tarmac, you will see the door to the plane is securely closed and the pilot is proceeding to taxi towards the runway."

Kane's fist slammed down on the counter making the radio jump. She frowned at him.

"Do you know who I am?"

"Yes, sir. You are a customer who came to the boarding area too late to board Flight 11."

He put his hands together and squeezed hard in lieu of choking some sense into this immovable woman. For an attorney who has made his living influencing courtroom judges and juries, why couldn't he sway this obstinate person in the same way? She didn't seem to care if he had a legitimate excuse for arriv-ing late to the airport and boarding gate. He blew out another angry breath knowing it would only make matters worse if he offered the real reason he wasn't on time. She wouldn't believe him anyway, that he allowed himself to be scammed by Morgan Proffitt, an angry consequence of Kane's unmatched prowess in the courtroom. Precious seconds were ticking away. His bully approach had gotten him nowhere.

"Please, listen to me," he said in a calmer voice. "I'm beg-ging you to stop the plane. Call the pilot and the tower. Tell them it is imperative attorney Oliver Kane, the DUI Doctor, be on this flight."

Kane slid a business card across the counter to the agent and waited for her stony expression to turn from couldn't care less to understanding his situation.

"Clearly, you are unaware I'm the celebrated attorney who represents clients arrested for driving under the influence. Someday you may need my services. How about this: if you get me on the plane, you have my promise I will work for you *pro bono* to get you acquitted. In essence, a get out of jail free card."

Unimpressed by what he was offering, her eyebrows knit together at the business card and sent it skating back to him without saying a word.

"Sir, you could be former Red Sox player Carl Yastrzemski or Boston Mayor Thomas Menino and it wouldn't make a bit of difference." She positioned her fingers on the computer keyboard again. "I could book you on a later flight. Best I can do."

"Screw it," he muttered, reaching into his pant pocket. Playing nice guy wasn't working either. He offered her a bogus smile along with a fat money clip in his open palm. "Everyone has a price, lady. How much will it take to get me on my flight?"

"Perhaps in your field kickbacks are an acceptable way of doing business. It's not permissible for airline employees to take tips or bribes." She seized her radio. "I'm needed at another gate. If you wish to continue this discussion, I'll call security. You can plead your case to them. However, it would behoove you, Mr. Kane, to freshen up so you don't have to explain your heavy scent of urine to them."

Kane peered down at the wet spot on his slacks. The gate agent sped away to her next destination as if the matter had been settled. Maybe it was for her, but not for him. He couldn't see if she was basking in victory. At least he wasn't in a courtroom full of people witnessing his humiliating defeat.

"You will pay for this, bitch!" he hollered. "I'm going to sue American Airlines and ground both of you permanently."

He went to the window overlooking the airstrip and stared at the plane's tail until it rolled out of view. His grouchy stomach voiced its sour opinion. It wasn't his fault he arrived late, but it sickened him to make a call that would fall on another unsympathetic ear. The Hollywood movie studio muck-a-muck had told him in no uncertain terms his interview was a one-time shot to convince them to create a movie script about the life of attorney Oliver Kane. In movie lingo, that meant he was viewed as a nonentity whose life story would most likely make the proverbial cutting room floor. One of the big guns was making his stay a few hours longer to accommodate the wishes of a higher-ranking studio mogul the DUI Doctor had saved from going to jail after being arrested for driving under the influence for a third time.

Kane placed a palm on the window for balance. His world was crumbling right before him and he was powerless to fix it. All he needed was a break. When a guilty client went to court, the chances of winning were against him, but he always beat the odds. Given the opportunity, he could impress the studio power-players with a dynamic, convincing argument. By missing his flight, he wouldn't be able to make that happen.

He removed a cell phone from his coat pocket, then peered at the Cartier watch decorating his wrist. He'd have to leave a message. Without a movie deal, his big payday to get him out of massive debt had turned into delusional shit. Then again . . . his head shot back as if he'd been given an electrical shock. Perhaps it wasn't game over. He jammed the phone back into his pocket. It was 7:50 am. Maybe the gate agent had come up with the solution to his dilemma after all. It was only 4:50 am on the West Coast. He still had a chance of making the meeting on another flight.

Kane raced to the area that listed flight destinations and departures. His eyes scanned the schedule three times before the numbers and letters blurred together. The later flights to Los Angeles wouldn't get him there in time for his meeting. His head dropped. There would be no presentation. Tammy Jo Moore, one of his mistresses and a wannabe actress, wouldn't get a role in the movie he had promised her. No movie, no huge payoff to get him out of his mounting obligations, and no celebratory trip to Hawaii with Tammy Jo.

Kane found an empty men's room. He stood in front of the sink and grimaced at a face in the mirror painted with rage. The reason he wasn't on Flight 11 was the fault of one person - Morgan Proffitt.

A day prior to driving Kane to the airport, Proffitt had traveled overnight from California to Boston with his heart nearing its last tick. Proffitt's mission was to assassinate Kane, thereby serving a dose of justice for the death of his daughter. She'd been killed by one of Kane's clients, a drunk driver the DUI Doctor got back onto the streets following a courtroom win for an alcohol-laced accident resulting in a death.

Proffitt's mission had nothing to do with revenge. Instead, he was clear that it was about protecting other sons and daughters from suffering similar outcomes at the hands of unrepentant drunk murderers behind a steering wheel.

From Kane's perspective, it was pure Proffitt bullshit. Proffitt wanted to blame someone for the loss of his daughter - why not blame attorney Oliver Kane? In addition, he was still puzzled why Proffitt, who was dying and had nothing to lose, changed his mind at the last second about killing him, as well as himself, by veering a commandeered cab away from a cement overpass.

Kane swallowed hard. He had never been so frightened in his life. Proffitt literally scared the piss out of him, along with making him miss his flight to Los Angeles. Perhaps that had been Proffitt's ultimate goal all along?

"I swear this isn't over." Kane held up his right hand like a witness before testifying in court. "Whether Morgan Proffitt survives or not, I will someday make that man and anyone close to him pay for what he did to me."

CHAPTER TWO (SEPTEMBER 10, 2002 ONE-YEAR LATER)

The vacant building's darkened doorway hid Bruno Santiago from view. A vigorous South Boston wind made him sniff several times to combat a runny nose. He rubbed his hands together, then shifted his weight from one foot to the other. He had an abundance of patience to observe a person or object for hours on end. On the other hand, or foot, he found it difficult to stand in a grocery store line to pay for a frozen dinner or wait in heavy traffic caused by the never-ending Boston's Big Dig Central Artery Project.

Across the street, a pudgy man in his late twenties wearing a gray suit turned the corner. He repositioned his black-framed glasses with a forefinger and stared down each side of the block before entering a neighborhood bar, unaware the private detective he'd agreed to meet was waiting outside in a doorway.

Bruno didn't have to check the man's ID to know it was Stanley, his appointment for the afternoon. The suit and tie stood out like a pair of white socks on a tuxedo-clad groom. The young attorney had information that Bruno had been seeking for years, but was reluctant to share it over the phone.

Bruno's pulse beat faster than normal. He rarely allowed his expectations to run amok, but the phone call from Stanley had left him with an optimistic gut that seldom led him astray. Why else would Stanley seek him out unless he was eager to impart inside intelligence? Tiny hairs on the back of Bruno's neck stood at attention, replacing his belly's upbeat mood. Was it possible Stanley contacted him under false pretenses? Could this meeting be a setup? Was Stanley sent as a spy to entrap him?

Bruno remained in the entryway several minutes to ensure no one had followed Stanley. He crossed the street and tugged open the pub's door, an act he'd performed more times than he cared to remember. His eyes narrowed as he moved from a late afternoon blue sky with patches of white and gray clouds into a dimly lit watering hole. Many of the patrons were seated in their usual spots. He tossed a pair of 30-yard line tickets to next Sunday's New England Patriots home game onto the bar top. The bartender deftly transferred the tickets to his shirt pocket, then hitched his head toward the hallway. Bruno acknowledged the gesture with a slight nod. He hurried past the golden oak bar, opened a "Do Not Enter" door and went into a room that doubled as one of his satellite offices.

The room reeked of stale tobacco. Pictures of Fenway Park, Freedom Trail sites, the Boston Garden, Ted Williams Tunnel - often referred to as the Ted - and autographed photos of famous New England sports figures adorned the walls. The opposite side of the office housed a desk with an adding machine, ashtray with dead butts, telephone, tissue box, and a pile of invoices. A black floor safe with yellow lettering was stationed behind the desk, surrounded by cardboard boxes containing various brands of liquor.

Stanley was already settled in the room. He sat at a small round table eyeing a brown bottle of beer. He combed a hand through his short dirty blond hair, unbuttoned a white dress shirt at the collar, and loosened a blue tie. From head to toe, Bruno was the antithesis of Stanley. He had a mass of dark brown hair, slim athletic build, olive-skinned complexion, a casual wardrobe, Air Jordan athletic shoes, and was at least ten years older.

Stanley stared up at Bruno. The room was chilly, but his pale face shined with sweat. He slugged down a gulp from the bottle before setting it on the table. Stanley looked like a patient about to have a root canal from a dentist with shaky hand syndrome.

Bruno removed a Boston Celtics windbreaker. He draped it over the back of the only other wood chair at the table. Stanley's Adam's apple jutted in and out after spotting the holstered pistol located on the belt around Bruno's jeans waist - a gun he was legally permitted to carry. He turned the chair to face Stanley and straddled it as if riding a horse.

"You look different than I thought you would," Stanley said in an anxious tone.

How many times had Bruno heard that before? Maybe it was his deep voice? He leaned his head toward Stanley.

"I never could figure how to match someone's physical appearance with their voice. What were you expecting, Stanley?"

"You're taller and thinner than your voice portrays, if that makes any sense. I pictured you wearing a double-breasted suit and a fedora - guess I watch too many old black and white movies." Stanley hitched his head to the side and smirked. "I bet you do well with the ladies."

Bruno's molars began to grind. Stanley's last sentence stabbed an open wound that hadn't ever healed. That wound - caused by Oliver Kane - was the loss of the love of his life. He pinched a forearm until it hurt, but it did little to remove his darkened frame of mind. This wasn't a good time or place to get maudlin.

"You look the way I thought you would," Bruno said, "but you're acting like a law student waiting for the results of his bar exam. Relax, Stanley, you passed. You're safe here, plus no one followed you. We're just two guys having a friendly conversation."

"My apologies, Mr. Santiago." Stanley placed both palms on the tabletop as he began to rise to his feet. "For numerous reasons, I'm having a serious case of second and third thoughts about contacting you. If I inconvenienced you, I'm sorry, but I can't do this."

Bruno grabbed a handful of necktie and yanked the attorney down to his chair as if he was a featherweight. If eyes are truly windows into one's soul, it was clear to Bruno that Stanley was suffering from a panic attack. Who did he fear the most? His boss Oliver Kane or a private detective named Bruno Santiago? Stanley was unaware that Bruno had been investigating Kane for years, attempting to uncover some way to stop him from practicing his tainted law tactics. Bruno's Plan B was a last resort that would make scumbag Kane permanently disappear from a courtroom and earth.

The choke hold on the tie made Stanley's cheeks turn red. Bruno eased the grip, but didn't let go. Morgan Proffitt's scheme to kill Oliver Kane had been an ideal scenario for Bruno. Proffitt, a successful, well-respected man with a bum ticker had nothing else to lose after his wife passed away and his daughter was killed by a drunk driver. His life's last mission had been to travel from San Francisco to eliminate the attorney whose legal specialty was to send arrested drunk and drug-influenced drivers back on the streets, putting the general public in harm's way.

Why didn't Proffitt terminate Kane when he had the chance? The only person who could answer that question is Kane. Proffitt, who had been seriously ill, had died the year before on September 11th, several hours after convincing Kane to get into a cab with him.

Bruno released Stanley's tie and focused on his face looking for a "tell" that would give him some insight. If Kane sent Stanley here on false pretenses, he hadn't tipped his hand thus far. Bruno wasn't leaving this room without knowing which side Stanley was on.

"Call me Bruno, Stanley. If you keep referring to me as mister, it'll make me feel old. I'm still a few years away from forty." He cleared his throat. "So now that we are on a first name basis, how did you get my name and number?"

"From the same former Oliver Kane employee who gave you inside information over a year ago." Stanley jerked his neck in several directions before adjusting the tie knot. "I'm not going to repeat his name, but you know who I'm referring to. I met him at a law seminar. When he learned I was an attorney at the Kane Law Firm, he described his former boss in this way: 'Evil comes in many colors and flavors, but Oliver Kane is the whole package. Kane comes across to clients like an angel. In truth, he's the Devil on steroids. Oliver Kane doesn't care who gets hurt as long as it's beneficial to him.'"

"Don't forget the devil was once an angel," Bruno offered.

"I can't picture Oliver Kane with a halo. This former employee vehemently urged me to contact you. Truth be told, I expressed my reluctance to get involved."

"What made you change your mind?"

"He said if I didn't go to you with what I know, I was no different than Oliver Kane." Stanley peered at a signed photo of

Red Sox star pitcher Pedro Martinez on the wall. "Being compared to Kane really shook me up, enough to persuade me to contact you."

"That sized up Kane perfectly. He also threw a major guilt dart at you, and it stuck. He advised you to do the right thing for the right reason."

"Sometimes it isn't in one's best interests to do the right thing for the right reason," Stanley said. "I'm afraid that my being here with you will come back and bite me on the ass."

Bruno stared at the young attorney, making no attempt to hide his contempt. Was he looking at another dead end after Stanley teased him on the phone? Or did Stanley have breakthrough information that could destroy Kane and his career as the DUI Doctor?

"I get why you're out on a shaky limb by talking to me." Bruno's eyes narrowed. "But vulnerability doesn't excuse cowardice. Let's cut to the short strokes here. You see, I'm having a difficult time understanding why you're still employed by a man you find so revolting. It just doesn't make sense to me. Didn't you research Kane Law before accepting a position with them? And once you discovered what Kane does, who he hurts, and the kind of man he really is, why didn't you have the cajones to tell him to screw himself and quit?" He pounded a thumb into his chest. "From where I'm sitting, you aren't a person I'd want to share a foxhole with, let alone trust. Convince me I'm wrong, Stanley."

CHAPTER THREE

Stanley pounded the bottom of his beer bottle on the office tabletop creating an attention-getting bang. Foam spewed from the top. He looked directly into Bruno's eyes and straightened his spine.

Bruno detected the difference in Stanley's demeanor. Maybe browbeating the young attorney had lit a fire under his ass to reveal what he knew about Oliver Kane. Or maybe the volley of intimidating words Bruno threw at him had a reverse effect that tightened the potential whistleblower's jaws.

"Don't sell me short until you know all the facts, Mr. Santi . . . Bruno," Stanley said. "You questioned if you could trust me. I'm going to throw that right back at you. What is your stake in pursuing Oliver Kane? I was told you have been after Mr. Kane for a long time. Are you in it for monetary gain like a bounty hunter? Or are you seeking retribution for something he did to you or someone you know?"

Bruno grinned. Stanley was spot-on. Score a point for the rookie attorney growing a set of balls. Was his newfound bravado real or for show?

"No one is paying for my services," Bruno said. "It's my time and my dime. I'm doing this *pro bono*. Morgan Proffitt was one of many who have been touched by Oliver Kane's evil law practice. My reward or payment will be to legally eliminate the DUI Doctor one way or another."

"If we were in a courtroom, I'd seek a more defined answer regarding your issue with my boss." Stanley put his hands together. "It's no secret around the office Mr. Kane holds a major grudge against Morgan Proffitt."

"Proffitt caused Kane to miss his flight to Los Angeles," Bruno said. "As a result, Kane lost a movie deal that would have highlighted his life as a high-profile attorney and personality. It was a package that was supposed to bring him boo-koo bucks."

"Makes sense. Kane has a massive ego, craves being a celebrity and the money it brings."

"Before his heart gave out, Morgan Proffitt flew from San Francisco to Boston to eliminate Kane for good," Bruno said. "One of Kane's clients caused a fatal crash that killed Proffitt's daughter. Kane got the kid off in court. If you have ever lost a loved one needlessly, try putting yourself in Proffitt's place. I don't have a sliver of doubt Proffitt believed if Kane continued to practice his form of law, other sons and daughters would suffer the same ending as his daughter Katie."

"Do you know what stopped Proffitt from carrying out his mission?" Stanley asked.

"If you ever discover the answer to that question, please let me know."

Bruno's features froze into a poker face. As much as he respected Morgan Proffitt, he regretted Proffitt's failure to take out Kane. Bruno had been patiently waiting for another perfect "Proffitt Moment" to present itself, hence the importance of this meeting with Stanley.

"After Proffitt's plane landed in Boston," Bruno continued, "he abducted a cab driver and his cab. I questioned the cabbie and learned there was an attractive young woman in the cab with Mr. Proffitt. The cabbie wasn't sure if she was an accomplice or what happened to her. Apparently, Proffitt drove Kane to the airport. I found a trooper who identified Kane rushing out of a cab on September 11th. The trooper recalled a man of Proffitt's description behind the steering wheel."

"You have definitely done your homework," Stanley said.

"Here's the ironic kicker, Stanley. Proffitt's actions caused Kane to miss his flight which, it turned out, to be one of the planes the terrorists crashed into a Twin Tower in New York. Morgan Proffitt saved Oliver Kane's life."

"Are you freaking kidding me?" Stanley adjusted his glasses. "Morgan Proffitt saved Mr. Kane's life? You'd think Mr. Kane would be grateful rather than being vengeful."

"Yes, any normal or semi-normal person would feel grateful rather than vengeful," Bruno said in a calm voice. "You may not understand how insane Kane really is. Think of him as someone having the opposite emotions and reactions to situations. You might expect him to put the whole Proffitt incident in the past, since it saved his life and since Proffitt died a few hours after he left Kane at the airport. But, according to my sources, Kane has spent the year figuring out how to exercise his revenge on a dead man." Bruno gazed up at the ceiling. The answer to his next question would test the reliability of his deodorant. "Does Kane know if someone assisted Proffitt with his mission?"

"Mr. Kane is positive that someone from Boston had been feeding Proffitt with background data. To my knowledge, he doesn't know who that person is. If you are privy to that information, please keep it to yourself. I don't want to know who it is."

Bruno exhaled the silent breath he had been holding. The person who helped Morgan Proffitt was sitting next to Stanley. But Stanley was right. He didn't need to know.

"Go on, Stanley," Bruno said. "You're doing fine."

"It didn't take long for me to understand why Oliver Kane had earned the DUI Doctor moniker," Stanley said. "The man is a genius at circumventing laws that were meant to protect innocent people. Every person does have the right to be defended, even those who are repeatedly caught driving under the influence. But Mr. Kane takes that right to a level that is criminal." Stanley's voice got louder with each word. "Kane's clients are guilty of driving intoxicated or being impaired from street or prescribed drugs, but he turns them into victims. I'm revolted by how he saves societal miscreants from prosecution, hard discipline, or no punishment and sends them back to the streets as potential menaces."

"So, you see how Kane turns things upside down and proceeds the opposite way most people might handle situations. Kane got his brains scrambled when his father was sent to prison for murdering people while driving under the influence. Instead of being horrified that his father killed three people - and almost killed his son - he put his father on a pedestal, thinking of him as a hero who got shafted. He doesn't think like the rest of us, which is why he's so dangerous." Stanley nodded to Bruno's insights. "You're a smart guy, Stanley. Why haven't you told Kane to jump into a lake of wet cement and quit?"

"You asked that question before, only you framed it differently. Allow me to share a Kane Law fact of life. When I passed my bar exam, Mr. Kane offered me top dollar as a first-year attorney. It seemed like an unbelievable opportunity to make a good salary and work with a famous lawyer like Oliver Kane. At that time, I figured I had nothing to lose and everything to gain . . . even with the unusual clause in my contract."

"What kind of clause are you referring to?" Bruno asked.

"When I signed my contract, I agreed to work at Kane law for a minimum of one-year. If I leave the firm on my own volition, or can't perform my assigned duties for any reason before my year is up, I lose a $40,000 bonus. What's more, every employee signs an NDA - legally binding non-disclosure agreement - to never disclose any sensitive law firm information. By meeting with you today, I'm breaching the contract I signed."

"I get why you're reluctant to reveal confidential information that would rat the son of a bitch out," Bruno said. "How much longer do you have before you can leave?"

"Four more months. It has been the worst eight months of my life." Stanley peeled a portion of the label off the beer bottle. "But it gets worse. I'm newly married. My wife and I are still paying off massive college and law school loans. Timing is everything, right? After I contacted you yesterday, my wife informed me she's pregnant. If Mr. Kane knew I was talking to you or any outsider, do you know what would happen to me? I'm not exaggerating when I say I'm putting my law career and possibly my life in jeopardy."

"You did the right thing by contacting me." Bruno patted Stanley's arm.

"That's easy for you to say. You're not the one who is taking the risk."

"Are your Jockey's bunching up on you again? C'mon, Stanley.

Get a grip. With your help we can save lives by turning the tables on Kane legally, like he does."

"*Legally*," Stanley blurted out. "Not exactly."

"What does that mean?"

"You don't know Oliver Kane as well you think, Bruno."

Bruno resisted snatching Stanley's tie again. Was Stanley screwing with him? The phrase "not exactly" was ambiguous. Did he mean not at all, not quite, not really, in no way . . .

"Define for me what 'not exactly' means?" Bruno formed air quotes with two fingers on each hand. "Or is that your way of telling me I've missed something?"

"Let me explain with a recent case," Stanley said. "Kane defended a woman who backed her car out of her driveway and knocked a boy off the skateboard he was riding on the sidewalk. She jumped out of the car to help the boy, but he died from head injuries."

"I'm familiar with the case, Stanley. Naomi Johnson was the woman who hit the boy. Her blood alcohol content was .07. Even though Mrs. Johnson was only one percent away from being legally intoxicated, she was charged with driving under the influence as well as manslaughter after she admitted being on a prescribed medication for depression. The label on the med bottle warned against operating machinery or a motor vehicle."

"Here's what you don't know, Bruno. The prosecution's case was relying on a key witness. That would be Ms. Johnson's seventy-one year-old next door neighbor, Mrs. Blake. She was going to testify that Ms. Johnson was slurring her words and wobbly on her feet when they exchanged hellos the morning of the accident. One day before the trial, Mrs. Blake disappeared from her rental house and so did her testimony."

"Oliver Kane is the only one who knows the whereabouts of Mrs. Blake, correct?"

"I don't know that for a fact, but I wouldn't bet against your assumption," Stanley said. "It only got worse for the prosecution. Mr. Kane's first witness was a man who observed the accident. He was walking his dog at the time. It shocked him so much, he released the leash, and his dog ran away down the block. He panicked and chased after the dog. A few days later the man apologized to the police for not coming forward sooner and said he saw Ms. Johnson look in both directions as she cautiously backed down her driveway. The man further asserted the boy wasn't wearing a helmet and was kneeling low on the skateboard while zooming down the sloped sidewalk at a high speed. It was impossible, in his opinion, for Ms. Johnson or any driver to see the boy. Next, Mr. Kane brought to the stand several neighborhood residents who experienced nearly hitting the reckless boy on his skateboard. Mr. Kane closed with a psychiatrist who offered his professional opinion that Ms. Johnson's medicine dosage most likely wouldn't have impaired her ability to drive safely. Since you followed the case, you know the jury's verdict found Ms. Johnson innocent due to mitigating or extenuating circumstances."

"I'm aware of the conclusion," Bruno said, "but the nightmare wasn't over for the boy's parents. Kane sued the kid's parents for damages incurred to Ms. Johnson due to the boy's irresponsible actions. She had to be hospitalized after having a nervous breakdown. She couldn't work and lost her job. The parents settled with Kane before going to court. They were forced to sell their house. They not only lost their son, but their home too."

"Are you familiar with the expression inside baseball?" Stanley removed his glasses.

"Absolutely. I'm a big baseball fan. You're talking about an expert's technical knowledge of how the game should be played right."

"I've got inside knowledge on how Kane's not guilty verdict from the jury was tainted," Stanley offered.

Bruno removed a microcassette recorder from his coat pocket and placed it on the table. Stanley shook his head. Instead of debating the issue, Bruno re-pocketed the recorder.

"You have my full attention, Stanley."

"The dog walker was paid off in cash. Mr. Kane's bodyguard, Rollie, found the guy after the accident and offered him a deal he couldn't refuse to tell a fictitious story."

"Can you prove the dog walker was paid to lie?" Bruno asked.

"Not likely. Cash doesn't leave a trail. If the dog walker admitted he lied in court, he'd go to jail. Plus, there would be physical repercussions from henchman Rollie."

"I presume those who swore they almost hit the skateboard kid on were also paid off?"

"Bingo," Stanley said. "Plus, you probably know Kane has used the same psychiatrist dozens of times to testify in court. The shrink regurgitates anything Mr. Kane wants him to say. The guy is a real whore." Stanley put his glasses back on. "In addition, the jury never heard Ms. Johnson had been charged with driving under the influence in two other states under a different name. Obviously, she never learned her lesson."

"Ms. Johnson should have plenty of money to move to another state," Bruno said. "I appreciate the inside intel, but without proof, it won't help me shut Kane down from ever practicing law again. To achieve that end, I need to know how I can stop Kane without killing the son of a bitch. In other words, tell me where Kane is most vulnerable."

"I can help you there," Stanley said. "If you concentrate on . . ."

Stanley's cell phone rang. After reading the caller's phone number, he appeared to be a few breaths away from hyperventilating. Bruno was ready to grab him if he passed out or tried to bolt out of the room. Stanley waved his hands before pinning a forefinger to his lips. Reluctantly, he raised the phone to his ear.

"Yes, Mr. Kane."

CHAPTER FOUR

Oliver Kane gazed through his seventh-floor office window overlooking the courtyard fronting downtown High Street. His forehead pressed against the cool glass. To most Bostonians it was another pleasant weekday afternoon, but this day was any-thing but pleasurable for Kane. The cloudy conditions of his life had transitioned into a catastrophic storm.

He resisted an urge to yell at a sign company worker occu-pying the bucket of a boom truck's lift to remove the Kane Tower shiny metal letters attached to the building. The guy in the bucket wouldn't be able to hear his salty rants, frustrating Kane even more.

His shoulders slumped. For years he had paid a hefty price to lease his vanity name recognition on the office building. The majority of Beantown's population was under the impres-sion Kane Tower was owned by wealthy attorney Oliver Kane. Nothing could be further from the truth, which had finally caught up with him after missing too many payments owed to the build-ing's actual owners.

He stepped back from the window and rubbed a scar from a childhood wound that cut a horizontal line through his eyebrow. It was a habit he couldn't break when his mood turned prickly. If he could have seen his creased features reflected in the glass win-dow, it would have shown how humiliated he was about losing the Kane Tower name. He removed his finger from his eyebrow. Maybe it wasn't as bad as it seemed. Maybe the public would assume he moved his law practice to a different location? A mock laugh snorted through his nose. Who was he trying to kid? There were no maybes about what would happen. When the rumor of his financial woes became breaking news it would spread like a deadly virus. The Boston Globe and Tribune newspapers, plus radio and TV commentators would spew malicious opinions about the DUI Doctor's demise. Once that ball started rolling, there was nothing he could do to stop it.

His forefinger went back to his eyebrow, then changed direction to smooth hair over the scar. A host of creditors were pressing him for past due payments, including the two mortgages on his Beacon Hill house. His bookkeeper had quit a week ago after asking, "how do you expect me to manage your money when there's no money to manage and you're behind on paying me?"

He eyeballed his spacious office. The Kane Law staff occupied the entire seventh floor. The plush furniture, office machines, law books, decorative artwork, rent, salaries, plus country and social club dues set him back six figures monthly. If he were to auction off all the items he owned, how much could he take in? He shook his head. It didn't take long to do the math. The greedy bastards would offer pennies on the dollar; that wouldn't put a dent in the millions he owed.

Kane kicked over a side table next to the couch. An expensive vase crashed onto the carpet. Now he could delete one less asset from his mental list. He'd spent and gambled away money as if he had access to the United States currency printing machine. It was too late to control his addictive nature and go on an austerity program to halt his lavish spending. He went down on a knee to pick up the broken vase pieces. How did he get in this situation? The image of Morgan Proffitt's face gave him a chill. Proffitt came to Boston from San Francisco almost a year ago to the day to take his life. Why did Proffitt decide not to kill him? And Proffitt had saved his life by making him miss the flight that hit the World Trade Center, but that didn't eliminate one ounce of revenge he wanted to inflict on anything Proffitt. Kane pronounced Proffitt guilty of fucking with him, and no one fucks with Oliver Kane and gets away with it.

Kane removed a thin money clip from his pocket and held it in his open palm as if to weigh the worth of the bills rather than the value of their numbers. He often wondered why someone would chance getting arrested and going to jail by robbing a bank. Now he knew how desperation could cause a person to become a desperado. Short of robbing a bank, how could he get his hands on enough money to erase the deficit he was facing?

He stared at his closed door and visualized a nicely clad middle-aged man bursting into the office requesting his services. The guy he saw in his imagination was nervous, twitching like he was scared shitless and guilty as hell of a crime he committed. It didn't matter what havoc this reprobate had wreaked while under the influence. He was at the DUI Doctor's mercy. *"I require a two-hundred and fifty thousand up-front fee and another quarter of a mil when I save your ass from going to jail. Furthermore . . ."*

"What the hell am I doing?" he blurted out, returning the money clip into his pocket. "Daydreaming irrational, crazy thoughts that won't solve the fix I'm in. I'd be better off going to the racetrack and betting every asset I have on a hundred to one long shot."

His eyes fixed on a framed photo positioned in the middle of the credenza. It was a picture of himself at seven years old with his late father and mother. It was the last picture taken from when they were a real family, over forty years ago and before he had an eyebrow scar. Today, he was the spitting image of his handsome, dark haired, blue-eyed father. The photo reminded him of what life was like before the accident. He'd never forget being in the front passenger seat when his inebriated father crashed their family car going the wrong way on a freeway, killing three innocent people. The incident sent his father to jail and he went to a hospital for stitches. His mother couldn't handle the shame and cruel insults from others and committed suicide. He peered up at the ceiling. His father wouldn't have gone to prison and his mother wouldn't have taken her life if they had the DUI Doctor as their attorney.

The bulky form of Rollie in the front courtyard down below caught his attention. His full-time bodyguard walked past cement planter boxes to stand on the sidewalk. He lit a cigarette as a cab pulled up to the curb to take him to the airport for a mission that had been in the works for a year. It was no secret Rollie enjoyed inflicting pain on others for his own gratification and to protect his boss. In a day, he would get his chance to help Kane avenge the audacity of Morgan Proffitt's actions by taking out the people who Proffitt cared about. Rollie would never be considered the sharpest bullet chambered in a Smith & Wesson, but his brawn compensated for his lack of smarts.

Rollie entered the cab's back seat and closed the door. Kane made a hand gesture like he was throwing a pair of dice as the cab pulled away. A year ago, he had been willing to pay an outside professional a five-figure fee to carry out this special assignment, but his money woes caused him to change plans. Instead, he sent Rollie, who had the wherewithal to do the deed for the mere cost of a round trip ticket. He also knew it was a big gamble that Rollie wouldn't screw up the mission.

Kane moved to his desk and riffled through six pending case files stacked on top. Only the Zeller case was close to paying off. The two sides were in a give and take negotiation mode, which usually meant a settlement would occur in the near future. He would soon step in at the last minute to close the deal. The firm's percentage fee wouldn't be as high as he'd have liked, but any money coming his way might help him stay afloat. Murray, his most experienced attorney, had to be replaced on the case after being hospitalized with bleeding ulcers. He had fired Murray and elevated rookie Stanley as the lead attorney to sink or swim in a pool against experienced alligators and sharks. Stanley was a talented rookie lawyer, but he was no Oliver Kane when it came to negotiations.

Kane buzzed Stanley's office. His fingers tapped on the desk waiting for a response. He pounded the buzzer again as if applying more pressure would give him a different result. Most likely Stanley was in the men's room or refilling his coffee cup in the attorneys' break room. He tried a third time with no success, then hit the button for his secretary.

"Where the hell is Stanley, Vera?" he barked. "He's not answering his phone."

"Stanley stepped out of the office to run an errand, Mr. Kane."

"Was the errand personal or business?" He gripped the letter opener like it was a dagger.

"He didn't say, sir."

Kane stabbed the desk mat with the letter opener. Was Vera covering up for Stanley? He expected each employee at the firm, whether it was an attorney, paralegal, process server, or secretary to be loyal to him and only him. Conversely, that didn't mean he had to share his loyalty in return. He would discipline or fire any one of them with no remorse.

"How long ago did Stanley leave?" he growled, pulling the letter opener from the desk mat, struggling to control his temper.

"About forty-five minutes ago." Her voice was shaky. "Did I do something wrong, sir?"

"Did Stanley have his briefcase with him?" Kane asked, ignoring her question.

"Maybe I . . . I don't recall seeing a briefcase."

"Did he say when he'd be back?"

"No, sir."

"That's because you didn't even ask. What's Stanley's god-damn cell number?"

Kane pushed in the numbers as if they were pins in Stanley's voodoo doll. Stanley never left the office, even when he was suffering from a bad bout of the flu. Running a personal errand was taboo, especially for a first-year lawyer. After eight months with the firm, he should've known better. Why did Stanley sneak off without permission?

"The last thing I need is for one of my people to go rogue." Kane squeezed the receiver until his hand hurt. Why isn't Stanley responding? The son of a bitch is going to pay . . ."

Stanley answered after the fifth ring.

"Why the hell did you leave the office without checking with me first, Stanley?"

"I uh . . . I didn't know I needed your consent, Mr. Kane. Since I never take a lunch break and normally work into the early evening, I thought it wouldn't be a problem if I stepped out to run an errand . . ."

"Consider yourself officially notified that I want to know where you and any of my staff are at all times. It's imperative that I can count on everyone when I need them. Is this registering, Stanley? I can't tell you how disappointed I am with you."

"I understand, Mr. Kane. My apologies. It was bad judgment on my part."

"What was so fucking important that you had to leave the office?"

"My wife is pregnant with our first child, Mr. Kane," Stanley explained. "Since I will be working well into the evening, I needed to grab a bite to eat and get to a florist before they close. I want to send a big bouquet of her favorite flowers to celebrate the exciting news."

"Let me be real clear here," Kane said. "What you need to do is get your fat ass back to the office. You should celebrate your prestigious job at Kane Law, not knocking up your wife. If we bring in a big settlement from the Zeller case, then you can rejoice." He rubbed the gash in the desk mat with a thumb. "Do you realize how lucky you are to be lead attorney on a large lawsuit in your first year? Murray's friggin' ulcers have given you an opportunity of a lifetime. Don't blow it."

"Again, I'm sorry, Mr Kane. It was my mistake not checking in with you first. I appreciate your confidence by allowing me to take the lead after Murray's illness. I won't let you down. I'll get my fat ass back to the office ASAP."

Kane slammed the phone receiver back to its base. Stanley could have called a florist. His apology didn't ring right. He'd never been close to insubordination, but all of a sudden he mysteriously leaves the office. He always brought a bag lunch from home so he could work through his break. Did Stanley's allegiance really disappear because of his wife's pregnancy? Or was this a betrayal? There was one easy way to find out.

"The last thing I need is a backstabber. When Rollie returns from his assignment, I will have him pay Stanley a visit to see if he's a team player or a traitor."

CHAPTER FIVE

Bruno didn't have to hear Oliver Kane's side of the conversation to comprehend the stern message being delivered by Stanley's boss. Stanley was frowning at his cell phone like it was a poisonous snake exposing its sharp fangs. He flicked the phone onto the table and slugged down the remaining dregs from his beer bottle, as if it were a serum to counteract Kane's venom.

"Man, I'm screwed," The color drained from Stanley's face. "Kane is suspicious. Do you think he found out I was coming here? I am thoroughly screwed."

"Chill out, Stanley." Bruno waited a few beats until he had the young attorney's attention. "I made sure you weren't followed, so you can relax. Think about it. Kane has no way of knowing your whereabouts. The only mistake you made was to do something out of the ordinary, like leave the office to run a personal errand without his knowledge. For a morally despicable person like Kane, that's like waving a blinking neon red flag."

Bruno's positive perspective seemed to calm Stanley down. But Kane's call couldn't have come at a worse time. It put Stanley in the middle of a Catch-22. Before the call, Stanley had been prepared to open a fresh package of Oliver Kane information. Would he still be a willing whistleblower? Or say "go suck a fig" and clam up? Bruno was certain of one thing: the odds of getting another chance to pump knowledge out of Stanley were poorer than placing a bet on a three-legged horse named Pokey to win.

"Obviously, your boss isn't pleased with you right now," Bruno quipped.

"That's an understatement." Stanley rolled his eyes.

"Has Kane ever hammered you like that before?"

"Mr. Kane has never talked to me in those words and that tone," Stanley said. "But I've seen him chastise others in the same way or worse." He fixed his tie knot. "I have to get back to the office before Mr. Kane changes his mind and fires me."

"Hold on." Bruno extended a palm out at Stanley in lieu of shaking some sense into him. "Open your eyes and push those blinders aside. You aren't seeing the whole picture. Don't leave until I make something clear to you. Believe it or not, he desperately needs your services; otherwise he would have fired your young fanny over the phone. Then you would've been black-balled to never work at any law firm in this state again. Or Kane would've have had his bodyguard Rollie scare or beat the crap out of you just on general principle so you and others would never forget what happens when someone screws with the great DUI Doctor." Bruno wasn't sure if his words were registering with glassy-eyed Stanley. "In other words, you're safe for now because you've got all the leverage."

Stanley rubbed the empty brown bottle with his fingertips. Maybe he was hoping the beer genie would appear and grant him a wish that his involvement with Oliver Kane and Bruno Santiago would disappear.

"Were you a used car salesman before becoming a P. I.?" Stanley asked. "You're trying to pressure me into buying into what you're selling without even a warranty." His angry eyes flashed. "It's not your ass that's on the line."

"I was a cop before going private. My ass was on the line everyday I was on duty."

"Let the record show you're making my case, Bruno. You left a secure job and the benefits of being a police officer because it was too dangerous."

"I left the police department for an entirely different reason," Bruno said.

"You fired a myriad of pointed questions at me. Now it's my turn. What made you quit being a cop?"

"Oliver Kane."

"Stop!" Stanley's Adams apple jutted in and out. "Don't tell me what your agenda is with Mr. Kane. It will only make me hate the man more, if that's possible. You were right about him needing me. The question is, can I stretch that need for four more months until my contractual obligation is fulfilled, and I get my bonus? You were spot-on with the foxhole comment. I'm not a hero. Never have been, nor do I ever plan to be."

"It took a lot of gonads for you to call me and then come here, Stanley. Kane will continue to abuse the law to his advantage, putting innocent people in jeopardy until someone stops him. That someone can be me. But I can't do it alone. If you provide me with insights to Kane's vulnerabilities, I will take him down one way or the other." Bruno pointed an index finger at Stanley like it was loaded. "Put another way, if you don't help me, right here and right now, how are you going to feel when the next person is killed by an Oliver Kane client? What if that other person is the child your wife is now carrying, God forbid?"

"Whoa. Forget what I said about you selling used cars, Bruno. You should apply for the open position of being my conscience." Stanley rubbed circles with his fingertips on the tabletop. "What the hell, I've gone this far, I might as well let it all hang out. I overheard a conversation between Mr. Kane and his bookkeeper that was obviously never meant for my ears. Mr. Kane has a temper he controls in a courtroom, but not in the office. He yelled at his bookkeeper after she reminded him about his mounting debt. Mr. Kane responded by saying Morgan Proffitt was responsible for putting him behind the deficit eight ball. He assured her another big payday was coming his way soon. She indicated soon may not be soon enough to stop him from filing for bankruptcy."

"Maybe Oliver Kane is finally getting what he deserves after ruining the lives of so many." Bruno could feel a rush of blood through his veins. "The son of a bitch has no one to blame but himself. I've known he's been in the red for a long time, but not as deep as you indicated. I have to give it to him. He has put up a great false front to keep his money troubles on the downlow." Bruno's body leaned towards Stanley. "So if I'm reading you right, are you saying Kane is close to self-destructing?"

"Before you do a happy dance on his grave, Mr. Kane may be desperate and down, but by no means is he out. He never stops believing he is one deal away from making a comeback. I wouldn't bet against him."

Bruno ran a hand through his hair as he considered Stanley's take on his boss. Kane was in massive debt and desperate for a deal that would wipe away what he owed. Bruno made a mental note regarding three D words: desperate, debt, and deal. He motioned with a hand for Stanley to continue.

"It's no secret Mr. Kane is a big-time womanizer," Stanley said. "The younger they are, the better. Word around the office is his marriage is on the rocks. I think it's his third or fourth." Stanley removed a handkerchief from his coat pocket and wiped his forehead. "Mr. Kane has dealings with people tied to organized crime, you know, guys in the underworld. He has a passion for expensive items like jewelry, clothes, furniture, country clubs - anything that make's him appear prosperous."

Stanley was on a roll. Bruno added women, out of control spending, and involvement with the mob to his list. He looked forward to connecting Kane's vulnerabilities into a strategy that could destroy him.

"It's no secret Kane loves to gamble. Given his money woes, is that still prevalent?"

"Absolutely. Mr. Kane likes the ponies and bets on other sporting events, but he's totally addicted to playing Texas Hold 'Em. He never misses his Thursday night poker game at one of his country clubs. Every Friday morning, we know if he has won big or lost even bigger just from his mood."

Bruno grinned. He also enjoyed the addicting lures of Texas Hold 'Em. Kane played Hold 'Em at the country club where Bruno was friendly with the club's general manager, Sid Parker. The weekly game was supervised by Sid, who was a childhood pal of Bruno's. Sid had offered to get Bruno a seat in the game even though he wasn't a member of the club. Bruno always declined because he couldn't afford the stakes they played for. Sid despised Kane as much as Bruno.

The word "addiction" wasn't nearly strong enough to describe the hold that Texas Hold 'Em had on some people. Bruno was reminded of a client who considered divorcing her husband after she discovered he had depleted most of their bank accounts and investments. The guy even sold his life insurance policy. The wife was certain he was romancing another woman and planning to leave her, taking the money they had saved. After tailing the husband for days, Bruno showed his client photos of her husband and his two-card mistress - pictures of him at a Texas Hold 'Em poker table. She was relieved and gave her husband an ultimatum: stop playing poker and join Gamblers Anonymous or she'd file for divorce. He chose Hold 'Em over her.

"There's more." Stanley tapped a nervous foot on the floor catching Bruno's attention. "A couple of days ago I was in a conference with Mr. Kane when his bodyguard Rollie burst into the office and interrupted our meeting. It was the first time I'd ever seen Rollie so flustered. He couldn't remember the name of the broad - his word not mine - at Proffitt Advertising in San Francisco he was assigned to take care of. Mr. Kane went ballistic and screamed profanities at Rollie before telling him to shut up. Then he ordered me out of his office. I assumed the assignment had something to do with Morgan Proffitt even though the man is dead."

"Before you left the office, did you hear the woman's name?" Bruno asked.

"Yes, but I don't remember. The message Rollie delivered must've been vitally important for Mr. Kane to send his bodyguard on the mission, leaving himself without security."

Bruno scooted his chair closer to the table. The less Stanley knew the better. Most likely, the woman in question was Virginia Webb, Proffitt's second in command. When Rollie said "take care of the woman" Bruno knew he wasn't referring to tender loving care. Virginia was in some serious danger and didn't know it. So were other employees and Mrs. Green, Mr. Proffitt's housekeeper.

"It's imperative that I know more about the assignment Kane gave to Rollie," Bruno said.

"I don't have that information, otherwise I'd tell you. But I wouldn't want to be in the shoes of the woman Rollie is after." Stanley bit down on his lip. "That man scares the holy crap out of me."

Bruno recalled his only encounter with Rollie. He was standing in the early morning shadows at Kane Tower's front courtyard when Rollie fired bullets at a cab with Morgan Proffitt in the driver's seat and Oliver Kane in back. Bruno surprised Rollie and made the thug drop the revolver on the pavement. He was there to protect Proffitt and help him carry out the mission to kill Kane. Folks in the New England area, as well as several individuals in San Francisco, would be a hell of a lot safer now had Proffitt succeeded in carrying out his plan to eliminate Kane.

"Any idea when this retribution scheme is supposed to take place?" Bruno asked.

"I believe Rollie said something about an anniversary."

Bruno smashed his palm down on the table making Stanley flinch. The beer bottle fell to the floor and broke into pieces.

"Tomorrow is Wednesday the eleventh of September, exactly one year after Oliver Kane met with Morgan Proffitt and the anniversary of the terrorist attack." Bruno jumped to his feet. "If what you're telling me is correct, Stanley, another 9/11 disaster is about to take place."

CHAPTER SIX

Stanley snatched his cell phone from the table and fled the tavern's office as if his life depended on it. Maybe it did. Before Stanley departed, Bruno was satisfied to know enough Oliver Kane vulnerabilities to knit into a strategy that would put Kane out of business for good.

Bruno went down to a knee to pick up beer bottle shards scattered on the floor before his bartender buddy popped in unexpectedly. The clean-up task would give him a few moments to determine how to approach a dicey chore he would rather avoid.

He noticed several red spots on the floor. Blood had dripped from a cut on his thumb, the hazards of being in a hurry and concentrating on a more important matter. He dumped the glass remains in a wastepaper basket, moved to the desk, and wrapped tissues around the wound tight enough to compress the bleeding. A rubber band held the makeshift bandage together.

Stanley left the office with a different kind of wound. He would have to deal with Oliver Kane's salty disposition and suspicions. Stanley's position at Kane Law should be secure for the time being since he was still considered necessary. The four additional months of his commitment were fraught with uncertainties. What if Kane pressured Stanley into confessing his whereabouts and the person he met with? The fortunes of Stanley, his wife, unborn baby, and a certain private detective would be in jeopardy. All the more reason Kane's insanity needed to be stopped.

Bruno examined the office one last time to make sure everything was in order. He checked his watch - a birthday gift that always reminded him of his fiancée, and the impetus for his actions against Kane. It was 5:05 pm in Boston and 2:05 pm in California. He flipped through his pocket sized address book until he found Proffitt Advertising. His forefinger punched in the numbers on his cell phone. How times had changed. Before cell phones became commonplace, he carried a pocketful of quarters for pay phones. His moral compass was forcing him to make this call whether he wanted to or not. It was his responsibility to alert the people closest to Morgan Proffitt. How do you persuade someone you don't know that their life and the lives of others are in peril without sounding like a raving lunatic?

"Proffitt Advertising," a female voice announced in an upbeat tone. "This is Mary. How may I help you?"

Bruno nodded after hearing Mary's voice. She had a slight Boston accent. Was the inflection a coincidence? Or was Mary the young lady who was with Morgan Proffitt in the cab?

"I'm calling from the East Coast, Mary. My name is Bruno Santiago. I need to speak to Virginia Webb about an urgent matter."

"Hold on for a second, Mr. Santiago, and I will check to see if Ms. Webb is available."

An unfamiliar song replaced Mary and her accent. Waiting with a cell phone pinned to his ear was just as bad as being stuck in Big Dig traffic. He drummed his fingers on the desk until he noticed a red stain had seeped through the Kleenex. If Virginia couldn't or wouldn't come to the phone, what was his plan B? Create a plan C to make a plan B.

"I'm sorry Mr. Santiago," Mary said, "Ms. Webb is in a meeting with a client. Was she expecting your call?"

Bruno pressed the phone harder against his ear. Was Virginia really with a client? Or was Mary screening her calls? Maybe he should have said: please tell Virginia I'm calling to give her a heads up that a hired assassin is coming from Boston to kill her and maybe you too, Mary? I'll hold the line while you pull Virginia away from her insignificant meeting with a client.

"Virginia isn't expecting my call, but she should be familiar with my name," Bruno said. "I'm a private detective. I worked with Mr. Proffitt for many years on a number of cases. Some disturbing information has come my way that involves Virginia and everyone at Proffitt Advertising. It's imperative that I speak to her right now."

Reaching Virginia was top priority. Otherwise, Bruno would have called Mary out if she had been the one with Proffitt the year before. He could hear a fax machine belching in the background. Mary's silence was disturbing. Was she trying to decide if this call was real, a crank, or a desperate attempt by a salesperson? Bruno would rather be posing as a deceiving salesman than a messenger delivering disturbing news.

"I'm sorry to say Morgan Proffitt passed away a year ago." Mary waited for the fax machine to stop. "Can I get your number and have Ms. Webb return your call?"

"I'm aware that Mr. Proffitt is deceased. Let me reiterate the urgency of this call. I don't care if Virginia's client is the governor of California. I need to speak to her as soon as possible."

"Please hold the line, Mr. Santiago."

Bruno rubbed his forehead. The end of Tony Bennett's song "I Left My Heart in San Francisco" was playing. Normally, he found that song pleasing to his ear. Not now. Was Mary having a difficult time convincing Virginia to take his call? What if Virginia didn't remember his name? If he was in their office pleading his case, he would have busted into Virginia's meeting with Mary pulling on his coattails. "Black Magic Woman" by Santana replaced Tony. How many songs would he have to listen to before . . .

"Mr. Santiago, this is Virginia Webb. I haven't had the pleasure of speaking with you before, but Mo spoke very highly of you and your work. Is this about an outstanding invoice I'm not aware of? Or did you somehow learn about tomorrow's one-year memorial at the gravesite honoring Morgan Proffitt's life?"

"My apologies for interrupting your meeting, Virginia. I realize this call is coming out of left field. Believe me, it's necessary. If only this was about an unpaid invoice. Just so you know, Mr. Proffitt paid me in advance and in cash for the last case I worked for him. He stipulated our agreement had to be verbal so there wouldn't be a paper trail that could lead back to me. In essence, he was protecting me. Mr. Proffitt recognized the position he was putting me in - a damned if you do and double damned if you don't. If the subject of my investigation ever discovered our connection, I'd be in life-threatening danger just like you are, Virginia."

"This is quite confusing," Virginia said. "Let me get this straight. If the nature of your assignment over a year ago was for Morgan Proffitt personally, rather than the Proffitt Advertising firm, why are you calling me now? And why would I be in danger?"

"Unfortunately, it does involve the Proffitt Advertising firm. I have it on good authority that you and possibly your staff are in grave danger."

"Is this some kind of joke, Mr. Santiago? If it is, I'm not amused. How in God's name could the people working for this agency be in danger?"

"It's no joke, Virginia. Are you aware of a Boston attorney named Oliver Kane?"

"Yes, I'm familiar with the name. We have a staff member who is from Boston. I found out, after the fact, that Mo flew to the East Coast to settle some kind of dispute with Mr. Kane. I don't know if that meeting ever occurred, but in doing so, Mo died from heart failure." Her voice cracked. "Obviously, going there was important to him, but it's a mystery to me as to why. What I do know, he never should have gone."

"On that matter," Bruno said, "Mr. Proffitt indicated his time was limited and told me he was taking on this mission alone. I believe he wanted to disassociate himself from everyone at Proffitt Adverting so they wouldn't be involved."

"Involved in what? It was never clear to me why Mo would risk his life to fly across country to meet with Oliver Kane. You obviously know more than I do."

"Mr. Proffitt blamed Oliver Kane for the death of his daughter Katie. Believe me, Mr. Proffitt isn't the only person who felt Kane was responsible for a disabling injury or death of a loved one."

"Are you saying Morgan Proffitt went to Boston to avenge Katie's car accident?" she asked. "If you are, I can't accept that premise. Oliver Kane wasn't the driver who made Katie crash her car. It's true that Mo was never the same after Katie's death, but what you just described doesn't sound like the man I knew and loved as a friend, boss, and gracious mentor. Mo was a kind, philanthropic person who didn't have a vengeful bone in his body."

"I provided Mr. Proffitt with information from several previous investigations of Oliver Kane, as well as updated material. He never told me he was on a mission to kill Kane, but it was obvious that was his intention." Bruno checked to see how much power his cell phone had left. "Like you, I don't believe Mr. Proffitt was motivated by revenge. He flew to Boston to bring an end to Kane - also known as the DUI Doctor - who has repeatedly represented people who drove under the influence and gotten them back behind their steering wheels to endanger others. It wasn't about payback, Virginia. Mr. Proffitt knew exactly what he was doing. In the time he had left, he was making a last-ditch attempt to save future innocent lives before they ended up in the morgue."

"Mo was our protector in so many ways," Virginia said. "I knew him better than anyone. He could never murder another person. What you are saying is crazy, Mr. Santiago."

Bruno's jaw clenched. He couldn't blame Virginia for defending her boss and dear friend. So far, his attempt to open her eyes to potential danger had failed badly, but he wasn't about to give up.

"Virginia, I'm not saying Mr. Proffitt was an immoral man. On the contrary, we both know he was extremely principled. He never asked me to do anything underhanded. Mr. Proffitt believed Oliver Kane was a societal menace - a depraved man who finds ways to keep dangerous individuals out of the justice system so they can continue to hurt and kill innocent people. By eliminating one life, Oliver Kane's, Mr. Proffitt hoped to save dozens of lives." Bruno transferred the cell phone to the other ear. "When it came to crunch time, maybe he didn't have it in him to take another person's life, even a despicable man like Oliver Kane. Maybe he figured out a different way to hurt Kane. The point I'm trying to get across to you is that Kane has never forgiven Proffitt for daring to interfere in his life. Since he can't take his vengeance out on Mr. Proffitt, he's going after the people Proffitt was closest to."

Bruno paused for Virginia to respond. Her silence could mean any number of things, most of them negative. It was time for him to open a can of candid.

"A few minutes ago," he continued, "a disgruntled lawyer who works for Oliver Kane told me Kane hired a hit man to target you since you were the person closest to Mr. Proffitt. That could also mean individuals at your advertising agency. Mrs. Green, Mr. Proffitt's housekeeper, could also be in harm's way."

"This sounds like something in a suspense novel or a thriller movie. I'm sorry, Mr. Santiago, but I just can't imagine what you are telling me is accurate. Did you approach this discontented employee? Or did he or she contact you?"

"He came to me. In doing so, he risked his job as well as retaliation from Kane."

"So you consider this person who contacted you to be honorable. Did you check out his credibility? Is it possible Mr. Kane wanted to get back at Mo through you by sending one of his attorneys with bogus information to dupe you into calling someone like me?"

Bruno blew out a frustrated breath. Virginia voiced his initial concerns about Stanley. He wasn't about to tell her his gut made the final decision about Stanley being the real deal. Yet, if Oliver Kane discovered he had been the private investigator working with Mr. Proffitt, it would make sense to try and deceive him into contacting any and all Proffitt people. It would make him look like an absolute fool whose mug imprint should be on an all-day sucker.

"I didn't give the whistleblower a polygraph test, if that's what you're asking," he said.

"I appreciate your concern, Mr. Santiago. I really do. With all due respect, I just can't accept the attorney's story as true. Conversely, I can't imagine calling the San Francisco Police Department and telling them I heard a rumor that someone from Boston is planning to kill me and my staff? Seriously, if you were in my position, would you believe what your informant said?"

"When you put it that way, I probably wouldn't. On the other hand, Virginia, if you were wearing my hat, wouldn't you warn the principals involved?"

"Touché, Mr. Santiago. I stand officially warned."

"I'm assuming a crowd will be attending Mr. Proffitt's memorial tomorrow?"

"Only four of us will be there. It's a private ceremony that includes Mary, the person who answered your call, her daughter, Mrs. Green, and me. Mo touched all of our lives in many different ways. He was explicit about not wanting any big memorial when he passed. I chose to respect his wishes. We can still respect him by meeting tomorrow morning at his gravesite in the Green Gardens Cemetery. It's in the city of Colma."

"I truly hope you are correct about my informant and nothing will happen. But be on the lookout for anything or anyone that looks suspicious. When you least suspect an attack, that's when it could happen."

"I will, Mr. Santiago. Thank you for your concern."

"One last question," Bruno said. "Have you told anyone else, especially someone you're not familiar with, about your memorial for Mr. Proffitt?"

"As a matter of fact, a man called saying he was a dear old friend of Morgan Proffitt and wanted to meet with me. You know, to reminisce and share stories maybe we weren't aware of. I told him about the ceremony, but it was private. He said he understood."

"Did you happen to get the man's name?"

"I think he said his name was Smith. I could tell he was calling from here. The background noise from traffic and a cable car bell made it seem like he was in a Market Street phone booth."

Bruno disconnected the call. Was Rollie dumb enough to give his last name or a suspicious alias like Smith? Then again, maybe he was clever enough to finagle Virginia's tomorrow whereabouts the next day at the Colma cemetery?

"The Proffitt people better hope I'm wrong or they are in big trouble," Bruno voiced to no one listening.

CHAPTER SEVEN

A shiver gripped Bruno as he hustled from San Francisco's airport terminal into an overcast morning. His gray sports coat and navy-blue turtleneck sweater did little to take the chill away. What ever happened to Northern California's vaunted warm and sunny Indian summers he'd read about? Mark Twain had been correct when he said the coldest winter he ever spent was a summer in San Francisco.

It took Bruno a few unsettled seconds to get his bearings, but the crisp air helped shake most of the redeye fog from his head. The flight had been uneventful and only half-full since this was the one-year anniversary of the 9/11 terrorist attack. His fellow travelers wheeled or carried various forms of luggage as they congregated to the arrival area anxious to find waiting transportation. Several horns honked at once. He didn't bother to seek out a parked driver to pick him up; he never told a soul about taking an unplanned cross-country flight.

Yesterday's phone conversation with Virginia Webb prompted him to pack a carry-on bag and catch a plane. Virginia wasn't heeding his alert about Oliver Kane sending someone to harm her. His warning should have set off loud alarm bells. If Virginia couldn't be swayed over the phone that she and her staff were in danger, perhaps he could persuade her in person.

Bruno buttoned his sports coat and hitched up the collar. He didn't have any second thoughts about his spontaneous decision to fly to the West Coast. It wouldn't be the first time he went beyond the call of duty to aid a person or client for their own good. If Stanley had been sent by Oliver Kane to deceive him, as Virginia suggested, the only damage would be to his ego, not an unsuspecting person.

A rolling suitcase brushed against Bruno's leg. The careless lady mumbled an incoherent apology and hurried off. He fought the urge to rub his shin. What a difference one day could make. Last year's terrorist attacks had changed everything about airports and flying. There was a lot more security, but less freedom and friendliness. Passengers of all ages and genders were suffering the indignities of pre-flight pat downs, x-rays, and interrogations. Procedures were in place to keep everyone safe, but many overzealous airport employees were acting more like the government gestapo. Bruno had left his revolver in his car's trunk at the airport parking lot to ensure he could fly at a moment's notice without any glitches. After all, why would he need to be armed to persuade Virginia to heed his warnings? Once he convinced her that an assault was a real possibility, and she promised him to secure protection, he planned to catch the next plane back to Boston.

Bruno gestured with a raised hand at the last cab in the lineup stationed at the curb. Airport cabs have their own priority system. So did he. The cabbie at the end would probably be the most flexible to his demands. The cab's engine purred to life after the driver signaled back with a wave. Bruno speed-walked to the rear door, threw it open, tossed his leather overnight bag on the seat, and settled in. Whoa. The cab's interior reeked of marijuana, causing him to cough and blink. He rolled a side window down a few inches, silently berating his choice of cab drivers.

The cabbie had a green Mohawk haircut and his scraggly beard appeared to attempt to cover his bad complexion. The photo on the taxi license attached to the passenger visor showed someone with normal hair and clean shaven.

"Where to dude?" the cabbie asked.

Bruno scowled at the driver. He didn't care if the guy smoked weed, but being called dude, buddy, pal, chief, bro, partner, boss, bugger, or any other moniker irritated him to no end, especially when voiced by someone much younger who he'd never met. The cab's digital dashboard clock reminded Bruno to reset his wristwatch to 9:29 am, three hours earlier. On the phone, Virginia had indicated the private graveside service for Morgan Proffitt would be held in the morning so Bruno assumed it could take place anytime before noon. Depending on how far the Green Gardens Cemetery was from the airport, he could be late already.

"Are you familiar with the town of Colma?" Bruno unbuttoned his sports coat, rolled the window down all the way, and sucked in the soothing cool air.

"I try not to go to Colma very often," the cabbie said. "The buried population far outnumbers the people who live there."

"There's a $20 tip in it for you if I'm at the Green Gardens Cemetery in ten minutes." Bruno spotted the driver's smirk in the rear view mirror. "Are we good?"

"You make it sound like it's a life and death situation, no pun intended." The cabbie cranked out a throaty laugh. "How about this, boss. If you bump up my tip to 30 bucks, I will get you there in eight minutes."

Bruno's brows knit together. The Colma cemetery had to be nearby. Nice try, dipshit.

"I see you like to negotiate." Bruno made the cabbie wince by squeezing his shoulder. "Because I'm in a good mood I'm going to counter your offer. You can kiss Andrew Jackson goodbye. I just lowered your gratuity to a sawbuck. My internal meter is also running. If I'm not at the cemetery in eight minutes, you get nothing and I'll show you what happens to cabbies who try to hustle out-of-towners."

The driver's shoulders bunched into his neck after Bruno released his hand. The cab peeled out, sending Bruno back into the seat. He buckled the seatbelt and hoped the green hair dye and dope didn't affect the guy's driving skills.

The cab ride took seven minutes. Bruno crumbled up a $10 bill with the fare and flipped it onto the front passenger seat. The driver eyed his tip as if Alexander Hamilton might bite his hand. Bruno grabbed his bag and stepped onto the gravel parking lot. As soon as the door closed, the cab rocketed towards the exit spewing tiny rocks.

Bruno counted six vehicles in the parking lot: a small Chevy rental car, a Dodge Caravan, an older model Ford with Massachusetts plates, a Jeep, a BMW, and a truck. Kane's bodyguard most likely came in the Ford or Chevy. He shouldn't have a problem identifying a group of three women and a girl. Gravel crunched under his shoes as he headed to the walkway. His breath caught once he moved into the grassy expanse of the cemetery. His last memory of a graveyard was etched in his mind. Would the empty feeling ever go away?

A paved road divided the cemetery in two. Morning dew made the grass shine. He couldn't tell if there was a difference from one side to the other - like going from one neighborhood into another. He proceeded slowly, surveying row by row from both directions. A man clutched a handful of flowers and spoke passionately to a headstone that wouldn't respond back. Two rows ahead, a young couple wearing matching sweatshirts stood silently in front of a grave with their heads down. To the far right, three groundskeepers tidied up an area. Moving forward, he observed a brunette woman with forehead bangs clad in a black skirt and jacket studying a sheet of paper.

Bruno arrived at the end of the cemetery grounds that were surrounded by a metal fence with an entrance for pedestrians. A black bird stood on the highest limb of a tree and sent out high-pitched messages to his feathered friends. Bruno turned around and headed back. Did the Proffitt group arrive early and leave? He had no choice but to wait until noon to find out. A new set of visitors had arrived. The sweatshirt couple had left. So did the man with the flowers. Some people find solace visiting cemeteries. He knew a few individuals who toured graveyards as a hobby everywhere they traveled. Others would loyally go to a burial ground at the same time and day on a weekly basis. He once had a case that involved a cheating wife meeting her lover at a cemetery every Sunday.

Two women and a girl marched towards him on the walkway. A short, older lady in a dark dress led the way, followed by a young woman in her twenties dressed in a navy-blue pantsuit. The girl was wearing a white dress. Bingo. They had no reason to pay attention to him as they passed. He waited several moments before tailing them to the gravesite where the woman holding a piece of paper stood in front of a headstone.

Bruno positioned himself next to a cypress tree to keep an eye on the Proffitt women. Virginia must have arrived first and was waiting to be joined by Mary, the young woman from

Boston who first answered his phone call yesterday, along with her young daughter, and Mr. Proffitt's housekeeper Mrs. Green. He recalled speaking to Mrs. Green on the phone a year ago just before Mr. Proffitt began his Boston trek to do away with Oliver Kane. The small party honoring Morgan Proffitt had no idea they were being watched, maybe by two people.

Bruno readied himself by reaching for the cold steel of his holstered revolver, only to find it missing. In hindsight, he should have gone through the airport security hassle by disclosing the gun and his permit to carry. He'd bet a dollar to a Dunkin' Donut that Rollie had been faced with a similar airport dilemma. The best-case scenario would have security holding Rollie in custody at Logan Airport after catching him trying to smuggle his gun on the plane. What were the odds Rollie would be that dumb? Bruno had to assume Rollie was hiding somewhere with or without a gun. He kept watch in four directions. Rollie's M. O. was to physically abuse his prey. But this time Rollie would need to make it look like a mugger's attack gone awry.

Bruno checked to see if he was being observed. A man holding a bag and standing next to a tree in a cemetery might look suspicious, but no one seemed to be paying any attention to him. Virginia could be tempted to give his position away if she knew he was here. His only advantage on Rollie was surprise. He was prepared to physically take him on if needed. Even if Rollie got the best of him, the women would have an opportunity to escape. If Rollie didn't show, he'd wait until the observance ended to approach them.

He was too far away to hear Virginia's words. Mary had a hand on her young daughter's shoulder, nodding. The girl entertained herself by dangling a small silver toy. Mrs. Green stood on the other side of the girl dabbing a handkerchief to her eyes. Virginia folded the paper in half and motioned to Mary; perhaps to say a few words.

A movement to Bruno's right caught his eye. His body tensed. The women had their backs turned to a man who was darting towards them. The guy was about fifty pounds lighter and five inches shorter than Rollie. What the hell?

Bruno dropped his bag at the tree trunk and took off to intercept someone he had never seen before. Did Rollie have an accomplice? Or was someone else after Virginia?

CHAPTER EIGHT

A few moments before, the cemetery had been calm and tranquil. The next second, Bruno was racing across damp grass to chase after a man making a beeline towards three women and a girl paying their respects to the late Morgan Proffitt.

Running into a stiff wind made breathing difficult for Bruno. The air wheezing in and out of his mouth sounded like an overworked engine. He hadn't sprinted this fast in years. His long strides helped him gain on the man. Did the runner even know someone was pursuing him? In high school Bruno ran track. Nineteen years later he still had a decent set of wheels, but age had robbed him of the extra gear that used to propel his legs to another speed. He would settle for catching a second wind before he ran out of gas.

Was the guy he was trailing an ally or an enemy? Hit men come in all shapes, sizes, and appearances. So do compassionate cemetery visitors. The runner was less than six feet tall, thin, around thirty, wearing jeans and a white t-shirt. His lengthy dark hair flew up behind him like a tail, exposing a black ink tattoo on the side of his neck similar to designs featured on prison inmates. There was no mistaking where the man was heading, but for what purpose? Was he a cold-hearted contract killer? Or was he someone arriving late to pay his respects as a sympathetic family member or friend?

As if he had taken in a blast of oxygen, breathing came easier to Bruno. His extra gear was still dormant, but a second wind had kicked in. The runner was only a few yards from his reach. Bruno leaned his upper body forward in anticipation. He stretched his hand out to grab the back of the man's shirt. Before his fingers could make contact, his shoe hit a sprinkler hole, throwing him off balance. He fought to remain upright. His arms flailed in the air for stability, but his shoes slid out from under him, sending his body down to the slippery grass.

Clinging wet pants gave him a jolt. Instincts from playing baseball made him perform a pop-up slide to stand and recoup his running stride. His fall may have left him with too much ground to make up. The lives of four unsuspecting people depended on his ability to find his missing running gear.

He looked past the runner. The women were still grouped in front of Morgan Proffitt's headstone unaware of what was taking place behind them. The young woman, Mary, was speaking without notes. He couldn't hear what she was saying. She gave a shaken Mrs. Green an empathetic one-arm hug. The older lady had served the Proffitt family as a housekeeper, Mr. and Mrs. Proffitt's care giver, and daughter Katie's nanny. Mary's youthful daughter continued to amuse herself by jiggling a small metal object. Why wasn't she at school on a Wednesday morning? Perhaps Mr. Proffitt's memorial took precedence over missing classes.

A line of sweat snaked down Bruno's forehead into his eye. The sting made him blink furiously. He was too far behind to catch the guy. If he had his gun and fired a warning shot, the sound might have drawn the women's attention and impeded the man's progress. It would have been a risky ploy, but maybe a life saving move.

"Virginia," Bruno shouted, unsure his voice would carry far enough. "Virginia, look out."

Virginia spun around to see who had called out her name. She cupped a hand above her eyes to shield the penetrating sun. The runner was nearing the gravesite. Virginia's head bounced back as if she was confused. Did she think the tattoo guy was the person who was trying to alert her? Or was she recalling yesterday's phone conversation signaling her of potential danger? A warning she dismissed as improbable.

Mary stepped in front of Virginia, squinting at the assailant. Her mouth opened in surprise. She pointed a menacing forefinger at the charging man.

"Oh my God, it's Larry!" Mary hollered. "How the hell did he find me?"

"Larry?" Bruno puffed out. "She actually knows the guy?"

Bruno willed his legs to propel faster. This scene was getting weirder by the second. Was Mary the target of Oliver Kane's revenge? Or was this a personal matter that had nothing to do with Kane and everything to do with Mary being the loser of an adult game of hide-and-seek?

Larry never slowed as he approached the women. Mary dashed towards him screaming like she had lost her mind. A crisis can make anyone appear crazy or act in a bizarre way. It can also throw caution and fear aside for a woman to attack a male assailant.

Mary's arm reared back, telegraphing her next move. She launched the punch at Larry's face. He deftly evaded the haymaker by lowering his head and knocking Mary out of his path with his shoulder. Mary skidded backwards on the slick lawn. Larry didn't bother to see if she was injured. Instead, he went straight for a different target: Mary's daughter. Larry picked up the girl with a one arm swipe and darted for the back exit.

"Mommy!" the girl shrieked, beating on Larry's face and chest. "Mommy. Help me."

"Let Rachel go, Larry." Mary struggled to her feet holding a hand on her midsection.

Bruno raced past Mary and the other two stunned women. Larry hadn't brandished a weapon because he wasn't an assassin. He was a damn kidnapper . . . not that there was much difference between the two evils.

Bruno was gaining on Larry at a rapid pace. Witnessing a defenseless child being carried away against her will released a flow of adrenaline that was every bit as effective as his extra gear. A tackle around the knees would take Larry down, but Rachel could get hurt when they hit the ground. Instead, Bruno grabbed a fistful of Larry's greasy hair to slow him down. Mary's frantic shouts from behind were as gut-wrenching as Rachel's cries for her mother. Bruno was determined to save the valuable package trapped in Larry's arm as if she was his own child.

Rachel kept squirming in Larry's arm. He slowed down to a trot. Bruno was careful not to yank too hard, only to be left behind with a handful of hair. Larry came to a standstill, out of breath, struggling to keep hold of Rachel with one arm. The fingers on his other hand covered his eye. Rachel continued to smack his face with the metal object she had been playing with. His cheeks were dotted with red welts and glistened from seepage leaking from a damaged eye.

Bruno snatched Rachel away from Larry with both hands, stepped back, and gave her a reassuring smile. He started to lower her to the grass, but Rachel wrapped her hands around his neck, signaling she was more secure in his arms.

"You're safe now, Rachel," Bruno said in a comforting tone. "I won't let this guy or anyone else hurt you and your mom. I promise to protect you. Okay?"

Rachel nodded. Bruno could feel her little hands tighten around his neck. She rested her head on his chest.

"I think you are a brave little lady, Rachel, just like your mother."

Larry reached to take Rachel back. Bruno smacked the hand away and shot a menacing glare, daring Larry to challenge him. Larry's good-eye widened in fear. Bruno twisted his body so Rachel was out of Larry's reach. He would have been content to beat Larry into a lifeless pulp and dump the body into the first unfilled grave he could find, but keeping Rachel safe was his main concern.

"Back off, assbite," Larry spewed. He extended a hand for Rachel again, then thought better of it. "This is none of your business."

"I'm making it my business," Bruno replied. "Kidnapping is a felony - a felony that will send you to the slammer for the rest of your life. You should have plenty of time to get a matching tat on the other side of your neck." Bruno's lips spread into a crocodile smile. "By the way, the last guy who called me a derogatory name couldn't speak for three months with a wired-shut jaw."

Bruno grabbed Larry's t-shirt, plus some flesh, and pulled him close enough to sniff a whiff of liquor on his breath. It was too early for someone to consume alcohol, unless that someone had a drinking problem. Maybe the scent was residue from the night before. Did Larry's courage to kidnap Rachel come from 90-proof whiskey?

"Rachel is my daughter, so it's not kidnapping," Larry said. "It's my right to see her whenever I want to." His fingers went back to his damaged eye. "The little bitch may have blinded me for life. You need to butt out and hand her over. This has nothing to do with you."

"Are you out of your freakin' mind, Larry?" Mary took Rachel from Bruno and hugged her daughter. She caressed Rachel's cheek and looked at Bruno. "No offense, but I don't know who you are, mister. Are you with my scumbag ex-husband who was just paroled from prison and is under a judge's restraining order?"

Stunned, Bruno's shoulders stiffened after being accused of being involved with Larry.

"For what it's worth, Mary, I can assure you that I had nothing to do with this guy."

"How the hell do you know my name?" Mary said.

"Mommy," Rachel said, pointing at Larry, "is this man my daddy?"

"Yes, Rachel. You were too young to remember him. He had to be sent away because he did some terrible things that were so bad he can't be in our lives."

"But I'm still her father," Larry fired back.

"You'd think spending several years in prison after running over a man on purpose in your car would have made you wise up, Larry." Mary's hand formed into a fist. "You never once acted like a responsible father or husband. You only want Rachel so I will get back together with you. If you really loved her, you would have stayed away."

Bruno swallowed hard. It didn't matter that Mary linked him with Larry. His heart went out to both mother and daughter. He was grateful to have been at the right place at the right time to nail a scumbag like Larry. But Larry had nothing to do with Oliver Kane. The Proffitt people were still in danger. Rollie could be lurking somewhere on the cemetery grounds watching this whole debacle.

"Did you call Proffitt Advertising yesterday, Larry?" Bruno queried.

"What? What kind of dumb ass question is that?"

Bruno released Larry's t-shirt and throttled his neck with one hand.

"All right, all right." Larry choked out. "Why would I call and tell anyone I'm here? Nobody's that dumb."

Mary's eyes narrowed at Bruno's question; an expression that was easy to read. She was wondering why he asked the phone call question. Mary didn't realize he was here for another reason that had nothing to do with her ex. He loosened his grip on Larry's neck.

"How did you know they'd be at the cemetery?" Bruno questioned.

"I followed them from the old lady's house." Larry glared at Mary. "Did you hire this punk for protection? Or are you just shacking-up with him like the little slut that you are? Have you forgotten there wouldn't be a Rachel without me?"

"No, Larry. I will never forget. How a precious child like Rachel could come from your evil seed is a miracle. How did you track me down?"

"Wasn't hard," Larry said. "It's no secret your old lady in Boston never liked me. When I paid her a visit, she got the impression I might harm her unless she told me. I swiped her friend's car and came here to take you and Rachel back." He produced an ugly smirk. "I warned you before they sent me to the joint. If I couldn't have you when I got out, then no one else will have you either."

"Nice - harassing women really is your superpower, Larry. You must have really frightened my mother. She didn't warn me that you had paid her a visit."

Bruno pressed harder on Larry's neck, making him grunt out strange sounds. It took all of Bruno's self-control not to dim Larry's lights for good. But Larry had been right about one thing; this was none of his business. Yet what would have happened if he hadn't been here looking for Rollie? Fate works in mysterious ways.

"In my coat's side pocket, Mary, you'll find a zip tie hand restraint," Bruno said. "Take it out and bind this dirt bag's hands."

"I have a better way of handling Larry. Let go of him," Mary ordered, questioning Bruno with intense blue eyes. "You heard me. Let him go."

Bruno paused, then removed his hand from Larry's neck. Mary gently placed Rachel down on the grass. She marched up to Larry and belted his jaw with everything she had. He went down as if all the bones in his body had been removed. She pounced on his lifeless frame and pulverized his face with countless punches.

Bruno wrapped his arms around Mary to lift her off Larry. With her feet peddling in the air, she struggled to free herself from his grasp. It surprised him how light, yet strong she was. Her perfume awakened warm memories. When all the fight left Mary, he set her down. Tears flooded her eyes.

"The bastard always did have a glass jaw." Mary's voice quivered. "Larry was never much of a fighter. That's why he ran over the guy with his car in a bar parking lot instead of duking it out. He was convicted of manslaughter and sent to prison. We were supposed to be notified if he got released. This is a nightmare."

Mary turned to Bruno.

"You saved Rachel and I'm grateful for that. But how did you know my name was Mary? What made you ask Larry if he called Proffitt Advertising yesterday?" She began pounding his chest with her forefinger. "Did you know Larry was coming for Rachel? Your accent tells me you're also from Boston. Why did you suddenly show up as Mr. Good Samaritan to save the day? How did you know my name and where I work? You best start talking, mister, before I find out if you can take a punch."

CHAPTER NINE

Larry was still sprawled across Horace Alowicious Wright's grave. A few feet away, Mary continued to shoot eye-daggers up at Bruno and poke her finger into his chest. Normally he wouldn't have tolerated the assault, but he was intrigued by Mary's tenacity in standing up to her ex-husband Larry. Something else perplexed him, but he couldn't pinpoint exactly what it was.

Being jabbed in the chest reminded Bruno of an incident several years prior. He'd been threatened by a woman loaded on whiskey while she aimed a revolver at him loaded with bullets. Unlike Mary, the woman's face was coated with enough paint to cover a barn, plus she reeked of tobacco. He negotiated a resolution before she could pull the trigger. Would Mary be as amenable?

"Yo, Mary," he said, "before you go into your Rocky Balboa mode again, you have me at a big disadvantage." His eyes purposely widened - an expression people render when their innocence is threatened. "I've never hit a woman in my life and I'm not about to start today. Since I unveiled this piece of information in good faith, would you please stop jabbing me in my chest? I'm not the bad guy here."

"So far, nothing you've said has changed my opinion. Maybe you should alter your approach by starting with your name and why you got involved."

Rachel tugged on her mother's arm. "Mommy, why are you being mean to the nice man?"

"Sweetheart, please listen to me." Mary's head tilted back, keeping an eye on someone much taller. "We don't know anything about this man. Who is he? How honest is he? Or why is he here? We don't even know if he's like the person who tried to take you away from me."

"No, Mommy, you don't understand. He promised to protect

me from the bad man. He said he wouldn't let anyone hurt me or you."

Mary's nostrils flared. She grunted out a word Bruno didn't catch, and then holstered the trigger finger hand into a pocket. He rubbed the pummeled area on his turtleneck sweater as if it was a battlefield wound.

"Well, you've managed to win over one of us," Mary said. "But you still haven't convinced me. Why would you tell Rachel you would protect her or me?"

"I meant every word." Bruno winked at the girl and noticed for the first time how Rachel's blue eyes and auburn hair were the spitting image of Mary. "I also told Rachel she is very brave, just like her mother. I watched you confront Larry. You knew he would try to take Rachel. And in doing so, you took a pretty nasty shot from him. When I saw what your husband was up to, I envisioned being a parent. If I had a child who was in jeopardy, I would hope someone would come to their aid if I couldn't."

"Correction, ex-husband." Mary wrapped an arm around Rachel. "I'd never let anyone take my daughter away from me without a fight. So maybe you can explain why you were chasing Larry before he grabbed Rachel? It looked like you knew what he was going to do. In other words, just who the hell are you and why are you here?"

"I think I can answer that question, Mary." Virginia approached, holding a cell phone in one hand and Mrs. Green's arm in the other. "By the way, the police are on their way to pick up your ex. One good thing about the city of Colma, the police department isn't far away." She turned her attention to Bruno. "Mary, if I'm not mistaken, this man who rescued Rachel has to be Bruno Santiago, a private detective from Boston. I'm not sure why you're here, Mr. Santiago, unless Larry is the person sent by Oliver Kane that you tried to warn me about?"

Bruno listened to Virginia, but Mrs. Green caught his interest. She couldn't be more than five feet tall. With untamed white hair and both hands on her wide hips, she was giving him the stink eye, as if he was the one who abducted Rachel. He realized the Proffitt family housekeeper, caregiver, and nanny had loads of authority. Between Mary and Mrs. Green, he was the recipient of their angry disapproval in stereo.

"Larry had nothing to do with my coming here, Virginia," Bruno said. "Our conversation from yesterday is the reason I'm here. How did you know it was me?"

"Even though I discounted your warning, your words were the first thing I thought about when I saw Larry and you running towards us. It had to be you chasing after what I thought was the person Oliver Kane sent. Now that I hear your voice, your slight Beantown accent is a dead giveaway." Virginia ran a hand through short brown bangs. "But I'm puzzled. You did your due diligence. So why are you here? To catch Mary's ex-husband, Larry?"

"Wish it was that easy," Bruno said. "Larry had nothing to do with Oliver Kane's plot. It's my belief the goon Kane sent is his bodyguard, Rollie. When I saw someone who looked nothing like Rollie running towards Mr. Proffitt's grave, I wrongly pegged him as an ally of Rollie's." He shifted his view to Mary. "That's why I chased after Larry and asked him if he called Proffitt Advertising yesterday. Rollie must have been the caller, not Larry."

"I'm completely in the dark, here." Mary threw a hand up in the air. "I get how you knew my name and where I worked. You're the guy who called the office yesterday all hot and bothered about speaking to Virginia. Are you some kind of bounty hunter? What does Oliver Kane and Rollie the bodyguard have to do with Virginia and Proffitt Advertising?"

"I'm at fault here." Virginia peeked at her phone and buried it in her purse. "Another man called before Mr. Santiago. I inadvertently told him about our memorial today."

"There's more, Mary," Bruno said. "If you're from Boston, then I'm sure you've heard the name Oliver Kane. He's seeking retribution for what Morgan Proffitt did to him in Boston. If what I learned from one of Kane's employees proves true, all of you are in danger whether you believe me or not." He ran a hand across chin stubble. "The reason I'm here, ladies, is to convince you in person that Oliver Kane's threat is real."

Bruno noticed the corner of Mary's mouth twitched every time Oliver Kane's name was mentioned. It was Mary who'd been with Proffitt in the cab. Bruno snapped his fingers when he realized what had puzzled him about her. She was cute, but wasn't wearing a smidgeon of makeup - not even lipstick - to enhance her attractiveness. If she was downplaying her looks, why would she wear such enticing perfume?

"I took a redeye flight last night after talking to Virginia," Bruno said. "It's understandable why she didn't heed my warnings from yesterday's conversation. Let me reiterate - Oliver Kane is a very dangerous man. It's possible he sent an assailant to harm those who were closest to Morgan Proffitt."

"What on earth could Mr. Proffitt have possibly done to this Oliver Kane character to seek revenge and send an attacker to harm any one of us?" Mrs. Green asked.

"Morgan Proffitt dared to challenge Oliver Kane's existence, and that is something Kane cannot let go of." Bruno's face contorted as if he was in pain. "If you knew about Kane's childhood, it'd be easier to put all the psychological pieces together. Maybe I can stop Rollie before he attacks. If the information I received was purposely bogus to make me look bad as Virginia suggested in our phone conversation, I'll gladly eat a humble crow sandwich on your sourdough bread before my flight back to Boston. At least I'll have erred on the side of caution."

"All I know, mister hotshot detective," Mrs. Green said, taking a step towards Bruno, "is that a year ago Mr. Proffitt left for Boston in such a hurry after your phone call, he didn't take the suitcase lying on his bed that I'd packed for him. Whatever you told Mr. Proffitt prompted him to rush to the airport. In my book, you are the reason he went to Boston and never came back alive. If you're such a great investigator, you should have known his heart and state of mind were never the same after his daughter Katie's death." She projected an incriminating finger at him. "You bet I blame you for his death. Mr. Proffitt was a kind and gentle man generous to a fault. He was all about helping folks, not hurting them. How do we know you didn't make up this story just to save your own derrière? How do we know the only reason you came here is to get paid for protection money when we don't need it? How do we know if you aren't that Rollie hooligan? That's my take on things and I'm sticking to it. Thank you."

"Virginia is aware Mr. Proffitt had been a client of mine for years, Mrs. Green," Bruno said. "I agree, he was a real gentleman and we had mutual respect for each other. From a business standpoint, he was above board with almost everything. It's vital that all of you understand how dangerous attorney Oliver Kane is, in or out of court. It was Mr. Proffitt who called me first to request intelligence regarding Kane. I returned his call with up-to-date Kane information. In fact, if my memory serves me right, it was you, Mrs. Green, who woke Mr. Proffitt to take my call. He shared a little bit about his condition . . . that time wasn't on his side for the mission he was planning. In all honesty, if I had it to do over again, I'd do the same thing to aid his endeavor."

Mrs. Green crossed her arms over an ample bosom. She shook her head emphatically. Bruno didn't need a word from her to know she wasn't buying what he was selling.

"You still haven't convinced me, Mr. Santiago, but he isn't making it up, Mrs. Green." Mary looked down at the ground and then back to Mrs. Green. "Mo was having trouble walking so I pushed him in a wheelchair after we landed. He was dead set on making his appointment on time with Oliver Kane at Kane Tower." She took a deep breath. "His strength was waning by the minute. I pleaded with him to go to the hospital. He was adamant we do it his way. I don't know if he met with Oliver Kane or not. I read in the paper the next day that Mo was found dead in a cab in front of Fenway Park."

Bruno nodded slightly. It was Mary who was with Proffitt.

"Mr. Mo gave me this hippo." Rachel smiled as she jiggled a silver hippo keychain for everyone to see as if she was at show and tell in school. "Mr. Mo told me that her name was Hope. And he told me to never lose Hope because she was special just like me. I take her everywhere I go, right, Mommy?"

"Yes, sweetheart. Mr. Proffitt was a very wise and generous man. We are both lucky and blessed to have met him when we did."

"Mr. Proffitt's daughter Katie gave him that keychain as a present." Mrs. Green dabbed her eyes. "It was so special to him. He passed it onto the right person, our dear Rachel."

"I realize each of you loved Mr. Proffitt in your own way," Bruno said. "Having said that, whether you want to hear it or not, Mr. Proffitt flew to Boston to eliminate Oliver Kane. He had the opportunity to follow through with his mission, but for some reason, let Kane live. Ironically, Proffitt saved Kane's life by making him miss his flight to L.A. That plane slammed into the World Trade Center. Still, Kane cannot abide anyone messing with his plans. He never forgave Proffitt, but waited patiently for a year - just like a terrorist - to carry out his retribution."

"I owe you an apology, Mr. Santiago." Virginia put her hands together. "Although I thought your call was sincere, I couldn't believe what you were telling me was true. I do now. For you to fly from the East Coast to warn and protect us is beyond the call of duty. Thank you. I want to reimburse you for your time and the plane tickets."

"No need to thank me or pay for my airfare. I have my own reasons to stop Oliver Kane." Bruno peered down at Rachel and smiled. "I'm good with knowing that Rachel is safe, Mary wasn't injured worse, and her scumbag ex-husband is about to be arrested."

"I was only with Mo for six or seven hours," Mary's cheeks flushed red. "He never told me what he was up to, but I knew it had something to do with Oliver Kane. I'm still not sold on you, Mr. Santiago, but you did save Rachel from God knows what. Sorry about getting physical with you. The thought of you being a stranger and Larry having Rachel - especially when he's on the bottle - made me lose it."

Bruno acknowledged Mary's apology with a head bow. He was mystified how Mary or any woman could get involved with a loser like Larry.

"You should be very proud of your daughter," Bruno said. "She saved herself by pelting Larry's face with her keychain to slow him down." He rubbed his chest again and glanced at Mary. "I wonder where she gets her fighting chops."

Mary wiggled her lethal forefinger at Bruno, making him raise his arms in surrender. She still harbored mistrust and hostility towards him, but hadn't lost her sense of humor.

Two Colma police cars with roof lights flashing and sirens blaring drove up the road towards them. A low moan came from Larry. He attempted to roll on his side to rise. Bruno kneeled down and restrained his hands together with the zip tie.

"You'd be wise to stay down before your ex takes one last shot at you," Bruno said.

"What does this Rollie look like?" Mrs. Green asked. "And where do you think he is?"

"I only saw Rollie once. He's my height and about forty or fifty pounds heavier. The thug sports a crew cut and usually has a toothpick or a cigarette protruding from his lips." Bruno put a foot on Larry's chest. "Maybe I figured wrong about the cemetery being the place Rollie would make his move. Or he could be here observing us now. Or he might be staked out at the Proffitt Advertising office."

"I'll call the office staff, and find a security company." Virginia removed her cell phone from her purse. "What else do you recommend, Mr. Santiago?"

"I'm not trying to frighten you, Mrs. Green," Bruno said. "I just want you to be aware of the possibilities. The man Oliver Kane may have sent could strike at any time or place, even your home."

"Oh my God, Rachel and I live with Mrs. Green." Mary stepped in front of Rachel and Mrs. Green as if to protect them from an invisible assassin. "It's happening to me again."

CHAPTER TEN

Larry threatened Bruno and Mary with a profanity-laced outburst before being escorted by two Colma police officers to their patrol car. In a short period of time, Mary's ex had accumulated a portfolio of felony charges by violating parole, as well as a judge's court order, stealing a car, assault and battery, and attempting to kidnap his own daughter.

If Bruno had been wearing a hat, he would tip it to Larry to give him credit where credit is due. The man was blessed with a wealth of natural ability to break the law and mess up his life.

The two remaining police officers were taking statements from Virginia Webb and Mrs. Green. Bruno caught the police-woman observing him as he checked his watch again. She was just doing her job, but the interrogation process was robbing precious minutes from his mission to find Rollie before he could carry out his assignment.

A woman's high-pitched sobs several rows away captured everyone's attention. Her body was shaking as she lovingly touched a headstone. A man stood next to her, looking perplexed and peering down at his shoes as he placed a hand at the small of her back.

Mary pulled on Bruno's sleeve and guided him away from the questioning officers. Her serious features were locked tight. She made a point of turning her back to the others and lowering her voice to a whisper. He craned his head down close to her lips to better hear what she was saying. He could feel the warmth of Mary's breath on his cheek as he took in her intoxicating scent.

"You told us," Mary said, "that you came here to warn Virginia in person about Oliver Kane's retaliation scheme and the assassin he sent. I don't understand why you didn't share that information with the police." She started to aim a thumb at the officers, and then stopped in midair. "Unless you have a good reason for not informing the officers, your omission tells me you are full of crap."

"It wasn't an omission, Mary. I didn't disclose what I knew, on purpose. Did you happen to notice the policewoman eyeing me every time I looked at my watch or lifted my bag?"

"You can't be serious." Mary aimed her finger at his chest without touching him. "That is your explanation. A female cop thinks you're hot and is flirting with you? You obviously didn't leave that massive ego in Boston. Tell me, Mr. Romeo, what does a policewoman looking at you have anything to do with holding back information from the police?"

Bruno gritted his teeth. Mary had misconstrued what he meant about the female cop watching him. Was she taking out her frustrations on him? Or was her past so tainted she disliked all men?

"The officer is working a crime scene looking for viable answers," Bruno said. "In other words, she's trying to discern if a Boston private detective is somehow involved with the kidnapping perp from the same city. Or is it simply a coincidence?"

"Your explanation doesn't make sense." Mary gripped his forearm again. "My ex knew the only way I would go back to him is if he had Rachel. Honestly, he didn't want her. It's me he's after. But Larry has nothing to do with your Oliver Kane insanity."

"Exactly my point," Bruno said. "If the police knew about Kane, they would have a different take in how to proceed. The two cases could get intermingled and convoluted. My stay here is limited. Rather than answering more of their questions, my time can be better spent finding and dealing with Rollie. I also want to make sure Mrs. Green's house, Virginia's residence, and the Proffitt Advertising office are as secure as they can be before I leave." He cracked a smile. "You know, it sure would make my job a hell of a lot easier if you trusted me, Mary."

"You're asking me to trust you. I don't have great luck with men who ask me to trust them. The only exception has been Morgan Proffitt. He gave me reason to believe in him and in myself. He offered me a chance for a life I never thought possible. Rachel and I are really comfortable here." Mary released his forearm. "Then, boom, you pop into the picture to tell us we're in mortal danger from a person we don't even know, sending Rachel and me right back to square one. If you were above board with us, the police should be informed about this Rollie guy and what he's been sent to do."

"Tell the police what?" Bruno said. "Unlike your ex, who perpetrated multiple offenses and was caught in a criminal act seen by witnesses, Rollie hasn't committed any crimes - at least not here. There's nothing the police can do, their hands are tied. If Rollie strolled up to us right now to say hey, and if we informed the police why we think he is here, they might question him, but there'd be no arrest. The last thing we want is cops questioning Rollie. It would tip him off that we know he's here."

"I hadn't thought about it in that way." Mary gave a half shrug. "I get why you're reluctant to share what you know with the police. But what are we supposed to do? Go into a witness protection program? Run for the hills? Wait for Rollie to attack us? This is like being in a tunnel and the only light at the end is a high-speed train coming at us."

Bruno had an urge to put a comforting arm around Mary's shoulder and tell her everything would be okay, but thought she might take the gesture the wrong way. She had every right to be frightened. It could push her over the edge if she knew what Oliver Kane could do. Kane would stop at nothing if he believed someone had wronged him. When Kane gives an assignment, that person will pay a hefty price if the job isn't carried out to his expectations.

"I don't blame you for being scared, Mary," he said. "But this is no time to panic. There's a flipside. The one time I dealt with Rollie was in front of Kane Tower in Boston. I took him down by surprise. I can do the same thing if I can get out of here and find him."

Bruno doubted his words made Mary feel any better. He purposely left out one key factor about the incident with Rollie. He had shown Rollie he was armed with a gun.

"Aren't you the one who thought Rollie would be waiting for us at the cemetery?" Mary said. "That doesn't assure me about your ability to calculate someone's next move."

"How do you know Rollie isn't here watching us right now? Maybe he got spooked when the police came to take Larry away?"

"I don't know. What if you're wrong about locating Rollie? You can't be everywhere at once. Plus you're leaving soon." Mary's eyes welled up. "I have no way of protecting Rachel. What about Mrs. Green and Virginia? We're all vulnerable to an attack."

"Don't forget, Rollie doesn't know we're on to him," Bruno said. "Plus we have another advantage. Rollie has a thick body as well as head, thus making him predictable."

"Have you forgotten your promise to protect Rachel?" She looked endearingly at her daughter. "I don't have a great bullshit meter. If you meant what you said, you'll stay here and safeguard my daughter for as long as it takes? How about it, Mr. Santiago?"

Being addressed as Mr. Santiago by someone a few years younger felt weird. He meant every word of his vow to keep Rachel and her mother safe, but Mary added a provision to his original promise. She turned the last part of his pledge "as long as I'm here" into an indefinite period of time. Smart lady.

Bruno's breath caught when he glanced at Rachel. Her white dress and patent leather shoes left the impression she was attending a playmate's birthday party rather than a memorial at a cemetery. She held the hippo keychain Mr. Proffitt gave to her in one hand and Mrs. Green's hand in the other.

"You have my word I will stay here to ensure Rachel's safety until Rollie is detained. I don't know if that gives me license for you to trust me or not, but my word is sincere."

"At this point I have no choice but to trust you," she said, with a dismissive wave of her hand. "That doesn't mean I have to like you."

Whether Mary liked him or not was immaterial. He would safeguard her daughter for as long as it took; something he never got the opportunity to do for his own child.

The policewoman headed towards them at a fast pace. Did Mary's emotional outburst catch the officer's attention? Or had Virginia or Mrs. Green alerted the cop about Kane?

"Is there some kind of trouble here, ma'am?" The police-woman stood a few inches taller than Mary. "I noticed you became a bit riled when conversing with Mr. Santiago."

"One of Mr. Santiago's comments upset me," Mary said.

"And that would be. . .

"Mr. Santiago said I shouldn't worry about my ex-husband anymore. Other people told me the same thing when Larry was sent to prison. Look what happened today. He almost got my daughter. How can I not worry that won't happen again?"

"I hear you," the officer said. "You have every right to think that way. However, based on your ex's previous record and the current crimes he allegedly committed, he should be incarcerated for a long time, if not a lifetime." She focused on Bruno with a hand on her billy club. "You have the look of a man who is already late for his own wedding."

"I never got the chance to be late." Bruno reached for his cell phone in his coat pocket. "I need to call a cab. I'm running out of time for a meeting in San Francisco."

"I will drive you wherever you want to go, Mr. Santiago," Mary said.

"Hold on, sir," the officer said. "Sorry to keep you, but I have a few more questions. In your earlier statement, you said you came to the cemetery to pay your respects. I find it interesting that you and the alleged kidnapper are from Boston. Did you know him?"

"Never saw the man before in my life. I guess you can chalk it up to happenstance."

"Happenstance?" the officer repeated. "Here's what I'm trying to ascertain, sir. You are a private detective. By the looks of things, you're probably good at your job. If you didn't know this man or anything about him, what prompted you to chase after him?"

"If I was wearing your hat, I'd ask the same question. Your logic is good, officer. However, there is no Boston connection between the kidnapper and myself. As I said before, I'm a former Massachusetts State Trooper. Now I'm a private detective. Put my hat on: if you were off duty and saw a man in a dirty white t-shirt with long greasy hair and a prison tattoo on his neck running balls out towards three women and a child at a cemetery, what course of action would you have taken?"

"This isn't about me, sir. I'm just trying to put all the pieces together. Did you come here from the East Coast solely to attend the private memorial service?"

"Officer," Mary said. "Ms. Webb informed Mr. Santiago that we were having a memorial service for the late Morgan Proffitt. Proffitt Advertising has used Mr. Santiago's SOS Investigation services for years. Mr. Santiago was paying his respects to Mr. Proffitt."

"Are you also here on a case, sir?" the officer asked.

"Yes, hence the urgency for me to leave."

"Thank you, Mr. Santiago." The policewoman gave him her card with a smile. "Please call me if anything pertinent comes to mind. I hope you make your meeting on time."

"If I don't," Bruno said, lifting his travel bag, "there will be big consequences to pay."

CHAPTER ELEVEN

From the passenger seat, Bruno took a quick look at the Mercedes' dashboard speedometer and cringed. He was sitting in what was often referred to as the death seat. He wouldn't admit it out loud, but Mary was scaring the hell out of him by speeding and weaving between cars on their short drive from the Colma cemetery to Mrs. Green's house in San Francisco. Mary's driving brought him back to the streets of Boston where survival was for the fittest drivers and pedestrians alike.

Bruno pulled on his seatbelt to ensure it was securely fastened. From the backseat, Mrs. Green and Rachel didn't seem bothered by the urgency of Mary's driving. So far, he had won over Virginia and Rachel's support. Mary seemed to tolerate his presence for Rachel's sake. Mrs. Green continued to blame him for Morgan Proffitt's death. He was batting five hundred; a great baseball stat, but a bad percentage as an approval rating.

Before they left the cemetery, Virginia alerted the entire Proffitt Advertising staff their downtown office was off limits until it was deemed safe for them to return. She learned how difficult it is to make believers out of an unbelievable situation. Would she take her own advice and stay away from the office?

Bruno's hand stayed glued to the dashboard. Mary didn't seem to notice. Perhaps she was used to nervous front seat passengers doing the hand thing. The Mercedes sped past a San Francisco city limit population sign. Mary zoomed by the sign so fast he couldn't read all of the numbers - possibly it was three million and something. She made a sudden left turn without slowing down, making her passengers sway to the right.

"I read somewhere San Francisco and Boston are a lot alike," Bruno said to Mary, hoping conversation would make her slow down. "What part of Boston did you live in?"

"I moved around a lot." Mary passed a slow moving van. "Mostly on the South Side."

"What prompted you to leave Boston?" Bruno learned she could drive fast and converse.

"Morgan Proffitt recommended me to Virginia for a job at the advertising firm a year ago to the day. It's my dream job. I've learned so much from Virginia. She's the only employer that has allowed me the autonomy to be creative. I'm the in-house graphic artist, account executive, backup secretary, receptionist, janitor . . . you name it."

"Ad biz people must do pretty well to afford such nice rides," Bruno said. "Virginia left the cemetery in a BMW and you're driving a Mercedes."

"If you saw the car I left in Boston, you'd have a different impression. The Benz belongs to Mrs. Green, but she doesn't drive. Guess I should add chauffeur to my resume."

"Why would Mrs. Green have an expensive car and not drive it?"

"Not that it's any of your business, Mr. Santiago," Mrs. Green said, "Mr. Proffitt left me his car as well as his house. There isn't a day that goes by that I don't miss the Proffitt family. Before he passed, Mr. Proffitt had the foresight to send Mary and Rachel to me. I'm so blessed to have them in my life."

"Rachel and I are the ones who are blessed, Mrs. Green. I don't know what we would do without you." Mary made a sharp right turn and chuckled. "I'm told Mo abandoned the Mercedes before catching his flight to Boston. I'm not sure why. Maybe he didn't have time to park the car in the long-term parking lot? Anyway, the authorities impounded the Mercedes. So, Mo's gift to Mrs. Green came with a price. She had to pay a fine to get the Mercedes out of impound."

The Mercedes entered a posh area of well-maintained older homes. It reminded Bruno of the Beacon Hill area in Boston where Oliver Kane lived. The only way Bruno could afford a house in this neighborhood would be to win the lottery. Crime must be minimal here. He didn't see one house with bars over the windows, but that wouldn't stop Rollie from carrying out his mission. On the contrary, it would only encourage him.

Mary removed her foot from the gas pedal and coasted at the same pace of the walking mailman. She pointed to a two-story white house three doors down, on the corner.

"Park across the street from Mrs. Green's house, Mary." Bruno detached his seatbelt.

"Why?" Mary had a puzzled expression. "I park mostly in the garage or in the driveway."

"From this point on, you have to trust my judgment until I consider Mrs. Green's house safe and secure." Bruno raised his voice and backed it up with a serious look until Mary pulled the Mercedes to the curb. "Everyone stay in the car until I check out the entire exterior of the house."

"Let's get something straight, Mr. Santiago," Mrs. Green said, unbuckling her seatbelt and opening her door. "It's my house and I'll enter it anytime I please. Thank you."

"I realize you're used to giving the orders, Mrs. Green, but this time you need to do what I say." He glared at her until she closed the door. "Thank you. Is Morgan Proffitt's name and address still listed in the current San Francisco phone book?"

"Yes. I preferred to keep it in Mr. Proffitt's name, rather than mine, as a safety measure."

"That was smart," Bruno said. "Is there an alarm system?"

"Yes. I always turn the alarm on before we leave."

"Do you have any nosy neighbors with hair-trigger cell phones dialed into the police if they were to see a stranger snooping around your front and backyard?"

"The backyard is fenced all the way around. This is a very respectable neighborhood, Mr. Santiago. The neighbors might call the police if they see a suspicious character like you."

Bruno exited from the front passenger seat. The overcast sky had evaporated, replaced by a light blue background with disconnected white clouds. A steady wind made his eyes water. He cupped a hand to his forehead to shield the sun's glare and studied the layout of the property. From his angle, the sculptured lawn made a sharp veer to the left around the corner. A girl's blue bike was parked on the porch, by the front door.

Bruno moved to the driver's side prompting Mary to roll down the window. Mrs. Green and Mary displayed grumpy faces after being told he was in charge. Rachel was captivated in a make-believe world, bouncing her hippo on her knee.

"Are there any animals I should be concerned about?" Bruno asked.

"We don't have any pets," Mary said, "If Rachel had her way, we'd have a puppy."

"It's not fair." Rachel produced a pouty lower lip. "I'm old enough to take care of it. And Mrs. Green said it would be okay with her."

"Count me in on you getting a puppy, Rachel." Bruno smiled.

"Thanks a lot, Mr. Santiago," Mary said. "No wonder my daughter likes you. Go through the gate on the left to check the back and side yards. There's no gate on the other side."

Bruno stepped towards the house, then jumped back. His backside slammed hard against the Mercedes driver's side door to avoid a speeding car. The car whizzed past him without braking. Bruno blew out the breath he'd been holding. He was almost California roadkill. Age may have robbed him of his extra running gear, but his reflexes were still intact.

"Are you okay?" Mary asked. "Oh my God, was that Rollie trying to run you over?"

"Rollie's face also flashed in my mind too, before I spotted who was behind the steering wheel: a blond teenage boy driving a souped-up black Mustang. Hell, the kid's driving a nicer car than I do." Bruno glanced at Mrs. Green. "I'm surprised you or your neighbors haven't complained about him. The only way that punk is going to slow down is when the police cite him for reckless driving or if he gets into an accident."

"We've complained several times, but the police haven't been able to catch him," Mrs. Green said. "It's like he's playing a dangerous game of cat and mouse."

"A game that can kill the cat and the mouse." Bruno pointed at a pair of cars parked on the same side of the street. "Before I check out the house, I want to take a look at those cars."

The blue Toyota had a child's car seat in the back. The other car, a Lexus, was sporting a San Francisco parking lot decal on its front bumper. They were local cars that Rollie wouldn't be driving. Rollie could have parked a rental car around the block or he may have hired a cab. The best-case scenario would be if Rollie never made it to California.

Bruno tested the house's front door and windows, then checked the attached garage. He followed a paved path leading to the gate and shook it before pulling the chain attached to the lock that propelled it to swing open. He entered the backyard and closed the gate. The yard was well-landscaped with different colored flowers and various trimmed bushes outlining a low-cut lawn. He noticed a swing set at the far end and imagined Rachel pumping her little legs on the swings or playing with a puppy. The cement patio was furnished with lounge chairs, a round metal table with an umbrella, and a barbeque protected by a canvass cover. It was sixty-two degrees according to the outdoor thermometer hanging on the wall.

Bruno didn't have to stand on his toes to peek into neighbor's yards. Nothing looked out of the ordinary. He inspected the windows and two doors, then turned the corner. He moved down an unpaved path on the other side of the house. There were visible shoe prints in the soft dirt that were too large to be those of a woman or child. He doubted the prints came from Morgan Proffitt. The last time Proffitt walked this property was a year ago. Maybe Mrs. Green had a gardener or a window washer. The last window he tried slid open easily, but the alarm never sounded. Either the security system had been sabotaged or the alarm had never been set.

Bruno stepped back and reached for his gun. Damn. He pushed aside the drapes and hoisted himself headfirst inside a dark room. He landed on a cushiony carpet and waited several seconds to navigate his way to the light switch by the doorway. There was no mistaking the room he occupied was a den. A large mahogany desk housed a computer and keyboard. The matching credenza top behind the desk held awards, pictures, and mementos. There was no dust on the furniture. A high-back executive chair meant for a tall person was positioned on a plastic floor mat in between the desk and credenza. The leather couch against the side wall looked comfortable. Hanging above the couch was a painting of Boston's Fenway Park. Morgan Proffitt must have been a baseball fan. Bruno retraced his steps and found bits of soil. The dirt could have come from him and not Rollie. Yet, if Rollie had entered the house, it was through this room.

Bruno left what appeared to be Proffitt's study to inspect the kitchen and adjoining laundry room. He opened the pantry door to find it well stocked with bottles, cans, and boxes. He found a bedroom off the kitchen with photos on the dresser of the three Proffitts, and another with Mary and Rachel. A small TV took up space on the opposite wall. This must be Mrs. Green's room. There was no place to hide in the dining room, guest bathroom, and living room. Mrs. Green kept a tidy house. The dirt on the study's carpet came after they left for the cemetery. Aside from the soil, there were no signs or sounds confirming Rollie had entered the house.

Bruno stepped slowly up the stairs. At the foot of the landing, he saw a child's bedroom decorated in purple and a herd of stuffed animals on the bedspread. Perhaps this had been Katie's room and was now Rachel's. He caught the scent of lavender. The bedroom had several framed ink sketches of Rachel on the walls. They were quite good. The next room must be Mary's room. He checked the bathroom, then the closet. She wasn't a clothes-horse. If Rollie was in the house, the only place he could be hiding in was the master bedroom. A slight creak sounded when he stepped onto the brown carpet. The closet and bathroom doors were closed. The other doors had been open. Adrenaline bees buzzed inside of him. Would Rollie hide in the bathroom or the closet? He opened the bathroom door and rushed in, ready to do battle. The only hiding place would be the shower, but there wasn't a large body behind a cloudy glass door. The back of his hand wiped sweat from his brow. A shower would be nice right now.

Bruno backed out of the bathroom and placed a hand on the cold closet doorknob. He pulled the door slowly, stared into the darkness, and waited for Rollie to jump out. A scent of tobacco alerted his nose sensors. Was Proffitt a smoker?

"I've got a gun with a hair-trigger, Rollie," Bruno said. "It's small in size, but just as deadly. Last chance for you to come out with your hands on top of your head. I'll give you the count of three. After that, if I see any movement or hear a sound, I'm pulling the trigger. Okay, you've been properly warned. One . . . two . . . three . . ."

Bruno emitted a self-conscious laugh. His gun forefinger went limp like a wet match. His dramatic warning had gone for naught. Mrs. Green and Mary would have had a good laugh if they'd witnessed his finger bluff.

Bruno reached for the closet light switch on the left and wished he hadn't.

CHAPTER TWELVE

Bruno's left arm recoiled from excruciating pain. The word that shrieked from his mouth would never be found in an English dictionary or any dictionary. He backpedaled away from the closet, unsure what had happened.

The red stain on his jacket sleeve was growing. His arm dropped down numb and lifeless by his side. Drops of blood leaked onto the bedroom rug. His breathing became shallow. Lightheadedness made him nauseous. He didn't need a roadside sign to realize he was entering a state of shock.

Rollie burst from the closet snarling like a wild animal and swinging a knife with a bloodied six-inch blade. His face looked like a clenched fist. From head to toe he was wearing a perfect outfit for a man trying to conceal himself in a darkened closet: black shoes, black pants, black sweatshirt, and a navy-blue stocking cap.

Bruno backed into a chest of drawers attempting to stay as far away from the blade as possible. Scent of tobacco emitted from the man trying to kill him. The knife attack had been soundless, but he doubted it was Rollie's first choice of weapons. Like Bruno, Rollie must have left his gun back in Boston to get past airport security without a hassle. As it turned out, it was a positive for Rollie and potentially the obituaries for Bruno.

"What's the matter, tough guy?" Rollie barked, moving towards Bruno while raising the knife higher. "Did your finger-gun run out of bullets? After I cut you to pieces, I'll do the old lady, and then the advertising broad."

Bruno slid away from the dresser with knowledge of Rollie's to-do kill list agenda. Did Rollie mean Virginia or Mary - or both? Bruno was surprised Rollie didn't recognize him from their first encounter in front of Kane Tower. Bruno had waited in the shadows and disarmed Rollie to provide protection for Mr. Proffitt on his mission to eliminate Kane.

Bruno inched back. Rollie raised the knife, pointing the tip down at Bruno's chest. Bruno had one good arm to protect himself. The reality of impending death was like a blast of oxygen to clear his head. Rollie plunged the knife downward. Bruno blocked the stab with a right forearm, knocking Rollie off balance. Bruno grabbed Rollie's wrist to keep the knife at bay. Rollie was strong, but Bruno matched the goon's strength. Rollie landed a punch to Bruno's temple. The blow rocked him. Bruno shook his head and tried to blink away the cobwebs. If he kept playing defense, Rollie would eventually wear him down.

Bruno retaliated by sending a knee into Rollie's crotch, depreciating much of the thug's family jewels. Rollie screamed in pain and struck back by smashing his fist into Bruno's head again.

Bruno lost his grip on Rollie's wrist. Rollie's lips spread into an ugly smirk . . .

A golf club struck Rollie across the face creating a "thwack" sound. Blood sprayed from Rollie's nose. Mrs. Green followed with another strike. Rollie made a swipe at the golf club and missed. He covered his nose with his fingers. Bruno took advantage by shoving Rollie back towards the closet. He banged Rollie's knife hand against the door frame.

"Run, Mrs. Green, before you get hurt," Bruno said. "Call the police. Go now."

Bruno could hear Mrs. Green's pounding footsteps leave the bedroom until the sounds faded away. She had gone against his orders. In doing so, she had saved his life. Bruno kept slamming Rollie's hand against the door frame until a portion of the wood smeared red. Rollie managed to throw a wild punch that grazed Bruno's cheek. It didn't deter Bruno from attacking Rollie's knife hand. The knife finally fell to the floor. Rollie dove for the weapon, leaving an opening for Bruno to stomp on Rollie's wounded hand. Rollie tried to defend himself until Bruno's shoe found Rollie's head.

Bruno retrieved the knife. Rollie's eyes widened in fear. In a matter of seconds their roles had reversed. Bruno, the heavy underdog, was now the favorite. Rollie rolled away from Bruno and labored to his feet. He hustled to the bedroom doorway.

Bruno chased after him holding the knife. Rollie scurried into the hall, then down the stairs. Bruno's useless left arm was slowing him down. A wave of dizziness made it difficult to navigate down the stairs without stumbling. He tried to suck in as much air as he could to keep from passing out. His strength was ebbing by the second.

Rollie landed on the first floor with a leap, fiddled with the lock, threw open the front door, and raced away from the house. By the time Bruno exited through the open door, Rollie was in the middle of the street heading towards the Mercedes. Bruno was pushing himself to the limit, but slowing down and losing ground to Rollie.

Rollie lengthened his lead. Mary left the safety of the car. She motioned a frantic finger at Bruno and shouted for his attention. If Rollie had staked out Mrs. Green's house before they left for the cemetery, he'd recognize the Mercedes. Mary and Rachel were in peril.

"Bruno! Bruno," Mary shouted, still motioning with a finger. "Look behind you."

Bruno turned his head in time to see a rocketing black car zeroing in on him. He dove for the curb. Squealing brakes created foul-smelling burning rubber to fill the air.

"It's Rollie." Bruno hollered. He tried to get to his feet and tumbled back down to the pavement. "Mary, get back in the car."

Mary jumped into the driver's seat and slammed the door shut as Rollie ran past the Mercedes. A blasting horn made him look over his shoulder. His mouth gaped open. The Mustang slammed into Rollie, throwing him forward in the air. He landed on the asphalt face down and motionless. A sickening thump, thump sounded. The Mustang couldn't stop in time before running over Rollie's maimed body.

Bruno managed to get to his feet, but was having trouble staying upright. The Mustang screeched to a stop. A portion of the front hood was crushed into a V. Neighbors on both sides of the street filed from their houses. The blond teenage driver bounded from the car holding a hand on his stomach. A greasy, stained, fast-food bag rolled off the seat behind him and onto the street where he soon lost his tacos.

Sirens rang out from a distance as Mary ran to Bruno. He placed his right arm around her shoulder to keep from falling back onto the pavement. Everything was whirling . . .

"Oh my God, Bruno, you're bleeding," Mary exclaimed, turning to a crowd that gathered on the sidewalks. "Someone call 9-1-1. He's been badly hurt and needs an ambulance."

"Is Rachel okay?" he huffed out. "Did she see what happened?"

"I told her to get on the floorboard. She didn't see anything. What did Rollie do to you?"

"As long as you and Rachel are safe," Bruno said. "I made good my promise this time."

Bruno's world went dark.

CHAPTER THIRTEEN

Bruno could hear voices in the background. He'd probably fallen asleep with the TV on. His eyelids seemed to be glued shut. Swallowing was difficult. His throat and mouth were as dry as a cracked desert floor. Something was wrapped tightly around his left arm. He moved his legs around under the covers to make sure they were functioning properly. If he was in the midst of a dream, this would be one reverie he'd want to forget after waking up.

He lifted his head from the pillow and regretted it. His head settled back onto the pillow. Soft fingers seized his right hand. The skin-on-skin connection had a calming effect. Maybe this dream would be worth remembering . . .

"Bruno," a familiar voice said. "Bruno, you need to wake up. Open your eyes."

One of his eyelids crept open, then the other. Mary was holding his hand. A taller Virginia stood next to Mary. Was he still in a state of sleep or was he awake? He tried to keep his stinging eyes open and failed. If Mary was holding his hand it had to be a dream.

"Bruno." Mary gave his hand a gentle squeeze. Her tone was more urgent and louder. "Wake up. Come on, open your eyes, Bruno."

"Okay. Okay." Bruno's voice sounded like it came from a stranger. He blinked several times until images of the two faces looking down at him came into focus. "Where the hell am I? Why are you holding my hand, Mary? Not that I mind."

"You're in a San Francisco hospital," Mary answered. "You passed out. Probably because you lost a lot of blood. You've got a concussion when you fell on the concrete. The nurses keep waking you up, but you keep dozing off. They want you to stay awake so they can monitor you."

"My head feels like it's being squeezed in a vise." The room's overhead lights weren't turned on, but sunshine through the window made Bruno squint. "What time is it? How long have I been here?"

"You were admitted yesterday," Virginia said. "It's half past four in the afternoon. Rollie stabbed your forearm near your wrist. You needed a blood transfusion. The doctor who stitched you up told us you were fortunate the blade didn't sever a tendon, a major artery, or bone. But there's a chance that you may experience numbness and weakness in your palm and fingers if there's nerve damage. Overall, Mr. Santiago, you are probably a very lucky guy."

Lucky wasn't a word he would have chosen at the moment. He wiggled his fingers on his left hand. The effort produced more pain. Was the throbbing sensation he was experiencing a good sign. Maybe he wouldn't have numbness or a lack of feeling from nerve damage? His tongue slithered over dry lips. He could hear himself swallow. Mary released his fingers and placed a paper cup with a straw in his hand. He raised his head with difficulty. Mary guided the straw to his mouth. He managed several sips of water, and handed the cup back to her.

"The last thing I remember is running from the house chasing after Rollie in the street," he said. "Did he get away?"

"Mary says you dove toward the curb at the last second to avoid a speeding car." Virginia gave Mary a soft elbow jab. "Rollie never looked back until it was too late. He kept running to get away from you, probably because you were holding his knife. The car couldn't stop in time and ran over him."

"Rollie's dead?" A wave of dizziness brought on a bout of nausea when Bruno raised his head again.

"Mrs. Green called the police, but Rollie was dead before they arrived," Mary said. "You caught Rollie inside the house and fought with him. If it wasn't for you, Bruno, Mrs. Green, Rachel, and I would have been alone with that killer. You saved our lives."

"It was Mrs. Green who saved the day. Rollie stabbed me and was about to finish the job when she bashed him with a golf club. She gave me a chance to take away the knife." His eyes blinked at a furious pace trying to clear his head. "Could you close the blinds?"

"Mr. Santiago, do you feel well enough to tell us how Rollie broke into the house?" Virginia asked, after closing the blinds. "Mary answered the questions from the police as best she could. What transpired inside the house?"

"I got in through the study window, but the security alarm didn't go off. Bruno closed his tired eyes for a few seconds. "The last room I checked was the master bedroom. Rollie was in the closet and stabbed my arm. He said after he killed me, he would eliminate you, Virginia, and Mrs. Green."

"Did I hear my name mentioned?" Mrs. Green entered the room with Rachel.

Bruno grimaced. Was Mrs. Green going to hammer him again about Mr. Proffitt's death? Or boast about saving his bacon against Rollie?

"I'm sorry you got hurt, Mr. Bruno," Rachel said softly. "Are you going to die?"

"No, Rachel, I'll be fine." He managed a smile. "And seeing your sweet face is the best medicine of all."

Rachel's presence did make him feel better. But his flattering remark caused her cheeks to turn crimson. She hesitated, moved to the bed, and handed him her hippo keychain. He cleared his throat, trying to dislodge a golf ball-sized lump.

"Thank you, Rachel, that's the nicest thing anyone has ever done for me. But I can't take her from you. Mr. Proffitt wanted you to always have Hope." Bruno's heart sank after disappointment registered in Rachel's blue eyes. "So, maybe we can negotiate?"

"What does gotiate mean?' she asked.

"Negotiate means you and I will discuss reaching an agreement that will make both of us happy. You're a very wise little lady, Rachel. You knew I could use Hope. Would you be willing to lend Hope to me so she can work her magic until I get out of the hospital, and then I will return her back to you?"

"Hmm." She pursed her lips and peered up at the ceiling. "You mean we can share her."

"Sharing Hope is exactly what I mean. Do we have a deal?"

Rachel looked at her mother and Mrs. Green. They nodded their approval. So did Rachel.

"Does anyone know when I can get out of here?" he asked.

"They might release you tomorrow," Mary said. "It depends on how bad your concussion is. But the doctor also said you shouldn't be flying for a while."

"I wish to say something." Mrs. Green stepped closer to the bed and placed both hands on her hips. "When you are released from the hospital, Mr. Santiago, you will recuperate at my house for as long as it takes. Thank you."

The room went quiet. Was that an order? Bruno could picture Mrs. Green as a sergeant in the Women's Army Corps earlier in her life. What had changed her mind about him? A question he would rather ask some other time.

"Thank you, Mrs. Green. That's very nice of you, but I should get back to Boston."

"Mr. Santiago, this isn't a negotiation with a child. You will stay at my house for as long as it takes for you to recover. I will be in charge of your care." She put a few strands of Rachel's auburn hair back in place. "Now that's settled, Rachel and I will wait outside."

"Hold on, Mrs. Green, one last thing." Virginia put her hands together and pointed them at Bruno. "When you are well enough, Mr. Santiago, would you be so kind as to make sure all of our homes and the Proffitt Advertising office are secure. We can discuss your compensation at a later time."

"That's a very generous offer, Virginia, but I don't think I will be much good for awhile."

"Please say yes," Virginia said, "otherwise I will sic Mrs. Green on you."

Everyone laughed, except Mrs. Green. She led Rachel from the room with Virginia following close behind. Mary made no attempt to leave. She waited until they were out of listening range before pulling the only chair in the room close to the bed.

"I know you're hurting, so I won't take long," Mary said. "We need to talk."

"If this is about Rachel giving me her hippo keychain, I probably blew it. I've never had the pleasure of being a parent. I think you've done a great job of raising her. She's a terrific kid. She knew what to do, but she wanted your approval as well as Mrs. Green's. You seem to have had rough patches in your life, but you should be proud of your daughter. And you should be proud of being a damn good mother."

"There are some things you don't know about me, but thank you." Mary looked past him as if she was in another world. "You were right. This is about Rachel and something else. You handled Rachel and the keychain perfectly. It's just that she's never been around many men before, but she's really taken to you. She even stuck up for you when I didn't. The problem is . . . the longer you're here, the more attached she will get to you."

"I admit to a soft spot in my heart for her. Is that a bad thing?"

"No, of course not. But what's going to happen when you leave?"

"I get why you're concerned, Mary. But isn't it possible that having an adult male presence in her life, even if it is for a short time, may have a positive affect on her? It's something to consider."

"Since that has never happened, I'm more fearful of negative repercussions."

"I understand. Especially when you are wary about a man you distrust and dislike."

"It's my prerogative to change my mind. I don't distrust or dislike you. After all, what would have happened to us if you didn't take the initiative to come here?"

"Would I be going out on a limb by saying you like me?"

"Don't push it, Columbo."

"I have a feeling there's something else you wanted to discuss with me?"

"This isn't over, is it?" Mary's features creased somber. "When Oliver Kane learns the man he sent is dead, he'll hire another person to finish what Rollie couldn't. It's even worse than before. You won't have inside information to warn us who is coming and when, ahead of time. Plus, you're in no shape to provide protection."

"Now I know where your daughter gets her smarts," Bruno said. "I won't lie to you, Mary. Kane won't give up his vow of revenge until it's carried out. Rollie's screw-up isn't going to sit well with Kane. He probably sent his full-time bodyguard since he can't afford a professional assassin. I doubt Kane knows Rollie is dead. Or that the mission wasn't fulfilled. It should give me time to come up with a strategy to take Kane out."

"When you say take Kane out, do you mean kill him? Would you actually kill him?"

"The thought has crossed my mind hundreds of times." Adrenaline was serving Bruno as a painkiller. "In lieu of murdering the son of a bitch, I'd like Kane to disintegrate on his own or for someone else to take him out. I have pieces of a scheme floating around in my head, but I haven't yet put all of them together. There's one thing I know for sure. The timing to get to Oliver Kane couldn't be better. His world is crumbling before him. And now he doesn't have Rollie to protect him or do his dirty work. If I wait for him to get back onto his feet, I may never get another chance like this."

"I understand now why Mo's dying wish was to eliminate Oliver Kane. If there is anything I can do to help you, Bruno, I'm in. It's my way of thanking Mo for literally saving my life. He believed in me. He knew I'd flourish under Virginia's guidance. He knew sending Rachel and me to Mrs. Green was the best medicine for all of us." Mary rose from the chair. "And maybe, just maybe, Mo somehow knew you would finish his mission of eliminating Kane."

CHAPTER FOURTEEN

The poker Gods were blessing Oliver Kane at his Thursday night Texas Hold 'Em game at the WMC. He leaned back in seat six as smug as a student with a cheat sheet of answers before the test. Different colored poker chips stacked in front of him amounted to over five-thousand dollars. The dollar total wouldn't put a dent into what he owed his creditors, but he would go home a winner with a pocket full of cash.

"Gentlemen, the bar will be closing in a few minutes," the attractive, dark-haired drink runner announced. Every eye at the table including the dealer zeroed in on her impressive cleavage. "Last call if you want a drink."

"You bet." Kane pointed at his empty glass. "Johnny Walker Black. Make it a double."

Normally he'd have only one drink when he was gambling, but his unexpected roll of luck tonight created a thirst to celebrate. The cab driver who delivered him earlier should be parked in front. By hiring a taxi, the DUI Doctor could never be stopped for operating a vehicle under the influence.

The dealer shuffled the cards. Kane was puzzled by his ability to outsmart players in a courtroom, but not players at a poker table. Circumventing the law into victories for his clients was a hundred times more difficult than winning at Texas Hold 'Em. So why did he lose most of the time? Did he lack the ability to understand the subtleties of a simple game like Hold 'Em? Highly unlikely. Maybe he had a "tell" the other players knew about? Again, that would be highly unlikely. He always brought his courtroom face to the poker table. It had to be sheer bad luck rather than lack of skill or smarts that determined his pileup of losses. Perhaps this was the beginning of a winning streak; a streak that could have a positive effect on his fortunes? John Madden, pro football coach and TV color commentator had the right idea when he said, "winning is the best deodorant of all." For Kane, it's like being injected with a shot of optimism . . .

"Here you go." The drink runner nudged her hip into his arm as she placed his scotch down on a small serving table. "Is there anything else I can do for you, Mr. Kane?"

Kane had to stop himself from grinning. Her name didn't come to mind, but he couldn't forget that she had been nails in bed only a few weeks ago.

"What's the matter, Ollie?" Big Tony in seat two puffed on a horrible smelling cigar that was as round as a cucumber. "Did ya glue together them happy chips down all the way to the green felt? I've never seen you play so tight."

The players laughed at Kane's expense, including Sid Parker the club manager. Kane kept a poker face. Very few people got away with calling him Ollie. He had been blessed with two God-given gifts: women gravitated to his handsome face and he was the smartest person in any room - especially a courtroom. Let them laugh. There wasn't one man here who would throw him a life preserver if he was drowning. He had been a social out-cast ever since the death of his parents, shuffling from one foster home to another. He was a loner who never had a best friend. Most school kids thought he was conceited, yet they'd come to him if they needed help with homework or an upcoming test. It's no different now. Folks tolerated the DUI Doctor because some-day they might need his services. He was like legal life insurance.

"Big Tony," Kane said, folding his arms across his chest. "I'm surprised you are aware of what playing tight is since you play about as tight as a reformed whore."

Big Tony chuckled. He loved to talk smack to the players knowing none of them would respond in kind. Kane could never tell if Big Tony was ahead or on tilt by his disposition or the tint of his cheeks. Big Tony won big or lost big, but his demeanor always stayed the same. He loved the game of Hold 'Em and played every hand, which made him a tough player to read.

Kane was careful how he jived back at Big Tony, although he'd never seen the large fellow get pissed off at anyone. In essence, Kane had a license of leeway ever since he saved Big

Tony's younger sister, Big Teresa, from going to jail after she was in a three-car accident while being smashed two times over the legal blood alcohol level limit. It was no secret Big Tony was well-connected to the Mafia. No one knew what he did for the mob, and no one dared to ask. Nor did anyone complain about Big Tony's stinky cigar smoke clouds lingering in the poker room. Kane couldn't have cared less about Big Tony's underworld activities. The only thing that mattered to him was to stay on the good side of the six-foot eight, 300-pound mobster. Big Tony owed him a huge favor and Kane knew he might have to collect on it sooner rather than later.

"Gentlemen, it's 11:58," Sid Parker announced. "This will be the last hand dealt before quitting time."

Kane confirmed the correctness of the time on the wall clock. The dealer finished shuffling and waited for players to ante up. Several players began to organize their chips into stacks that fit snug into plastic racks, making it easier to cash out. The game officially ended at midnight. No hand would be dealt after twelve, no exceptions.

Sid was officially the club's general manager. He was also the unofficial poker game judge and jury for any disputes. His rulings were final. Sid served as the banker, too. He converted players' cash into chips before the game and handled buy-ins during the game. After the last hand, Sid exchanged the chips back into cash.

Kane gave Sid a hard look. The general manager either didn't notice or care. When Kane first entered the poker room, Sid had approached him about being three months behind with his club dues. Kane didn't show any emotion, but the debt reminder pushed another loathing pin into Sid's voodoo doll. Last year, Kane eliminated Sid from his Christmas card list and added him to his shit list when Sid ruled against him on a huge pot. Kane believed Sid's judgment was influenced by cronyism rather than the rules. Kane never expressed his resentment to Sid. Why give the son of a bitch another reason to rule against him? He'd considered sending Sid a message through Rollie, but that would've scared Sid away and terminated the Thursday night poker games. The club's board of directors turned a blind eye to the weekly high-stakes poker game being played in one of their activity rooms. The club's honchos knew Sid was getting a piece of the poker action. The poker group was a club within the club on the Q.T.

Sid stood behind Kane holding a stack of plastic chip racks to pass to each player when the last hand concluded. The dealer distributed two cards face down to each player. The rest of the cards would be dealt face up in the middle of the table. Kane intended to push his cards towards the dealer without looking, and then changed his mind. He took a quick peek and found two tens. Not a great hand, but a hand he'd typically play. Fold or play? His internal debate irritated the players who liked to play fast. Kane reluctantly slid his cards face down to the dealer, silently praising himself for being disciplined. Once the dealer touched his discards, his hand was automatically dead.

Kane waved away some of Big Tony's stinky cigar smoke. If only he could show the same restraint with his personal and business finances. Creditor phone calls and letters were mounting up. Just as troubling, the one person he'd been anxiously waiting to hear from was missing in action. Rollie hadn't checked in and wasn't answering his cell phone. Normally, his bodyguard would provide regular unsophisticated updates. Did Rollie complete the mission? Maybe the dumbshit got in some kind of trouble. If anyone could screw up a plan, it would be Rollie. Or maybe Rollie was fed up with being put down by his boss and found another gig. Rollie's absence irritated Kane to no end.

Sid placed a rack onto the table next to Kane, the only player who folded. He began stacking his chips into the rack and noticed heavy betting from the rest of the players before the flop. Some were probably betting on their two powerful hole cards. Others were attempting to get back some of their losses, hoping for a dumb luck win on the last hand. For once, he had the wherewithal to forgo a hand that might have taken away a good portion of his winnings.

The dealer turned over the flop; three exposed cards that played for all who were in the hand. When Kane noticed the cards in the middle of the table, the chips he was transferring to a plastic rack fell to the carpet. He thought his heart might stop beating. The dealer had turned over a seven of clubs, ten of hearts, and ten of spades. His two hole cards had been the other two tens. If he had played instead of folding, he would have had four of a kind. Only three other hands could have beaten him - a higher four of a kind, a straight flush, or a royal flush. The betting was heavy again. None of the players seemed to notice Kane bending down to pick up his chips off the floor. The next two cards the dealer exposed were the two of hearts and three of clubs. There was no way Kane could have lost. Even worse, the hand that won the enormous pot was a full house - three sevens over two tens. Kane had been on a roll the entire night. He should have played. The pot would have more than doubled the value of his chips.

Kane's fingers were shaking when he inserted the chips into the rack. Acid burning the lining of his stomach had risen to his throat. He swallowed at a furious pace, fearing he might toss his cookies. What was happening to his decision making? The old Oliver Kane would have played a pair of tens without a single thought. And what about Rollie? Had he screwed up by sending a street punk like Rollie to deal with the Proffitt matter? He should have hired a professional. If Rollie was in trouble, would it come back to him?

Sid peeled off fifty-three hundred-dollar bills in front of Kane. The bundle was about a half inch thick. Kane pocketed the Benjamins. He couldn't bring himself to say thank you to Sid. Courtesy was never one of his strong suits, especially now.

"Ollie," Big Tony said, pointing his cigar at Kane. "You look like a man who just swallowed a wad of chewing tobacco." His body shook with laughter. "Are ya feelin' raunchy, dude? Do you need a medical doctor to attend to the famous DUI Doctor?"

Big Tony's cutting taunt blindsided Kane. Did he look as bad as he felt? He was in no mood to be mocked by any of the players, particularly Big Tony, who had won the last hand.

"A case of heartburn, Big Tony," Kane spit out. "Or maybe it's the stench from that friggin' stogie between your fat lips."

Whoa. The room went silent. Kane held his breath. Big Tony threw him a menacing scowl that would scare the shit out of the Grim Reaper. Kane had crossed a line.

"Listen, Big Tony, I'm really sorry." Kane offered a sheepish smile and put a palm on his chest. "I was just kidding. The heart-burn must've given me a case of agita."

It took several painful seconds for Big Tony to accept Kane's apology with a nod. Kane had overstepped his bounds with the big guy, but he couldn't afford to pussy-foot around anymore with his life. He didn't become the DUI Doctor by being timid. His hourglass was down to its last grains of sand to escape the money crunch of debt. If it meant going against the odds to venture into an irrational, yet potentially profitable big deal, he'd be more than open to the risk. His problems couldn't get much worse. Or could they?

CHAPTER FIFTEEN

Wife number three didn't stir after Kane climbed into bed when he got home from the poker game. The former beauty queen's soft snore hinted she was amongst the living and under the influence of sleeping pills. Their marriage was as unresponsive as his lifeless wife, but a divorce at the present time would put him deeper in debt.

His wife didn't budge when he left their bed the next morning. She would probably accuse him of being out all night and never coming home. He would rather do battle with a judge or an opposing attorney in court than wrangle with his wife. The results often turned out to be like a hung jury.

After Kane showered and dressed, he waited on the front porch for a taxi to take him to his downtown Boston office. He'd never once sat behind a steering wheel. His bodyguard Rollie usually chauffeured him in the Jaguar sitting in the garage. But Rollie was still nowhere to be found. Plus, the Jag was days away from being repossessed. For a moment, he considered rousing his sleeping drug-saturated wife to drive him. But how would it look if a cop stopped this bleary-eyed, groggy woman with her DUI Doctor husband sitting in the passenger seat? It was more prudent to call for a taxi before his wife woke up and the bickering began.

"Where you go," the driver asked when Kane entered the taxi's backseat.

"Two . . . four . . . High . . . Street," Kane announced, as if he was talking to a child.

The cabbie turned to Kane with squinting eyes, and palms up, shaking his head."

"Kane Tower, you fucking idiot," Kane shouted. "Kane Tower, 24 High Street."

The driver's head bobbed up and down as if he understood.

The cab passed Kane's bank; a depository that housed not one red cent of his money, but a large amount of his debt. Taking out another loan was out of the question. No one would take a chance on him in the lending world; he was a pariah. He could only imagine his credit score . . . probably minus something. Maybe this was Proffitt's plan all along: to make him suffer in total despair by allowing him to live.

Kane gripped his unattached seatbelt with both hands. If it sounds too good to be true, then what's being offered is likely a screw. That had always been his motto. How could he have been so gullible to let Proffitt deceive him? The deal Proffitt offered seemed infallible. Kane had nothing to lose and everything to gain, or so he thought. Proffitt had reeled him in by saying he was desperate for a consultation with the DUI Doctor. So desperate, that Proffitt had commandeered a taxi to drive him to the airport. What attorney wouldn't jump at an offer of $25,000 upfront in cash to listen to a potential client's situation? Proffitt said he'd double the fee if Kane convinced this prospective client during their consultation that his supposed crisis would disappear. The large cash proposal was Proffitt's Trojan horse. If it got close enough, it would kill him.

A pain in Kane's stomach said hello. He recalled Proffitt delivering him to the Logan Airport departure area to catch his plane to Los Angeles; a flight he'd missed by mere minutes. A flight he would have died on. Proffitt then passed from heart failure, parked in front of Fenway Park. Was it sick to wish Proffitt was still alive so he could have the satisfaction of eliminating him? He'd wanted to seek retribution against the people in Proffitt's life ever since. He could only hope they were as dead as Proffitt, and that Rollie was heading back to Boston.

The driver snuggled the cab against the curb in front of the building that had once been called Kane Tower. Kane hurried into the lobby after paying the driver and punched the elevator button for the seventh floor. Before the car door closed, Joan slithered through to join him. He acknowledged the firm's paralegal with a nod, unwilling to partake in idle chatter. She was unaware this would be her last day at the firm. Joan tended to be a crier.

He intended to fire Joan and offer her a box of tissue as sever-
ance pay. Stanley would have to assume Joan's duties whether
the young attorney liked it or not. Stanley would be the next one
to go before his rookie bonus money kicked in. He didn't give a
diddly squat if Stanley's wife was carrying a set of triplets. This
captain wasn't going down with his ship at the expense of others.
Survival was all that mattered.

Kane marched into the office and went straight to his secretary's station. Vera's fingers left the keyboard and pointed to a
neat pile of messages on the corner of her desk. He sifted through
the pink slips: Taylor Mortgage Company, Joy Jewelers, WMC
Country Club, Detective Prescott from the San Francisco Police
Department . . .

"Vera, did Detective Prescott from the San Francisco Police
Department give a reason why he called?" Kane's voice was calm
belying a pounding pulse.

"No, sir. The call came late yesterday afternoon. Per your
instructions when you are out of the office, I told him you were
in court and wouldn't be back in the office until today. He said it
was important that you return his call as soon as possible."

Kane went to his office and closed the door. No doubt a call
from the San Francisco Police Department had to do with Rollie
and why his bodyguard was incommunicado. Did the police
catch him in the act of eliminating one or both of the Proffitt's
women? Or did the police nab Rollie for something else? If so,
would Rollie incriminate him? Kane's eyes rolled. Why else
would the detective want to contact him? Should he return the
call or ignore it the way he'd been dodging all his creditors? There
were positive and negative reasons for each move. The buzzer on
his phone startled him.

"Detective Prescott from the San Francisco Police
Department is on the line," Vera said. "Will you take the call, sir?"

Good question. It was 7:00 am on the West Coast. The detective must have a good reason to think he was involved with
Rollie. It would look bad if he kept avoiding him. Then again,
why would a busy attorney take the time to speak to an unknown
person from a different state? If he ignored the detective's calls,

would they stop contacting him? Or would it send up a big red flag? He never should have sent Rollie.

"I'll take the call, Vera." Kane punched the blinking button. "This is Oliver Kane, Detective. I'm due in court in fifteen minutes. What can I do for you?"

"I appreciate you taking my call, Mr. Kane. I'll try to be as quick as I can. Are you familiar with a man named Roland Smith?"

A fine way to learn Rollie's legal first and last name. Rollie must have ratted him out. Maybe he shouldn't have taken this call. It's too late now. He had to be careful how he worded his answer.

"Roland Smith," Kane repeated, writing the name on the first line on a legal yellow pad of paper. "I don't believe I'm familiar with anyone that goes by that name, detective. Is there a reason I should be?"

"Are you saying Roland Smith isn't employed as your bodyguard?"

"You mean Rollie. I never knew his given first and last names. Sure, he serves as my bodyguard. He's on vacation."

"Sir, we are trying to ascertain if you sent Mr. Smith to San Francisco or if he came here on his own volition."

Kane cleared his throat. Rollie had paid for the airline tickets on his own credit card after Kane said the firm would reimburse him when he returned. That would justify Rollie taking a vacation to San Francisco.

"Detective, I'm not aware if Rollie is in Boston or vacationing in Hawaii. Why are you asking me about Rollie?"

"We found your business card in Mr. Smith's pocket, along with a Massachusetts driver's license showing a Boston address."

Kane squeezed the letter opener. Did Rollie fink on him? Or did Vera, his secretary, stupidly disclose Rollie was his bodyguard?

"Detective, hundreds if not thousands of people carry my business card on their person. I specialize in DUI cases." Since he was speaking to a cop, it wouldn't be wise to use the DUI Doctor moniker. "When someone is arrested for driving under the influence anywhere in New England, I'm the first attorney they call."

"I appreciate you providing that information, sir. That might explain why Mr. Smith or someone would have your business card in their pocket. Mr. Kane, I'm sorry to break this to you, but Roland Smith is dead."

"Dead!" Kane responded, genuinely surprised. "How? Where? When?"

The detective said Rollie was dead, not murdered. Did they find Rollie before or after he died? A question he couldn't ask the detective. Dead men don't talk. Live men sing any song that may take the onus off of them. He was now out a bodyguard, chauffeur, and enforcer. On the positive side, he had one less expense.

"Mr. Smith was hit by a car last Wednesday in San Francisco," the detective said. "Are you familiar with a man named Morgan Proffitt?"

Kane's jaw dropped open. Damn it. Rollie must have squealed. Should he admit his experience with Proffitt? Any lie usually came back to bite the prevaricator on the ass. Then again, were there any witnesses other than Rollie who could link him to Proffitt? He closed his eyes. Should he roll the dice or not?

"As you can imagine, detective, I'm terribly distressed about Rollie's death. The name you mentioned doesn't ring a bell. Is this Morgan fellow also carrying my card? Again, my time to talk to you is waning."

"Mr Kane, it was brought to our attention that you sent Roland Smith to San Francisco to murder several people as retaliation for what Morgan Proffitt did to you."

Kane ran a finger along the blade of his letter opener. That scumbag Rollie must have spilled his gut. It was time to take a different tack.

"Seriously, revenge for what? Before this phone call I had never heard the name Morgan Proffitt. Is this some kind of joke? Wait. Is that you, Harry, performing one of your dumb ass stunts?" Kane offered a sarcastic laugh. "You know damn well I'm too busy to be a sucker for your sick sense of humor."

"Sir, I can assure you this call is no practical joke. If you need to verify who I am, call the San Francisco Police Department and ask for Detective Frank Prescott."

"I would, but you're out of time," Kane said, notching up his voice. "If you are who say you are, you're mistaken about my being involved in some kind of reprehensible action. As I said, I'm due in court. You've wasted enough of my valuable time. Detective, I plead guilty of being ignorant enough to take this call and probably being late to court."

Kane banged the phone receiver down, disconnecting the call. He put his hands together to control the shake. Did Rollie implicate him before dying? If not, how would anyone in San Francisco know about Rollie's mission, who sent him, and the name Morgan Proffitt? Maybe it didn't come from San Francisco. He stabbed the desk pad with the letter opener. "Maybe it leaked from Boston?"

CHAPTER SIXTEEN

R achel took her batting stance next to a brown paper bag serving as a makeshift home plate on the backyard lawn. As much as Bruno enjoyed teaching Rachel how to hit a Wiffle ball, his thoughts were on Oliver Kane . . .

It has been five days since Rollie was killed. How is Kane going to compensate for the loss of his bodyguard?

Rachel gripped the plastic bat and raised her elbows a bit after he motioned with his head. Her eyes zoned in on the holey white Wiffle ball balanced in his palm . . .

What's Kane's next move? Who would he send, and when? Mary was right; there won't be a warning from someone like Stanley. The ladies are in more danger than ever.

Bruno lobbed the ball underhand like a slow pitch softball pitcher in the direction of home plate. Rachel's eyes narrowed as she followed the ball . . .

Detective Prescott from the San Francisco Police Department questioned everyone involved about Rollie's breaking and entering Mrs. Green's house and attempting murder with a deadly weapon. The detective called me after he questioned Oliver Kane. Without definitive proof, he can't charge Kane with a crime since Rollie and Morgan Proffitt are deceased and there are no other witnesses.

The tip of Rachel's tongue jutted out between her lips as she took a vicious swing. The hollow sound from the bat smacking the ball resonated . . .

Prescott impressed me, but how much of his valuable time can he devote to investigating Rollie's crimes and death? More than likely, the case will land in a cold file.

Bruno followed Rachel's hit as it sailed over the fence into a neighbor's yard.

"Wow! Way to go, Rachel. You just hit a homerun." Bruno pumped his pitching hand in the air. "See what happens when you watch the ball meet the bat. I'm proud of you, kid. If you keep practicing, you might be the next Babe Ruth."

Instead of trotting around invisible bases, Rachel ran to him with a beaming smile. She jumped as high as she could to give him a high five, being careful not to bump into his injured left arm still wrapped in gauze and an Ace bandage. If possible, he enjoyed the blast more than she did. Mary had told him Rachel was doing well in school, not that he needed convincing. She asked good questions, listened to his answers, and applied what she learned. Too bad her mother wasn't here to see her daughter's first home run.

"What team does Babe Ruth play for, Mr. Bruno?" she asked. "Maybe I could watch her on TV or see a picture of her in the newspaper."

"The Babe played for the New York Yankees a long time ago, Rachel." Bruno chuckled. "Those two names together are confusing. Babe is *his* nickname. *His* full name was George Herman Ruth. He was also called The Great Bambino and the Sultan of Swat. The Babe was considered the greatest home run hitter of his time and maybe ever. A lot of people don't know that he started out as a pitcher before he hurt his arm."

"Maybe I can see what he looks like in one of Mrs. Green's encyclopedias." Rachel skipped back to home plate, picked up the bat, and took her stance. "Can we keep practicing so I can be the best home run hitter ever?"

"You can practice after you do your homework, young lady." Mrs. Green had both hands on her wide hips. "As for you, Mr. Santiago, it has only been three days since you were released from the hospital. The doctor said you should rest for at least a week with your concussion." She straightened her apron. "What's more, I seriously doubt your doctor would condone any exercise that could split open your stitches. Thank you."

Rachel stomped her foot and dropped the bat on the grass. She knew better than to put up a fight. So did Bruno. There was only one boss in this household. Bruno found being with someone Rachel's age a new and enjoyable experience, even if it was against her mother's mixed feelings about it.

"I think she's got us, Rachel." Bruno bent down and plucked the spare Wiffle ball off the grass. "Mrs. Green is right, you know. Homework and chores come before play. I also have some work I could be doing." He looked at Mrs. Green. "Maybe we can squeeze in more practice later if we finish our work and when Mrs. Green isn't looking."

Mrs. Green's head twisted away from Bruno to hide her grin. Rachel sauntered to the kitchen door in a pout and entered the house. Bruno flipped the ball up in the air and caught it with one hand and turned to Mrs. Green.

"I wouldn't be here now if it wasn't for you, Mrs. Green," Bruno said. "I want to officially thank you. We both know I was losing my fight with Rollie until you clubbed him with a six iron. Plus, you've done a terrific job as my caregiver. I will always be grateful for your assistance, along with allowing me to stay in your home while I heal. I'm not feeling any effects from the concussion. But you do give me a headache by referring to me as Mr. Santiago. You can call me Bruno."

"I will take your request into consideration." Mrs. Green picked up the Wiffle bat and paper bag from the grass. "Don't think I haven't noticed how good you are with our precious Rachel. And her mother, too. They're both very special. I haven't forgotten why you came here and that you risked your life to save us from that hoodlum. Maybe I was premature in judging you. So I thank you for what you have done for all of us."

What a comeback. Compliment's from Mrs. Green after she despised him. Perhaps she had finally stopped blaming him for Morgan Proffitt's death.

"Oh, by the way, tonight's dinner will be served at six rather than five," she said. "We are having Mr. Proffitt's favorite meal: salad, steak, Swiss chard, mashed potatoes, and homemade chocolate cake." She waved the bat like an orchestra conductor as she listed each dish. "Every Monday night Virginia joins us after work."

"You're spoiling me, Mrs. Green. I usually dine on frozen dinners or greasy spoon diners." He touched his stomach. "I'm going to miss you when I go back to Boston."

"Am I the only one you will miss?" she asked, with a hint of a smile.

Mrs. Green didn't try to hide her wisdom. He would miss all of them. She had found her place in life as a caregiver for the Proffitt family and now for Rachel and Mary. He wasn't offended when Mrs. Green kept calling him Mr. Santiago. After all, she still referred to Morgan Proffitt as Mr. Proffitt. Bruno had been honored when she offered him Mr. Proffitt's master bedroom, but he declined. Instead, he slept on the couch in the den. They treated him like he was a member of their family. Maybe he was a novelty to them, like bringing home a new puppy from the pound. Even if he had all his shots and was house broken, how soon would the newness wear off?

Bruno headed to the house. He planted his feet and dropped the ball when the gate's chain was pulled. The gate inched open. A man's boot became visible, then khaki pants and shirt. The man entered cautiously, as if looking for something. Bruno darted to the man and pinned him against the gate with his right hand. Whatever the man was carrying fell to the lawn. His shirt pocket contained a canister with a red top. The guy kept mumbling letters. Bruno ripped the canister from the pocket and bunched the front of the intruder's shirt, ready to throw him to the ground.

"No, no, Mr. Santiago," Mrs. Green shouted, running as best she could. "He's the meter reader from PG&E. Please don't hurt him."

"Sorry, buddy." Bruno placed the canister of Halt Dog Spray back into the meter reader's pocket. He picked up a brown leather-covered book off the grass and handed it to the shaken gas and electric employee, softly patting his chest. "I'm from out of town. Hey, better me than a neurotic German Shepherd."

* * * * *

Bruno scooted the cushioned office chair closer to Morgan Proffitt's maple desk in the den. His office in his Boston apartment consisted of a folding table, folding chair, and a filing cabinet. He stared down at written notes he recalled from his meeting with Stanley. There was enough ammunition to make Oliver Kane's life miserable, but that wouldn't do. He needed to shut down Kane permanently. His fingertips rubbed his chin. The info pieces were frustrating him, like one big word with its letters scrambled. He still wasn't close to putting the clues in the right sequence for a viable scheme.

Mary entered the study wearing another work pantsuit. Today's color was gray. Normally, she'd seek out Rachel when she returned home for an update of her daughter's school day before changing into jeans or sweats to assist Mrs. Green. Bruno put his pen down on the notes and offered her a chair in front of the desk with a wave of his hand. He'd seen her determined features set on serious several times before.

"I hear you and Rachel played Wiffle ball in the backyard after she came home from school," Mary said, getting right to the point without a civil hello. "She couldn't wait to tell me about her heroics of hitting a homerun like Baby Ruth."

"That would be Babe Ruth the baseball player." He smiled. "Baby Ruth is a candy bar."

"Whatever. I don't mind you playing or helping Rachel. I'm a little jealous that I don't have as much time with her. But I do mind when play gets in the way of schoolwork."

"Mrs. Green already scolded both of us about Rachel doing her schoolwork first."

"Your involvement has become a problem, and I don't know what to do about it." Mary leaned forward. "Do you recall the conversation we had before? Rachel really likes you, Bruno. She trusts you. Maybe I'm a little jealous of that, too. She has never gravitated to a man like that before. Mrs. Green said you can live here for as long as you want. In all sincerity, it's nice having a man in the house, but for how long? You're eventually going back to Boston. I'm worried Rachel won't understand when you leave her."

"I haven't forgotten what you warned me about," he said. "I'm as conflicted as you are, Mary. This is uncharted territory for me. I've never been around kids Rachel's age. She's smart, fun, and such a breath of fresh air compared to the miscreants I deal with. Like I said before, you've done a great job raising your daughter by yourself."

"Thank you, but you don't know my history. Look, I'm not blaming you, Bruno. I think you are a good influence on Rachel." Mary peered down at the coupled hands in her lap. "Here's what you don't know. Rachel doesn't remember Larry as her father. Thanks to you, hopefully, she never will. The other night Rachel told me she would like you to be her daddy. The longer you're here, the more she'll grow fond of you. She thinks you are like Babe Ruth . . . the player not the candy bar."

"Would it help if I talked to Rachel about it? Or maybe we can talk to her together?"

"I don't know the best way to handle this. If you quit being Rachel's friend or stopped paying attention to her, it might have a worse effect than you leaving." Mary squirmed in the chair. "This boils down to being my fault. I don't have good luck with men, as you witnessed by dealing with my ex. There hasn't been a man in my life for a long time. I have resigned myself to keep it that way. We are so fortunate to have Mrs. Green and Virginia in our lives. But to Rachel, most of the other kids have a mommy and a daddy living together as a family, and she really likes you."

"Are you proposing to me so Rachel can have a daddy?"

"Not funny, Bruno. I don't want my daughter to get hurt."

"Sorry, I don't want to see her hurt either. Nor do I want you to be hurt. But you need to lighten up. I think you'll find the problem will solve itself in a positive way. I don't mean to get personal, but I just can't see you with a man like Larry."

"I was at a girlfriend's apartment. Her husband invited his friend Larry over. He seemed like a nice guy. We drank a lot. Had a good time. When my car wouldn't start, he offered to drive me to my place. One thing led to another and we had sex. We began dating platonically, but I quickly realized he was an alcoholic and stopped the relationship. Then I found out I was pregnant. I didn't have a fulltime job and my credit cards were maxed out. When I approached him with the news, he offered to quit drinking and would take care of the baby and me if I'd marry him. Well . . . you know how that turned out."

"Is that why you don't wear makeup? So men won't be attracted to you."

"Don't pat yourself on the back, Dr. Freud. Virginia and Mrs. Green came to the same conclusion. Believe it or not, there was a time I used to wear too much makeup."

"I realize men aren't at the top of your list, and I'm a card-carrying member of that sect, but you are a very attractive woman without makeup. With a touch of makeup . . ."

"Whatever you're thinking, those days are over. Good night, Bruno."

CHAPTER SEVENTEEN

During the steak dinner feast, Mrs. Green gave a hyperbolic rendition of how Bruno responded when the meter reader entered the backyard – unannounced - looking for the gas meter. Virginia, Mary, and Rachel laughed long and hard. Bruno did his best to keep a straight face. Laughter can be every bit as contagious as a yawn. Who knew Mrs. Green had a sense of humor?

"Once more you proved to be our protector, Bruno," Virginia said, after she caught her breath. "Those meter readers can be tough hombres, but that poor guy met his match. Mrs. Green should nail a sign on the gate: 'Beware of Vicious Boston Detective.'"

"In my defense," Bruno countered, "the meter reader was armed with dog spray."

Bruno planted a hand on the dining room table, rose to his feet, and loosened his belt a notch after consuming Morgan Proffitt's favorite dinner. It would be difficult for him to go back to frozen dinners and diners. Rachel began clearing the table and delivering dishes to Mrs. Green in the kitchen. Mary and Virginia followed Bruno into the den. He settled in one side of the couch with Virginia claiming the other. Mary occupied the same chair she'd sat in earlier, fronting the desk.

"In all seriousness, Bruno," Virginia said, "I can't thank you enough for providing off-duty police and former cops to guard the Proffitt Advertising office and my condo." Snapping her fingers, she added, "Instead of going back to Boston after you mend, why don't you stay in San Francisco and start up a security service?"

"Detective Prescott was most helpful in my setting up your protection," he said "I would never consider leaving my S.O.S. Investigations in Boston to move here as long as Oliver Kane is still practicing his lunacy in the courtroom."

"I haven't heard from Detective Prescott. Do you know if he interrogated Kane?" Virginia asked.

"The detective called Kane." Bruno straightened out a wrinkle bunching the Ace bandage. "Kane denied sending Rollie to California or having any knowledge of Morgan Proffitt. No surprise there, right? Turns out Rollie paid for the roundtrip ticket with his credit card. So the only link to Kane is that Rollie was employed by him as a bodyguard. Unless Prescott uncovers definitive hard evidence implicating Kane, he's going to skate."

"How could that be?" Mary said. "Rollie broke into Mrs. Green's house and attacked you with a knife. Your informant told you Kane would be sending Rollie on a revenge mission for what Mo did to him. What more do the police want, Bruno?"

"Actual proof, not hearsay. My informant would deny everything, fearing what Kane would do to him or his family. It took a lot of guts for the guy just to seek me out."

"If the police won't do anything about Oliver Kane, we're back to where we were before. Or worse." Mary pulled on a stand of hair. "Even with you being here, Bruno, and added security, Kane may have already sent another goon to attack us."

"I don't think so, Mary." Bruno uncrossed a knee. "Kane doesn't have the means to send another assailant. That's why he sent Rollie. Plus, the police are aware he may have been involved in Rollie's attack even if they can't prove it. Kane will lay low until he believes he's off the radar. That gives us time to create our own plan of attack."

"When you say us, what do you mean?" Virginia asked.

"I can't pull this off without help. I've been going about this the wrong way. I can't take down Kane by being passive. Mr. Proffitt had the right idea. For the past year, I've been waiting for another Proffitt opportunity to surface. The odds of that happening again are against me. With Rollie dead, Kane is vulnerable and more desperate than ever. There's a good chance he may self-destruct on his own. Rather than wait for that to take place, why not speed up the process with a creative scheme of deception?"

"It sounds like you want us to play some kind of con on Kane. Isn't that illegal?"

"Not if we don't get caught, Mary. And I'm thinking it would be more like a sting."

"Whether it's a sting or a con, isn't what you're planning still against the law?"

Rachel stepped carefully into the den carrying a silver tray with three petite crystal glasses filled with dark-colored liquor. Without spilling a drop, she placed the tray down on Morgan Proffitt's desk. She served Virginia and Mary first, then Bruno. Rachel then moved to the side of the couch and whispered something in Bruno's ear. He grinned and nodded. Rachel retrieved the tray and danced out of the room with a smile.

"Here's to Morgan Proffitt," Virginia said, raising her glass. "Grand Marnier was Helen and Mo's favorite after-dinner drink. It has become mine as well. Cheers."

Bruno observed them sipping their drinks. Mary's features scrunched into a big wrinkle as she waved a hand in front of her lips. Virginia enjoyed the bitter orange burn of the brandy, emitting a soft murmur of contentment.

"What are you and Rachel cooking up, Bruno?" Mary asked, after clearing her throat.

"I don't think Rachel would mind if I shared what she whispered. She asked if we could practice Wiffle ball tomorrow, after she finishes her homework. Rachel also wanted me to talk to you about getting a puppy since you're the only person in this house who isn't in favor of it." He raised an eyebrow. "If you're unwilling to get a puppy, why not get a grown German shepherd or Doberman? That would be more prudent for security."

"We can talk about both subjects later, Bruno," Mary responded in a stern voice. "You were saying something about needing our help?"

"People in the advertising business are creative," Bruno said. "You build ad campaigns that make products or services appetizing to prospective customers. I want both of you to help me assemble a campaign around Oliver Kane's weaknesses."

"Thank you for the kudos, but we are out of our element here," Virginia said. "Mary and I have no experience generating deceptive plots to trap scumbags like Oliver Kane."

"That's exactly what I'm looking for; totally different view-points. Are you with me?"

"With all that you've done for us, how could I not be with you, Bruno?" Virginia said.

"What do you have in mind?" Mary asked.

Bruno handed them a pen and a sheet of paper listing ten words before reclaiming his spot on the couch. He waited until each lady raised her head from reading.

"The words listed are in no particular order and emphasize Oliver Kane's weaknesses," Bruno explained. "The words – DEBT, MOVIE, MOB, DESPERATE, VULNERABLE, WOMANIZER, SPENDING, ADDICTION, ROLLIE, and POKER are a roadmap that might steer toward Kane's demise." He studied his notes. "Before I explain their significance, if you have any thoughts that seem unconventional or too far out-there to verbalize, blurt them out anyway. Anything goes."

"Is there one Kane weakness that is more noteworthy than the others?" Mary asked.

"That's what I've been trying to figure out. Do we focus our campaign on one of Kane's vulnerabilities? Or do we connect all or most of Kane's weaknesses into a scheme?"

Bruno looked at his watch. Tomorrow was a school and a work day for his conspirators. He needed to cram as much information as possible into this conversation before they had to attend to other duties.

"Kane has squandered a trove of wealth and spent an additional fortune to go into massive debt, possibly in the millions," Bruno said. "He's desperate to keep the lifestyle he's accustomed to which leaves him open to engage in a risky big dollar deal even if it sounds too good to be true. He's also vulnerable because Rollie's dead."

"How did Kane get into so much debt?" Mary asked.

"Kane has an addiction problem, not just cocaine and booze, but buying the very best money can buy whether he has the cash or not. That includes his downtown law office and the rights to have his name on the building. He lives in the ritziest Boston neighborhood and belongs to several country clubs. Kane can't help himself around a young, attractive woman. He's been married three times and pays huge monthly alimony to two of his exes. He gambles big dollars on sports teams, the ponies, and especially playing Texas Hold 'Em poker."

Bruno noticed Mary's grimace when he said Kane was addicted to attracted women. She must have known her share of sleaze bags like Oliver Kane.

"What does movie and mob mean?" Virginia asked.

"It's rumored Kane deals with mobsters. Kane believes he lost a movie deal about his life because of Morgan Proffitt. That's the reason he sent Rollie after you."

"But why come after us?" Mary asked. "Shouldn't he be satisfied that Mo has passed?"

"That's not the way Oliver Kane thinks. Each of his courtroom wins avenges the death of his father and mother. He won't be satisfied until he evens the score in proportion to what he thinks Morgan did to him. Since he can't hurt Proffitt, the next best thing is to go after the people Proffitt was close to." Bruno downed the rest of his brandy. "As a side bar, Kane is so twisted he can't even imagine being grateful to Proffitt. The plane Kane missed was the one that hit the North tower of the World Trade Center."

Bruno saw Mary exchange a glance with Virginia. Mary rubbed her arms as if she had a sudden chill. Morgan Proffitt had created havoc in Kane's world. On the flip side, maybe Mary wondered what her life would be like had Proffitt not traveled to Boston.

"Good night, Aunt Virginia and Mr. Bruno." Rachel stood in the doorway in her pajamas with little pink roses.

"Excuse us, everyone, time for our bedtime reading," Mary said, joining Rachel.

Virginia went to the credenza behind the desk and slid open the middle door. She reached into the back and removed another bottle of Grand Marnier. After filling both their glasses, she put the bottle back into its secret hiding spot.

"Mo and I used to chat about work and life every Monday night." Virginia's glass clinked against Bruno's. "Sometimes Helen joined us. Mrs. Green frowns upon more than one social drink." Her lips made a smacking sound after a sip. "Looking back, Bruno, I never understood why Mo would take a spontaneous flight to Boston with his bum heart. You knew about his condition and what he intended to do to Oliver Kane even if he didn't tell so in exact words. You said he paid you up front in cash. Were you helping him because you needed the money? Or were you assisting him out of your hatred for Oliver Kane? Weren't you concerned about aiding and abetting Mo in a crime?"

"Virginia, we could waste time debating this fine gray line about my being involved. Money wasn't an issue. I would have helped Mr. Proffitt *pro bono*. He paid me in cash because my license and reputation were at stake. He knew his time was limited and was hell-bent on killing the menace that played a role in his daughter Katie's death. I won't bullshit you. No one wanted Kane dead more than me. I've thought long and hard about killing Oliver Kane. Mr. Proffitt's intentions provided a perfect scenario that fell right into my lap - a gift I wouldn't have to unwrap. If he succeeded, there was no way I'd have been implicated." Bruno hitched his shoulders. "When Mr. Proffitt allowed him to live, it made me want Kane dead even more."

"What did I miss except that Mo's decision made you want to kill Oliver Kane?" Mary said, picking up the paper and pen from her chair.

"You missed another round of after dinner-drinks." Virginia finished her drink and rose. "It's getting late. I have an early morning appointment. Maybe I can mooch another of Mrs. Green's dinners tomorrow and we can do some serious brainstorming with you, Bruno. I've got several ideas swimming around in my head, but I'll let them marinate for the time being."

"Before you go, Virginia," Mary said, "while I was reading to Rachel, did Bruno ever give you a reason why he wouldn't kill Oliver Kane?"

"As a matter of fact, he didn't. What stopped you, Bruno?"

"If I murdered the bastard," Bruno said with no hesitation, "I'd be just as evil as he is."

CHAPTER EIGHTEEN

Bruno could hear Virginia in the kitchen saying goodbye to Mrs. Green, but his eyes never left Mary. Her shoe tapped nervously on the rug when he explained why he hadn't takened Oliver Kane's life. He placed his notes about Kane's weaknesses down on the couch. It was time for them to put their cards on the table.

"I know my relationship with Rachel is a problem for you," Bruno said. "That's your prerogative and I will do whatever you want regarding Rachel, but I won't leave until there's an end-game strategy to deal with the Oliver Kane situation."

"I've changed my stance on your involvement with Rachel after conferring with Mrs. Green. We've never seen Rachel so excited about anything. She wants to sign up for girl's softball, soccer, and basketball. We agree your interest and care for Rachel has been beneficial, and will continue to be good for her even if it's only for a short period of time. I still have concerns how it will affect her when you leave. Maybe we should talk to her together."

"Thank you, Mary. That means a lot to me." Bruno leaned towards her. "Now, tell me what else is bothering you besides Rachel's welfare? I noticed my answer about why I wouldn't kill Kane had an affect on you. What are you holding back?"

"Good catch, Bruno. You'd make a great detective." Mary put her hands together. "I told Morgan Proffitt the same thing you said about why he shouldn't kill Oliver Kane before I left him. I knew what he was planning to do to Kane. I've never told anyone that I was with Mo when we got off the plane that morning. He needed a car, but the car rental agencies weren't open yet. My car wouldn't start so he commandeered a cab from its driver with a useless gun that had no firing pin."

"So that's how Proffitt ended up with the cab," Bruno said.

"I interviewed the cab driver a few weeks later. He said there was an attractive young woman in the cab with him. You obviously were the young woman, but the cabbie didn't think you were involved with Proffitt."

"I drove the cab to where my mother and Rachel were staying. That's when Mo gave Rachel the hippo keychain his daughter Katie had gifted him. Mo was determined to make his meeting with Kane, but he chanced losing that meeting to ensure my safety."

"I wonder if something you said to Proffitt might have deterred him from taking Kane's life," Bruno said.

"I never considered that." Mary lifted her drink, wrinkled her nose, swallowed, made a face, and placed the glass back down on the desk. "This is the first glass of alcohol I've had since I met Larry. I can feel the effects already." Her cheeks flushed rosy. "Perhaps that's what Mrs. Green was going for? She's never offered me liquor before."

Bruno smiled. He looked towards the kitchen, then back at Mary. She appeared relaxed for a change.

"Why didn't you say anything about being with Proffitt after leaving the plane?"

"Guilt." Mary's voice quivered. "I'm ashamed of what I didn't do. I shouldn't have left Mo. Maybe he would still be alive today if I'd gone with him to meet Oliver Kane."

"Mary, don't blame yourself for Morgan Proffitt's death. Believe me, he knew his days were numbered. If anything, you added hours to his life."

"Great of you to say, Bruno. Wouldn't it be nice if words could melt away shame?"

"Earlier, Virginia didn't hesitate to say she'd join team Bruno in taking Oliver Kane down," Bruno said. "But you didn't. Why? Don't you remember saying you would help me get Kane as gratitude for what Morgan Proffitt did for you?"

"You caught me again, Bruno. I did say that. The reason I'm reluctant, is that I'm afraid you will ask me to play the girl I left in Boston. I'm not that person anymore."

"I've never doubted how smart and talented you are, Mary, but I wasn't aware you had ESP. Are you with me or not?"

"Careful what you wish for. I need to tell you one more thing." Mary closed her eyes and blew out a breath. "I divorced Larry after he went to prison. Larry threatened if he couldn't have me, then no one else would either. He said he'd hurt or kill me and Rachel if I was with someone else. Then I met Zack who was working temporarily at his company's office in Boston. Before Zack returned to San Francisco, he gave me an engagement ring and wanted me and Rachel to move into his house. He wanted to adopt her." Mary bit down on her lip. "Zack had a great job and wanted more children. I wasn't in love with Zack and told him so, but marrying him was perfect timing. I knew Larry might get out of prison with early parole and by taking Zack's last name, I figured Larry would never find us. When I flew to San Francisco to make arrangements for the wedding, I discovered vile pictures of Zack with other men. It all made sense then. He'd never pressured me for sex. I thought he was shy. The pictures indicated just the opposite. He was gay and wanted to use me and Rachel as a false front for appearances. I was so angry I wanted to kill him, not because he was gay, but he wouldn't tell me the truth."

"What did you do to Zack, Mary?"

"You don't want to know, Bruno, but I didn't kill him. I got on a plane back to Boston. I kept thinking what a failure I was as a person . . . as a mother. Rachel deserved better. I had no doubt Larry would find me when he got out of prison. If I wasn't around, he wouldn't look for Rachel. He just wanted me. I emptied a bottle of sleeping pills I'd swiped from Zack into my hand after boarding the plane. Before I could put them in my mouth, Morgan Proffitt grabbed my wrist and stopped me from killing myself. I told Mo about Zack and Larry. I told him no one believed in me as a creative artist, but I showed him a sample of my work. I'll never forget how impressed he was. Mo called Virginia from the plane and recommended me for a job at Proffitt Advertising, adding that we could stay with Mrs. Green."

"It must have felt like Morgan Proffitt was your guardian angel?"

"Yes, by the time we left the plane, Mo had proven I could trust him. I still think of Mo as my guardian angel." She peered up at the ceiling. "He had tremendous foresight. He saved me from doing something disastrous. He sent me to Virginia as a raw student and knew Rachel would be the best thing to happen to Mrs. Green since Katie's death. Virginia said Mo lost his desire to care about life after Katie died. But he never lost his compassion for others, or I wouldn't be here right now. This sounds crazy, but I think he transformed me into his daughter, Katie."

"Maybe Proffitt didn't go through with his mission for fear of disappointing you, Mary."

"We will never know for sure, will we?" Mary aimed an incriminating finger at him.

"Okay, Bruno, I've shared plenty with you. Now it's your turn. What prompted you to become a self-appointed, one-man vigilante to rein in Oliver Kane?"

Bruno didn't change expression, but his heart pounded at an uneasy beat. His eyes moistened, forcing him to look away from her. Mary had struck a nerve by pressuring him to explain why he was so determined to stop Kane from practicing law, or if need be, from ever breathing. He usually kept his emotions to himself; incapable of unleashing pent-up feelings festering inside. His body rocked back and forth. It was easy for Mary to reveal the skeletons in her guilt closet. Was he being a coward by not reciprocating?

"I get it, Bruno," Mary said. "Your silence tells me it's none of my damn business why you have a vendetta against Oliver Kane. But please, answer another question that has been eating at me. Do you remember what you said before passing out in the street?"

"I have no memory of passing out or what I said, Mary. Do I owe you an apology?"

"No, Bruno, there's no need for you to apologize." Mary laughed. "You said, 'I made good my promise this time.' What did you mean by that?"

Bruno reached for his glass and realized it was empty. His eyes fixated on the carpet. He didn't need to recall what he had said to know the meaning.

"Maybe someday you'll be able to tell me." Mary dipped her head slightly.

"Morgan Proffitt wasn't the only one who lost a loved one because of Oliver Kane," Bruno said in a low voice. "A man named Hunter Gill was a Kane client. Gill was cited for drunk driving twice. Kane got him off both times." A tear rolled down Bruno's cheek, landing on his pant leg. "Gill never should've been allowed behind a steering wheel again. Six weeks after Gill's last court appearance, he was drunk and speeding in downtown Boston. When he attempted a right turn into an alley, he cut it too sharp and crashed into the backend of a parked car. The parked car spun around, jumped the curb, and landed on the sidewalk just as a young woman approached her vehicle. The car's momentum pinned her against a brick storefront building. She didn't have a chance."

Mary gasped. "Oh my God, how awful, Bruno. Who was the young woman?"

"Her name was Wendy." Bruno still couldn't look Mary in the eye. "She was my fiancée. We met when I was teaching a self-defense class for women in Boston. Wendy signed up for the class after being attacked by a street mugger. The experience was traumatic for her. At the end of the class, I asked for feedback. Wendy raised her hand and stated, 'Thank you. I feel much better prepared to handle a creep like the one who assaulted me. But in all honesty, Trooper Santiago, I would feel even safer if you were there by my side.' It got a big laugh from the class. Later, as we walked out to our cars in the parking lot, I asked her out. We became inseparable. When I proposed to Wendy, I promised to be by her side for the rest of her life." His hand formed into a fist. "We were supposed to go to the jewelry store to have her engagement ring sized smaller, but I had to work overtime. She went to the jeweler alone. I broke my promise."

"I'm so sorry for your loss, Bruno." Mary left her chair to sit next to him on the couch. "You've been carrying this burden inside of you all this time. You knew exactly what Morgan Proffitt was trying to achieve by going after Oliver Kane. No wonder you were so frustrated when Mo didn't follow through with his initial objective."

Bruno finally gazed at Mary. Where was the release he was supposed to experience from spilling his gut? The vacant sensation in his stomach continued to gnaw at him.

"I didn't know it at the time," he said, "but Wendy was carrying our baby when the car hit her. A girl." He could hear himself swallow. "I will never know for sure, but Wendy may have been reluctant to tell me about the baby since we hadn't set a wedding date yet. Maybe she was afraid I wouldn't marry her because she was pregnant."

"Come on, Bruno. You gave her an engagement ring - a commitment to be married." Mary took his good hand into hers and squeezed. "Wendy was probably waiting for the right time to tell you. She knew how good a man you are. Now I understand your fondness for Rachel and eagerness to protect us. Please forgive me for doubting you."

"I've thought about why I was drawn to both of you," Bruno said. "When I saw Larry knock you down and then take Rachel, there was no way he was going to get away."

"Oh dear." Mrs. Green stepped into the den. "I didn't mean to interrupt. I wanted to know if Rachel will eat anything other than a peanut butter and jelly sandwich for her lunch."

"You aren't interrupting, Mrs. Green." Mary released Bruno's hand. "I once tried sneaking a cheese sandwich into her lunch box and was scolded when she got home. Let's stick with peanut butter and jelly." She glanced at the face of Bruno's watch. "I didn't realize how late it is. Thank you for making Rachel's lunch."

"It's my pleasure, Mary." She backed out of the den with raised eyebrows. "Carry on."

Bruno and Mary exchanged grins. The more he was around Mrs. Green, the more he appreciated her. If he wasn't mistaken, she'd just given them her nod of approval.

"Thank you for trusting me," Mary said. "My heart truly goes out to you. I've never experienced that kind of loving relationship. I probably never will." She returned to the chair and wiped her eyes. "Before I totally break down, let's talk about puppies. I do believe Rachel is mature enough to take care of a pet. It's one more responsibility and expense for me and I have a lot on my plate already. Also, this is Mrs. Green's house, although she treats it like it's our home too. If Mrs. Green didn't have a dog before we arrived, maybe she really didn't care to have one. I would never want her to think we're taking advantage of our situation or that we don't appreciate her loving generosity."

"Mrs. Green needs you and Rachel just as much as you need her, Mary. I didn't take into account what getting a pet would entail. I shouldn't have butted in."

"Maybe your butting in isn't a bad thing at all. I . . . I better say good night, Bruno."

CHAPTER NINETEEN

Sitting behind the wheel of a Mercedes made driving in down-town San Francisco more tolerable. Bruno likened it to getting an upgrade from coach to first class. He was learning which hilly or traffic-filled streets to avoid, and ignoring the constant clangs of trolley car bells.

He delivered Mary to the Proffitt Advertising office after they dropped off Rachel at her school. Later, his driving duties included taking Mrs. Green grocery shopping and picking up Rachel. He was getting a hint of what being in a family was all about.

Virginia would drive Mary home after work, and then she, Mary, and Bruno would meet for a fourth night. It was time for them to hear the scheme Bruno had pieced together that could take Oliver Kane down. He had abandoned his lone wolf approach about eliminating Kane. It would take his two cohorts' involvement to implement it.

Bruno's cell phone chimed. He pulled the Mercedes to the curb and answered.

"Sid Parker here, Bruno. Sorry I haven't returned your call sooner. A big special event I'm organizing at the WMC Country Club has taken up much of my time. The reason is legitimate, but it's not much of an excuse. Did you call with good news, buddy?"

"Is the winner-take-all Texas Hold 'Em tournament happening? If so, do you still want me to provide security for it?"

"Not only is it in the works, Bruno, it's a go." Sid closed the door loud enough to be heard. "You know I don't trust outsiders . . . someone I don't know. We've been buddies since grammar school. I've kept the job open just for you. Are you on board?"

"I've got a couple of questions, Sid. First, what the hell does WMC stand for?"

"You're not supposed to know, Bruno. WMC was established in the 50s. It stands for Wealthy Man's Club. If you aren't worth millions, don't apply."

"I'll never have to worry about that," Bruno said. "Is Oliver Kane one of the players?"

"I have ten members signed up. We can take up to twelve. Kane isn't one of them. Hell, the asshole is three months behind in club dues. There's a rumor he's flat broke. Kane is despised by club staff, members, and me. Most of the Thursday night poker players hate playing with the cocksucker. However, Kane would be more than welcome in the tournament because he's such a shitty player. You've been after Kane for a long time. The Hold 'Em tournament is on the up and up. Be honest with me, Bruno. Why are you asking about Oliver Kane?"

"Bear with me, Sid. I'll get to that. What are the stakes?"

"Each player puts up a quarter-million in cash," Sid said.

"Holy shit. If my math is correct, the winner's take is two-and-a-half million."

"Three-million if we get twelve players. Believe me, these gentlemen can afford it. They are multi, multi, multimillionaires. They can afford to lose it. There's a rich man's code here: millionaires want to be multimillionaires and multimillionaires want to be billionaires. But this game isn't just about money. It's about winning. All of them are top-notch players. I'd compare it to being a pro golfer in a major PGA golf tournament. The winner is the one who gets hot at the right time."

Bruno smiled. This tournament was every bit about money - money in Sid's pocket. After expenses, he'd probably walk away with hundreds of thousands in non-taxable cash. Sid would be holding all the cash. If for some reason something went awry, Sid would need a hell of a lot more for legal fees to stay out of jail. He would also lose his job. The players weren't the only ones gambling big.

"Are there any unusual tournament rules?" Bruno asked.

"We will start with two tables for five or six players on each. When a player loses a quarter mil in chips he's out. There will be no buy-ins. We will go to one table when there are five or six players remaining. Unlike most Hold 'Em tournaments, this baby will go quick because of the limited amount of players and high progressive antes – maybe it won't last even an hour."

"I take it you're hiring at least two dealers and probably a backup dealer just in case. Or maybe you can be the third dealer?"

"That wouldn't work. If there are any conflicts, I have to be available to make a ruling. At the moment I still haven't found a second dealer."

"I may be able to help you there," Bruno said.

That would be great if he's experienced with tournament play. Betting is limited to the value of chips in front of a player. When a player loses his chips he's out of the game. The antes start at ten thousand. There will be no splitting the prize money. The game is over when one player ends up with all the chips."

"When is the tournament taking place?"

"In Seventeen days. Now, tell me why you asked me about Oliver Kane? By the way, I just heard one of his lawyers got mugged and beaten up pretty bad."

"What's the name of the attorney that got mugged?" Bruno asked.

"Something like Bradley. Or Stanley?"

Bruno's fist pounded the steering wheel. It wasn't a mugger. It was a Kane retaliation.

"You still there, Bruno?"

"Sorry, Sid. If Kane came up with the entry fee, would you accept him?"

"If Oliver Kane handed me the entry fee in cash and there's an opening, he's in. I know you hate Kane even more than I do. I hope you're not up to something nefarious, Bruno?" Sid cleared this throat to back up his question. "Most likely, we won't have to worry about it. If the rumors are correct, there's no way Kane can come up with the money."

"I'm working on that. If Kane is in the game, I'll handle your security to make sure your game is safe and secure."

"I just had a scary thought," Sid said. "What if the son of

a bitch wins? Tournament play is different from a regular Hold 'Em game. Anything is possible. Kane has numerous tells as a player, but he could get on a lucky roll."

"I'm betting he won't."

"But theoretically he could."

"Theoretically, he won't," Bruno affirmed. "Let's assume there will be twelve players. Not counting the players' ability, the odds of any players winning the tournament is under nine per cent. The odds Kane won't win are worse. It's like betting on a long shot at the track with a 300 pound jockey on its back."

"Even long shots win every once in a while," Sid argued.

"Remind me never to go to the track with you. Does Kane know about the tournament?"

"He may not. Kane doesn't have any friends here except for our well-built drink runner. The tournament is simply limited to the first twelve players to pay the entry fee in cash. If the last two spots are taken, or if Kane can't come up with the entry fee, he's shit out of luck." Sid coughed. "By the way, I've budgeted $5,000 for your security services. You're the person I want to do the job. Will you do it, buddy?"

"I'm in if you agree to a few small caveats."

* * * * *

Oliver Kane strolled into the club's poker room confident his hot streak would continue. He sat in seat six, the same as last week, and was wearing the same lucky tie. The drink runner placed a glass of scotch next to him without being asked. He couldn't help but smile. Winning made everything look brighter, smell more aromatic, and taste better.

"There's a good possibility you will get lucky tonight, Oliver," the waitress whispered, after nudging her hip into his elbow on purpose. "I'm not just talking about poker."

Kane winked at the drink runner. Why not? His wife was visiting her sick mother in New York. He didn't have to be concerned what time he got home or deal with an argument if she was awake. He was on such a good roll; his wife might stay away permanently.

Big Tony filled the doorway and stopped, blocking the whole entrance. He turned to speak to someone. From Kane's vantage point it was impossible to see who Big Tony was conversing with, but the person had the big guy's complete attention.

Big Tony finally entered the room and took a seat at the poker table. Sid Parker followed him and quickly got another player's ear. Kane sipped his drink wishing he could read lips. Something was going on.

"What did Sid say to you, Big Tony?" Kane asked in his courtroom voice.

"I don't recall being sworn in on the witness stand, Ollie. None of your business."

"Let's not forget I saved your sister, Teresa, from going to jail; *pro bono* no less."

Big Tony glared at Kane. He rubbed a forefinger under his nose, looked around the room to see if anyone was listening to their conversation, and leaned across the table.

"You didn't hear this from me, Ollie," Big Tony said in a low voice. "Sid has set up a mega-buck Hold 'Em tournament like no other for twelve club members seventeen days from now. It's not publicized, if you know what I mean. He still has two open seats. Man, the total prize could get up to three million Samolians and the winner takes all."

"Who the hell is sponsoring the tournament?" Kane asked.

"The twelve players. The entry fee is a quarter of a million. Sid asked me if I wanted in." Big Tony lifted his massive shoulders. "My bankroll is a bit shy of the entry fee, know what I mean? But I know where I can get the G's. Don't know how I could pay it back plus the vig if I don't win. The way I play I could be out of the tournament in one hand. Then again, I'm talking about a chance to win three-million bucks in cash. That's one fucking golden carrot, know what I mean?"

Kane had never seen Big Tony so demonstrative and scared. It was obvious to Kane that Sid didn't want him to play in the tournament, but that didn't stop his heart from jackhammering in his chest. Three-million dollars would solve all his problems. He was on a hot streak. All he had to do was beat eleven players.

At this point he'd sell his soul to get into the tournament. Where could he find a worthy buyer?

* * * * *

On the fourth night of brainstorming, Bruno raised his glass of Grand Marnier and saluted his two allies. He shared his conversation with Sid Parker about the Hold 'Em tournament being a go and what had happened to Stanley.

"The assault on Stanley is just another example of why Oliver Kane has to be eliminated," Bruno said. "The tournament is the seed for my strategy to do away with Kane. He will do *almost* anything to get the entry fee money, *maybe* even risk his life. I want to take the words *almost* and *maybe* out of the equation. I need help from both of you to take part in my scheme. We have a little over two weeks. Virginia, tomorrow I want you to make a phone call to Kane and impersonate someone in the movie business. Ask Kane if he's still interested in having a movie made about his life. Say you have backers, but could use more. If he isn't interested, you will move on to another project."

"I get it," Virginia said. "You're adding another carrot to make Kane beg, borrow, or steal the entry fee for the poker tournament. The prize money will get him out of debt and offers the prospect of the movie he lusts for."

"Exactly." Bruno turned to Mary. "You're the key for pulling off this mission."

"Does my not wearing makeup have anything to do with my role?" Mary said.

"Smart lady. I believe Kane is so desperate for the tournament's prize money that he will go to the mob for the entry fee. He also knows if he can't pay them back, he's dead meat. We're aiming to force Kane to get the money from the mob so he can enter the tournament. When he loses and can't pay them back, not even Oliver Kane can overcome the heavy gavel of mob justice."

"What if Kane has a sane moment and doesn't go to the mob?" Mary asked.

"That's where you come in, Mary. I've arranged for you to meet with Kane at his office tomorrow afternoon. I'll prep you on the plane how to handle him."

117

"You want me to be the bait, all alone, with a notorious womanizer?"

"I'll be in the waiting room," Bruno said. "He won't make a play knowing I'm with you. Your role is to guarantee Kane that you can make him win the tournament."

"I think that drink has gone to your head, Bruno." Mary had both hands on her hips.

"Hold on, Mary," Virginia said. "Bruno is onto something. If Kane believes the fix is in for him to win, he should have no problem going to the mob for the entry fee."

"How am I supposed to convince Kane that I can do all of this?" Mary asked.

"You, Mary, are now one of the dealers in the tournament and a gifted card mechanic."

"It still doesn't make sense to me. Why would I be doing this for Kane?"

"Because you will be offering Kane your dealing skills in exchange for a percentage of the three-million dollars."

Mary sipped her drink, then her features brightened.

"I can't go to Boston. What about Rachel and my job?"

"We'll cover for you at work," Virginia said. "Rachel is in good hands with Mrs. Green."

"Bruno, you know I want to help, but I'm not sure I can pull off my part. What about Virginia? She's capable of doing anything, including role playing."

"If I had your looks and figure, Mary, I'd gladly do it," Virginia said. "You are the perfect person for this role. You know how much I care about you, but I have faith in Bruno and the plan he's concocted to stop Oliver Kane for good."

"I must be crazy to agree to do this. Both of you don't realize how scared and uncomfortable I am going back to Boston and being a part of this crazy scheme."

CHAPTER TWENTY

Before Oliver Kane stepped out of the office building's elevator, he touched his suit coat to feel last night's poker winnings in the inner pocket. He was on a winning roll like never
before. It was like an injection of speed. The total score was less
than the previous game, but it gave him a newfound confidence.
He was amazed how much the cards had turned in his favor. He
couldn't imagine ever losing again.

He smiled at his secretary Vera on his way to his office. She
blinked several time after seeing such a rare, pleased expression from Kane. A tear-storm started to flow from her eyes. She
grabbed tissue to combat the flood and gasped for air. Was she
that sensitive?

"Isn't . . . it . . . just . . . awful?" Vera stammered. "I just can't
believe it."

"Can't believe what, Vera?" Kane offered his best quizzical
expression.

"Our Stanley was mugged last night and badly hurt." Vera
pulled more tissues from the box and dabbed her eyes. "He's in
the hospital. Dear God, his poor wife. She's pregnant. What's she
going to do? How could something like this happen to such a
sweet person like Stanley?"

"I couldn't agree with you more, Vera. What a damn shame."
Kane shook his head and headed to his office, then he stopped to
turn to her. "Did they find the guy that attacked Stanley?"

"Not to my knowledge. Hope they get the guy and string
him up by his . . . you know."

After Kane closed his office door his lips spread into a satis-
fying grin. He knew exactly how Stanley was assaulted and who
the culprit was. All it took was a phone call and five-hundred
dollars to one of Kane's former clients to perform the deed.

"No one fucks with Oliver Kane and gets away with it."

119

He dropped his briefcase on the credenza as if it had been the offender. "No one."

Nerves had gotten the best of Stanley ever since he left the office without permission. It was easy to finger him as the snitch after he was questioned. Stanley denied any wrongdoing, but the nerd was a horrible liar. Sweat on his forehead made it look like he'd just taken a steam bath. How did he find out about Rollie's going to San Francisco and who did he tell? Rollie would be alive today if it wasn't for this traitor and the Proffitt people would be dead. Stanley is lucky he's still alive.

Kane sat at his desk, removed most of the hundreds from his pocket, and locked them in a bottom drawer . . . his method of governing his spending. It might be too little too late, but he was trying to stay afloat for as long as he could. He believed the WMC Texas Hold 'Em tournament prize was the answer to his financial woes. It didn't matter that he'd never played in a poker tournament before. He was on a winning streak that could carry him out of his money miseries if only he could resolve a pair of issues: find a way to come up with the entry fee fast enough before the last two seats were taken.

He removed a yellow legal pad from his desk's middle drawer and drew a line down the middle of the page. He wrote $3 million on the top line on the left side. It felt good just making all those zeros. On the right side, he listed his debts. When he totaled the amount owed it came to almost two million. The cash prize would propel him out of the red and into the black with a million dollars to spare.

He went to his file cabinet and brought back a folder listing the former clients he'd saved. With a yellow highlighter, he marked the wealthiest ones who could easily loan him money. How many of them would be willing? What answer should he give if they asked the reason for the loan? The reason certainly couldn't be to back him in a poker tournament. Nor could he tell them he was trying to avoid bankruptcy.

"Shit." Kane threw the folder halfway to the sofa. By the time he hit up enough people on his list for a loan, there wouldn't be any open tournament seats. The money had to come from one source that could raise a quarter million in cash instantly. He knew of only one person who could make that happen.

He riffled through his Rolodex until he found what he was looking for. He placed the card on the blotter and stared at it. Was he that desperate?

"Mr. Kane," Vera announced through the intercom. "There's a woman on the line who says you will want to speak to her. It's regarding a movie venture you had been interested in. Her name is Marilyn Harrison. What should I tell her?"

"I don't know any Marilyn Harrison . . . hold on. I wonder if she's related to Royce Harrison, the movie mogul client who wanted to do a movie about me. I'll take the call."

"This is Oliver Kane. How can I help you, Ms. Harrison? I don't believe we've met."

"We haven't met Mr. Kane. I'm Royce Harrison's niece. Uncle Royce passed away five months ago." She paused to allow him a chance to offer his condolences. "I worked closely with my uncle for many years. You saved him from going to jail after his third DUI. Unfortunately, Uncle Royce didn't learn his lesson or need your services for his fourth DUI. He wrapped his car around a tree trunk drunk as a skunk."

"Too bad," Kane said. "If he had lived, I could've saved him again."

"That's not why I'm calling you, Mr. Kane. You amazed my uncle with your expertise in the courtroom. He believed a movie of the DUI Doctor's life would have been a box office hit. Are you still interested in having a movie made about your life?"

Kane ran a hand over his mouth. Was she really interested in creating a movie about his life? Or was she fishing for him to finance the movie?

"How much money would I have to invest in this movie, Ms. Harrison?"

"Mr. Kane, I have financial backers, but I'm not opposed if you want to invest in the movie. I'm interested in developing a great script and finding the right actor to play your role. Does a movie about you still appeal?"

Damn it. If her pitch is on the up and up, it was coming at the worst time. He was close to bankruptcy. When word got out, rather than a rag to riches story, his tale would be about a man's riches to rags. The good news was Royce Harrison's niece wouldn't be calling him if she knew he could only afford a movie ticket.

"I need more information," he said. "How much time would it take to create a script?"

"Not as much time as you think, Mr. Kane. I have another take on this project that differs from my uncle. He thought you could play the DUI Doctor role. No offense, but being a successful attorney in court is different from emoting in front of a camera with real actors. I'm looking for a name actor who will make your character significant."

"Ms. Harrison, I was looking forward to being the star of a movie about me. There is only one DUI Doctor."

"Mr. Kane, from what I know about you and your ego, that comes as no surprise." She laughed. "Please bear with me for a moment and listen to how I want to play this. First, you need to write a memoir that includes your childhood."

"Whoa, I don't have the time for that. Nor do I have the wherewithal."

"I expected that answer," she said. "I can ghostwrite your memoir anyway you prefer, meaning I can embellish it as much as you want. In fact, I've already contacted a major book publisher. They were very interested in publishing your story. We both believe a memoir from the DUI Doctor would do very well."

"Why do you want me to write a memoir? Don't movies make more money than books?"

"Of course. But a best-selling memoir would be a great pre-promotion for your movie."

"Just so we understand each other, Ms. Harrison, you know my time is extremely valuable. If I were to agree to devote time to a memoir, I'd expect to receive an advance from the publisher and all of the royalties."

"Please call me Marilyn. Just so we understand each other, Oliver, my time is also valuable. If you require those conditions, you'd have to pay me in advance for my ghostwriting services. You will also pay me upfront for the movie script I'd write with both our names listed as co-writers. This isn't my first rodeo."

"Now we both know who we are dealing with, Marilyn, tell me about *your* film credits."

"That should have been your first question. I'm sure my uncle sent you his film resume. I've worked on most of his projects in a number of roles. Three independent films have received great reviews, which is why I have several backers. I've done too many TV ads to count. I'm also working on a project like yours that could be big if everything falls into place, which leads me to ask again, are you still interested in doing a movie about your life? I don't need a commitment from you today, but I do need to know if you're *not* interested. Why waste each other's time?"

"I'm interested," he said. "Of course, we would have to work out an agreement on paper. Listen, Marilyn, my schedule is real tight for the next two weeks. We should meet in person. Get to know each other. How can I get back to you when I see some daylight?"

"Don't wait too long, Oliver. What I'm offering you has a shelf life. Here's my cell phone number. . ."

Kane jotted down her cell phone number. At a different time he'd demand that he'd get to play himself. He also had an expiration date. She wasn't aware her offer was predicated on his winning the Hold 'Em tournament. His fortunes away from poker were also changing for the better. It was imperative he get a seat in the tournament. Then he'd have money to negotiate being the star of the movie. If his hot streak continued for two more weeks, the DUI Doctor was back in a big way. He picked up the receiver and dialed.

"This is Oliver Kane. I'm calling in the favor you owe me, Big Tony."

CHAPTER TWENTY-ONE

Mary's head rested comfortably on Bruno's shoulder. Her breathing was deep and steady. He avoided moving for the longest time fearing it would disrupt her peaceful slumber. His joints ached. Riding coach wasn't meant for tall passengers.

The plane hit an air pocket. The slight drop didn't affect Mary, but it reminded Bruno how leaving Mrs. Green's house in San Francisco affected Rachel. He still had a large lump in his throat after Rachel hugged him and cried, voicing the fear that she would never see him again. He promised to return.

Bruno had set the hands on his watch to East Coast time. Their red-eye flight got a late start and would get them to Boston around 9:30 am. As of yesterday afternoon, Sid Parker still had two seats open to the Hold 'Em tournament. Bruno was confident a desperate Oliver Kane would do anything to come up with the entry fee to be one of the twelve players vying for the three-million prize . . . even get a mob loan.

A cabin bell sounded, followed by the captain announcing the plane would be landing at Boston's Logan Airport shortly. Bruno nudged Mary slightly until her eyes crept open. She removed her head from his shoulder, blinked to get her bearings, stretched her arms, and fastened her seatbelt after noticing the lit sign.

"Sorry about using you as my pillow," she said, with a sheepish grin. "How long was I out? I hope I didn't snore."

"You slept for about two and a half hours. Does slurping and drooling count?"

"Very funny." Mary focused on his face. "I just noticed. Are you growing a beard?"

"I have been for a couple of days. The only time Oliver Kane may have seen me I was in a courtroom clean shaven and wearing a suit. Whiskers and casual threads can change a man's appearance. Kane may not recall my face after two more weeks of growth." He scratched his neck. "What do you think?"

"My honest opinion: it makes you look sort of sinister." She continued to study his face. "I doubt Mrs. Green would approve. However, Virginia would still think you're hot."

"I'll take sinister. Keep in mind I'll be providing security at the Hold 'Em tournament. We're scheduled to meet with Sid at the country club at noon. We should have plenty of time to pick up your luggage, take a shuttle to my car in extended parking, and get to Sid on time." He cocked his head to the side. "Did you just say Virginia thinks I'm hot?"

"Hold your water and ego, Studly," Mary said. "Virginia's heart belongs to someone else. I'm convinced she doesn't have a significant other in her life because she compares every man to Morgan Proffitt. To Virginia, that mold was broken when Mo died."

"Based on the way you revere Mr. Proffitt, you probably feel the same way."

"As much as I love that man for what he did for Rachel and me, I was only with him for six hours. My love for him is more like the father that I never had." She put a hand on his arm. "I know you care about me, but how much?"

"Is that a rhetorical question? I don't let just any woman sleep against my shoulder."

"I'm serious. You know I'm not comfortable with my part of the strategy you came up with to get Oliver Kane. I agreed to do my part to protect us. I want to be involved, but not in the role you've thrust upon me. If you really cared about me, Bruno, you'd take into account what I'm saying."

"If you're worried about your safety, Mary, you should know by now I will protect you."

As soon as the words flew out of Bruno's mouth his stomach jumped. He made the same promise to Wendy before she was killed, something he had revealed to Mary. Was she worried the same thing would happen to her?

"I know I'm safe with you, Bruno. That's not the problem. It's me. I never should have agreed to come back. I never wanted to return to Boston again and face the memories I'd prefer to forget. You've put me in a vulnerable situation. Oliver Kane is going to see right through me."

"You'll be fine, Mary. You've got the dialogue down. Remember, we're approaching Kane when he's at his weakest. I've studied the man for a long time. I know what makes him tick. You are the absolute perfect person to approach him." Bruno held up a palm before she could object. "I'm not going to sugarcoat what you will be up against. You're young and attractive. He's going to hit on you. He's smart and cunning. He's going to see your nervousness. Your hands will probably shake. Your voice might quiver. Believe it or not, those emotions are going to convince Kane you're being square with him. If you approach him anxious but confident about your ability, he won't get the sense he's being set up."

Bruno paused to see how she was processing what he was saying. So far, his comments made her bite down on her lower lip.

"He's going to be suspicious of you and your story," Bruno continued. "Stick to the script and above all, remember you are in the catbird seat. You're offering him his fail-safe. If he still rejects your proposal, you know what to say. Then leave your cell phone number and walk out the door."

Bruno's pep talk ended as the plane's wheels touched down on the runway. Mary white-knuckled the armrests. It was obvious she was feeling the pressure of a proverbial five-hundred pound gorilla on her shoulders. Bruno leaned back into his seat and gazed at her. Something else was troubling Mary besides coming back to Boston and having to interact with Oliver Kane.

* * * * *

Bruno wasn't shocked when he caught sight of Sid Parker's office desk. It was a junk drawer's delight. Stacks of country club paperwork, clipboards, T-shirts, files, newspapers, magazines, and a half-eaten lunch were piled on the desktop. How could someone this disorganized pull off a major three-million coup? Looks can be deceiving. As a teenager, it was no different. Sid's bedroom, school locker, and car were disorderly messes. When he played a card game, he never sorted his hand. His brilliant, jumbled mind knew exactly where each card was or where it belonged. Just like his desk.

Mary sat next to Bruno in chairs fronting the desk. A metal-framed photo of Sid with his wife and kids took up a tiny uncluttered corner. The photo had been shot several years before. The Sid Parker sitting behind his desk was 25 pounds heavier and he didn't have enough hair to be parted.

"There are Texas Hold 'Em tournaments everywhere, but not like this one," Bruno said. "How the hell did you come up with the concept and get the players to buy into it?"

"Actually, it wasn't my idea." Sid pushed some of the mish-mash into other mishmash. "Two of our Thursday Hold 'Em players have played in the Las Vegas World Series of Poker. Most Hold 'Em tournaments are marathons with a lot of players and the prize money is split proportionally with the final winners. They wanted to create a "mega- buck" Masters Hold 'Em tournament with several other players who were their equal in poker and in money status. They had in mind a tournament that would have a max of twelve players, one winner takes all, but were confronted with three problems: Where to hold the tournament, where to secure the cash money, and where to find an impartial person to organize it. They contacted me."

"But you aren't coordinating this super game out of the goodness of your heart, Sid." Bruno's lips spread into a wide smile.

Sid stared at Mary and then pointed a celery stick at Bruno. His eyes told no lies.

"Mary wouldn't be here if you couldn't trust her, Sid. If you trust me, you can trust her."

"This is all on the down-low. My cut is five percent, not counting a tip from the winner."

"With twelve players, your take is about two-hundred thousand," Mary blurted out.

Bruno double blinked. Mary was quick with numbers. What other talents was she hiding?

"It's not all gravy," Sid said. "I'm responsible for all the expenses. If something goes wrong before or during the tournament, it's my butt on the line." He lifted a carrot stick, made a face, and put it back on the plate. "I make a decent salary here to make ends meet. The extra lettuce I make from the Thursday night game goes to my kids' private schools. This tournament, if it goes well, is my chance to get ahead and stay ahead."

"They must really trust you if you're responsible for three-million in cash," Mary said.

"They trust me, but not with that much dough." Sid pointed at a safe behind him. "One of the players supplied a safe. He owns a safe company and he's also a board member of the club. I'm not privy to the combination, but he must be present when I stuff the cash in. The winner will have a nice problem of laundering the winnings."

"So will you, Sid, when you collect your percentage." Bruno leaned forward. "Did Oliver Kane come up with the entry fee?"

"Sorry to be the bearer of bad news. Eleven players have come up with the fee. Kane isn't one of them. However, one potential player called me this morning from England - of all places - on a business trip. He wants to lock up the twelfth seat. I told him it was first come, first served. He's flying back here to scoop up that last seat. He's legit."

Bruno and Mary exchanged a look. Her swallow was audible. Before she chickened out, he needed Mary to change into a different outfit for her meeting with Kane at his office.

"I have no idea what you had planned for Kane," Sid said. "The odds of him winning the prize against these players are astronomical. In horse racing terms, Kane is a hundred to one shot. What's more, the odds for Kane to come up with the entry fee are worse."

"What do we do now?" Mary said, her eyes widening at Bruno.

"We're going to push ahead exactly as planned. You're going to meet with Kane."

"Bruno," Mary said, shaking her head. "We talked about this."

"Were you scared before interviewing with Virginia for the Proffitt job?" Bruno asked.

"You bet I was."

"But you went through with it. How did you get over your fears?"

"Morgan Proffitt believed in my abilities."

"I'm no Morgan Proffitt, but Virginia and I believe you can push Kane over the edge."

"You two can settle your differences somewhere else," Sid interjected. "Bruno, you'll be working security alone, right?"

Bruno leaned back. Sid almost sounded desperate. Something didn't smell or taste right.

"There will be four of us, Sid."

"That doesn't please me, Bruno. I'm trying to keep the tournament and money on the down-low." Sid bit into a celery stick. "I know Kane is a big prick. Sorry about my language, Mary. What is your interest in him playing in the tournament?"

"No apology necessary, Sid," Mary said. "I couldn't have said it better myself."

Bruno shared Stanley's story about Kane being responsible for the mugging and the deaths that resulted from allowing miscreants under the influence to get back behind the wheel.

"I didn't realize how dangerous Kane is." Sid picked up a piece of paper. "By the way, I've arranged for Mary to start dealer school tomorrow like you asked, if need be."

Mary threw Bruno a disapproving look. "Do they teach cheating at dealer school, Sid?"

"No way. This poker tournament is legit."

"Let me know when Kane delivers the entry fee." Bruno rose, avoiding Mary's stare.

"Don't hold your breath, Bruno," Sid said with a chuckle.

CHAPTER TWENTY-TWO

Bruno stepped down from the curb on the road in front of the club. Mary grabbed his jacket sleeve before an approaching Cadillac hit him. He gasped out a word that sounded like "*whoaoaoaoa.*"

"Thank you, Mary. My mind was somewhere else. You're nice to have around."

Mary's phone rang. Her mood brightened seconds into a call that lasted a minute.

"Virginia wanted to tell me about her performance portraying movie mogul Marilyn Harrison," Mary said, after hanging up. "Oliver Kane is re-interested in doing a movie of his life, as long as he can play himself. That cracked both of us up. Obviously, your plan worked, Bruno. Virginia had to leave for a meeting, but she would call some other time with Detective Prescott news.

They walked to the parking lot in silence. Mary's auburn hair fluttered in the wind. She gave up trying to put each strand back in order. Bruno's green 1996 Chevy Camaro appeared out of place next to several posh European cars. He reached for the passenger door handle, but she pulled his arm again and gazed up at him.

"What's bothering you, Bruno," she said.

"I can't understand Sid's reluctance to have extra men safe-keeping three-million in cash, even if it's secure in a safe. Sid is a sharp guy. He should know better."

"I was hoping you'd be overly concerned about my meeting with Kane in a few hours. So you're not worried about Kane forcing himself on me? Or I'll screw up the mission?"

"Just remember, Kane needs you more than you need him. You hold all the leverage." She didn't resist when he took her hand into his. "Kane is the one who should be worried if he lays a hand on you."

"Is that your rah-rah pep talk to make me less nervous about Kane? Or do you really care about me?"

"Are you blind, lady? I haven't felt this way about a woman since Wendy. Does that answer your question about my caring?"

"Yes!" Mary rose on tiptoes and kissed him. "Mrs. Green and Virginia believe you are my Mr. Right. I've been trying my darnedest not to fall in love with you, Bruno, but I can't help myself. Our problem is you're staying in Boston. Rachel and I are in a good place. Mrs. Green and Virginia are family to us. I'm so grateful for what we have and don't want to lose it. A relationship with thousands of miles between us wouldn't work. And if we get too close it will be that much more hurtful."

"We'll figure it out, Mary." Bruno opened the passenger door for her. "We have to."

* * * * *

Bruno's phone rang just as he unlocked his apartment door. Mary entered with her suitcase as if she lived there. He leaned against the hallway wall to answer the call.

"It's Sid, Bruno. The dude who's in England just called. His flight is delayed due to mechanical problems. England is five hours ahead of us. He's confident he can get to me in time with the entry fee. If that doesn't happen, he'll have to get his money to me tomorrow. The guy's really eager to play."

"Thanks for the heads up, Sid. Have you heard from Oliver Kane?"

"Nope, not a word from Kane. I think that ship has sailed." Sid cleared his throat. "It's good to have you on board, Bruno."

"Did you have a backup if I had declined the job?"

"In all sincerity, you were my first and only choice for security, buddy."

Bruno flinched. If Sid wasn't lying, he was crazy not to have several backups. Something was going on with him.

"I appreciate your confidence in me. When I was in San Francisco, I contacted three ex-cop buddies here in Boston to assist with security. That's the only way it will work for me. All the exits will be guarded. The poker room will be my station."

"Bruno, we really don't need your ex-cop buddies. The less people involved the better. Guards would be a big red flag. We have to make it look like a normal club activity."

"I get that. On the other hand, what if it looks like a normal club activity that has gone terribly wrong? Let me do my job, Sid." He paused for a response that didn't come. "We never talked about the money in the safe. I want a final count in my presence. I want –"

"Don't worry about it, Bruno. I've got that part taken care of. I'll call you when the twelfth seat is filled."

Bruno frowned at the phone after Sid ended the call. When it came to security, he worried about everything. Sid did know his business, but guidelines were needed.

Bruno stepped into his apartment's living room. Newspapers were scattered on the couch. Moccasin slippers were over by his folding table desk. Stacks of files were on the tabletop. His Boston Celtics' jacket was draped over the desk chair. The trash basket was full. He wandered into the kitchen. Several plates rested in the sink waiting to be washed, dried, and put away. His place wasn't a complete disaster.

He moved into the bedroom. Mary's suitcase was propped open on the bed. She was transferring her clothes into the empty bottom drawer and into the closet.

"If you need more room," he said, "I can empty another drawer for you."

"What I need is for you to get outta here so I can change into the *uniform* Virginia picked out for me to meet Kane. What time is my appointment with the letch?"

CHAPTER TWENTY-THREE

Oliver Kane stared at the Rolodex card between his thumb and forefinger. The phone number on the card left him two choices: damned if he did and damned if he didn't. He tossed the card on a stack of overdue invoices piling up on his desktop.

Kane unlocked the bottom drawer and removed a clear plastic packet. A snort of stimulating nose candy could help him make a decision that would affect his life one way or another, forever.

He eyed a yellow legal pad lying next to his mountain of debts. Maybe he should make a list of why he should or shouldn't make the call. Then again, it would only be an exercise in futility. He knew which side would win.

The phone buzzed, startling him. He closed his eyes and made two fists. It was probably another greedy bill collector. He ignored it. His secretary buzzed again.

"Yeah, Vera," he said after picking up the receiver. He ogled the packet of white powder on bills he couldn't pay. How ironic. He could buy a cocaine farm with what he owed.

"Your appointment is here, Mr. Kane."

His finger ran down the appointment calendar and stopped at the name Mary McGrath. Vera must have scheduled her when he was busy. The name didn't look familiar. What kind of trouble was this woman in? More importantly, did she have a shitload of money to make his troubles evaporate? Probably not, but some money was better than no money.

"Tell Mary McGrath I will greet her in the lobby shortly, Vera."

He sniffed hard through his nose and ditched the packet and overdue bills into a drawer. His feet slipped into black loafers under the desk. He shined them on each pant leg for a quick polish. By habit, he put his suit jacket on and opened the office door.

The lobby was about fifty steps away. He had less than a minute to pull himself together to put on a song and dance the woman was most likely expecting. She should know what he looked like since his picture had been in newspapers and on TV for years. Entering the lobby, he noticed an unshaven, dark-haired man sitting with his long legs crossed, leafing through a magazine. He'd seen this man before, but couldn't recall when or where.

Kane received an unexpected surprise. Sitting next to the man, Mary McGrath was probably in her mid-to-late twenties, and an absolute babe. Kane was probably twice her age, but that was never a concern. She was wearing a tight black skirt and dark nylons that showed more than a hint of nice gams below her knees. The top two buttons of her green blouse were unfastened: just enough to tease his trained eye. Her vibrant blue eyes were enhanced with just enough makeup to not look slutty. As it turned out, he didn't need the white blow to be stimulated.

"Oliver Kane." He offered his hand and a smile. "You must be Mary McGrath."

She stood and accepted his hand briefly, but didn't return his smile. Her skin was like silk. He could hear her swallow, a sign she was nervous. He liked that. She'd be more reliant on what he could do for her. He wondered what she might do for him. It wouldn't be the first time he was offered sex for his courtroom talents.

"Please hold all of my calls, Vera." He pointed with an open hand towards his office. "Can we get you some coffee, tea, or water, Ms. McGrath?"

"No, thank you."

As they walked down the hallway, his nose sensor picked up her enticing scent. Kane closed his office door when she took a seat in front of his massive desk. He sat down in the chair opposite her, something he didn't often do. Thus far she'd only said three words, but he found her voice pleasing. Most potential clients were chatterboxes, spouting out the situation they were in. He was stunned by how different she was from most of the people who needed him. She could be shy or maybe in awe of his presence.

"How may I be of service to you, Ms. McGrath?" His eyes shifted from her face to her chest.

"Am I correct in assuming that anything I say to you is privileged?"

"Yes. Anything you say to me shall remain confidential between us."

"If I was arrested for killing a person with my car while under the influence of alcohol, what would it cost for you to defend me?"

"For starters, a quarter of a million," Kane said, stretching to snatch the yellow legal pad from his desk. "I need to know the particulars of who, what, where, and when this incident occurred."

"Would I be accurate in saying the cost could climb to say a half a million?"

"It depends on the number of hours needed to work your case. That figure is feasible."

"I want to be totally up front with you, Mr. Kane. I don't have half a million dollars."

"Ms. McGrath," he said, slumping back into his chair, "you must understand why they call me the DUI Doctor. I'm the best at what I do and my services are in great demand."

"Mr. Kane, I said I don't have that kind of money. I didn't say I don't have access to a half a million dollars. Allow me to correct you on something else. It isn't how you can be of service to me, but it's how we can be of service to each other."

Kane's head shot back. This was getting interesting. He straightened the knot of his tie that didn't need straightening. Her voice didn't have one hint of being seductive, but he was aroused. He adjusted how he was sitting. What kind of service was she suggesting?

"Would you clarify your last statement, Ms. McGrath?" He leaned towards her.

"I'm here to offer you some life insurance." She put her hands together in her lap. "In other words, I can provide something you badly need."

"You want to sell me life insurance." He laughed long and hard. "Surely, Ms. McGrath, you're joking."

"No joke, Mr. Kane."

"You've got some nerve, babe." No longer smiling, he stood up. "I'm not interested in your little hustle. This is the big leagues. Go play your game with someone else."

"Sit down, Mr. Kane." She elevated her voice. "I understand your skepticism. I'm aware you have massive debt. You are going to lose everything unless you make a big score. That's why you're desperate to secure the last seat in the rich man's Texas Hold 'Em tournament. The three million dollar prize is your only way out. You could secure the entry fee for the last seat, but that doesn't assure you winning the three-million." Her tongue ran across her lips. "The life insurance I can offer you isn't on a policy, but it's a guarantee that the jackpot will be yours. If you're interested, we can speak further. If not, I will leave and the life insurance will be off the table."

"Who the hell are you?" Kane sat down delivering her a defiant stare.

"Like I said, my name is Mary McGrath."

"Will you show me some proof to verify that?"

She removed a Massachusetts driver's license from her purse and held it out for him to see. Her hand was trembling, making it difficult for Kane to read. He squinted at the license, at her face, then at the license again. The expiration date, picture, name, blue eyes, auburn hair, five feet five inches tall, one-hundred-and-fifteen pounds all seemed to be on the square. Her words had come out confidently, but her voice didn't convey the same meaning. Her hands were clasped together to control the shake after returning her license into her purse. Were her nerves a positive or a negative?

"How can you guarantee me or anyone else to be a winner of the Hold 'Em tournament?"

"Mr. Kane, the tournament is rigged."

"How are you privy to that knowledge?"

"Initially, the tournament will have two tables. I was selected to be one of the two dealers for a specific reason. My hands are my business. I'm a card mechanic, although you wouldn't know it. My fingers are shaking because I'm anxious about what I just voiced to you. It's illegal and could get me thrown in jail." She notched her head at him. "You noticed my hands when you weren't ogling my tits. The twelve male players don't expect a woman to be a card manipulator. Like you, they'd rather stare at my boobs and face."

"You must be working with that bastard Sid Parker, the club's manager."

"Sid is the one who put the tournament together and approved me as a dealer, but he's not aware the game is fixed."

It took a few seconds for Kane to close his mouth. Who was the mastermind rigging the game if Sid wasn't involved?

"If there are two dealers, how do you know I will be at your table?"

"Eventually the two tables will be condensed to one table as the players drop out. You will always be at my table."

Two soft knocks made both of them look at the door. Kane ran a hand through his hair. He'd told Vera to hold all his calls. That meant do not disturb. He jumped up and swung the door open.

"I'm sorry Mr. Kane," Vera said. "My son was hurt at school. I have to leave. There is-"

"All right, go." He flipped his hand at her. "But I'm only paying you for half a day."

Kane slammed the door in her face. Vera was the least of his problems. He sat down behind his desk this time and pointed the sharp end of the letter opener at Mary McGrath.

"Let's get real, Ms. McGrath. You were picked to pitch to me because you are one hot number. Who sent you?"

"Sorry, Mr. Kane. You're better off not knowing."

"Or could it be you are better off not telling me?"

"Touché."

"What's in it for you, Ms. McGrath?"

"I've been waiting for that question. It should have been your first. In essence, we will become partners. My take from the three million you will win is five-hundred-thousand dollars. I believe that is a fair amount. I'm not greedy, Mr. Kane. I could ask for much more."

"Why would you come to me? I'm not even in the tournament." He pushed out his palm before she could answer. "Hell, I'll answer my own question. You pitched me because I'm desperate for the jackpot money. But your timing here is telling. You came to me, today, after I made a phone call yesterday about funding my entry fee."

Her eyebrows arched up. Mary McGrath was easy to read. She didn't know about the call.

"I'm not the first player you have contacted, am I?"

She cocked her head to the side and for the first time smiled.

"Of course, I'm not the first player you approached. It would be someone who already has a seat in the tournament. The player in question wouldn't need the money like I do. This is a man who probably loves to win and hates to lose, the very reason he amassed all of his wealth in the first place." He aimed a forefinger up at the ceiling. "The other player nixed your half a million payout. How much was he willing to give you?"

"Mr Kane, we are getting nowhere with your theories." Her eyes focused on his. "Here is what I meant regarding life insurance for you. Winning the tournament prize is your only way out of your financial dilemma. However, if you obtain the entry fee but fail to cut a deal with me, you're wasting your time trying to secure the money to play in the tournament. *You can't win!* Your only option is to partner with me."

Kane pressed the letter opener point into a finger, breaking skin and producing blood. Everything she was saying was logical and made sense. What other choice did he have? It was a perfect plan; he was the ideal patsy. That was the problem: the setup was too perfect. Beads of moisture formed on his forehead. He wiped his brow with the back of his hand. He was used to making other people sweat.

"What would happen if I won and decided not to pay you, Ms. McGrath?"

"Was that a rhetorical question? I believe you know what will happen to you, Mr. Kane."

"Your life insurance is more like blackmail, Ms. McGrath. We have no deal."

"I'm sorry you feel that way, Mr. Kane." She rose to her feet, placed a card on his desk, and then headed for the door. "We both just lost a lot of money - you more than me."

Mary McGrath didn't look back at Kane as she headed for the door. Did he just make a fatal mistake?

CHAPTER TWENTY-FOUR

Oliver Kane wrapped a handkerchief around his bleeding finger while he admired Mary McGrath's curvy derriere as she headed for the door. She had given him an opportunity to erase most or all his debts and troubles. The scheme seemed too good to be true and he declined. Now he wasn't sure. His stomach was grumbling signals to him. Had he just thrown away any chance to turn his life around?

"Wait!" Kane bounded from his chair as Mary opened his office door to leave.

She turned around to find him rushing towards her. Her hand went straight into her purse. Holy shit, was she about to pull a gun on him? He fell to his knees on the carpet. She stared down at him with steely eyes, sending a surge of panic through him he hadn't felt since he was Morgan Proffitt's passenger when he drove a speeding cab towards a cement overpass. Proffitt had let him live. Would Mary McGrath do the same?

"Hold on," he cried, waving his hands. "I was only trying to stop you from leaving so we can negotiate." His throat and mouth were parched. "Please, don't do anything both of us will regret. I'm sure we can calmly and peacefully come to an acceptable agreement."

"I didn't come here to dicker with you. I'm offering you a plan that will be beneficial to both of us. You either accept the conditions I laid out to you before or we have no deal."

Kane's brows knit together. He considered himself a power broker in court and in this office, but Mary McGrath wielded all the muscle away from him. She hadn't dislodged her hand from her purse. The expression on her pretty face was unyielding. If she possessed a gun, he hadn't a sliver of doubt that she'd use it. The DUI Doctor was now a defendant in her court, a deja vu of what Morgan Proffitt had done to him a year ago. He never thought he'd have to defend his life again this way.

He rose slowly from the floor, eyeing the hand in her purse. She took two steps back. He hated this woman for humiliating him, but couldn't help lusting after her even more. He threw the bloodstained handkerchief in the trash and sat in his chair behind his desk.

"Ms. McGrath, what would you do if someone you had never met before cold-called to propose rigging a three-million dollar prize in your favor? You'd have major apprehensions just like I do." He pointed to the chair she had been sitting in. She shook her head. "Don't get me wrong, I'm impressed with your scheme. Whoever developed this scam is dastardly brilliant, but it's also full of risk. I need assurances."

"What kind of assurances, Mr. Kane?"

"First and foremost, do you have a gun in your purse?"

"You'll find out real quick if you make a move on me," she said firmly.

"Ms. McGrath, I'm offended if you'd think I'd make advances towards you."

Her response was a sneer. Why didn't she reach into her purse when she observed him admiring her figure? Plus, if she had a gun, it would have been pointed at him when he had rushed to stop her from leaving. He leaned forward and envisioned her minus the black skirt and green blouse. His lips spread into a smile. He shook his head and pinched his wounded finger hard. The pain it provided brought him out of his reverie.

"Who are you working with, Ms. McGrath? How many people are involved in this plot?"

"You rephrased a question you asked me before, Mr. Kane. I'm not a witness in court."

"Your answer wasn't an answer," he said. "May I remind you, partnerships are formed on trust? How can I depend on you if I can't trust you?"

"It comes down to this and only this: if you win, I win. Put another way, you can only win with me as your partner. You can't win without me, but I can still win without you."

"Yes, but you won't get nearly as much money as you'd like." He leaned back in his chair with open palms. "That's why we should have equal say as partners."

"That is not the way this game is going to be played, Mr. Kane. You have no say in how this will go down. It's my way or no way." She removed her hand from the purse. "Do you know what will happen to you if you don't relinquish my five-hundred-thousand once the three-million is in your possession?"

"I get your point. Just so you know, every dollar I come away with will go towards what I owe. This may sound ridiculous, but with your half mil and what I will owe from borrowing the entry fee, it won't cover all my debts." He rubbed the side of his face. "If we are partners, I'd appreciate it if you would be open to negotiating your portion."

"Mr. Kane, I have no sympathy for your money woes. It's nobody's fault but your own. Nor do you give a rat's ass about my going to jail if we get caught." She put a trembling hand back into her purse. "You should be aware of something else. Since you don't drive, a car will be provided for you to transfer my portion of the money to the driver after you win the tournament. The driver will take you wherever you want to go after that."

Kane's head tilted to the side. How did she know he didn't drive? She must be aware he has no security since Rollie is dead. What else does she know?

"You can't be serious about how we exchange the money," he said. "What's going to stop the driver or anyone else in the car from taking the money or my life?"

"Your trust in me, Mr. Kane. You are lucky to have this opportunity. You either accept my conditions or we have no deal" She pointed a finger at him. "Are you in or out?"

"What other conditions am I not aware of?" he asked.

She had him cornered and wasn't giving him an inch. He never came away from a negotiation without getting something. She wasn't willing to part with her portion of the money. What else could he get?

"Assuming I can still obtain the entry fee, I want to throw in one little caveat. Since I'm your partner, Ms. McGrath, I want you to be part of the deal."

"I'm bringing you guaranteed luck, but that doesn't mean you will get lucky with me. This is strictly business. Yes or no, Mr. Kane?"

"You should have been a lawyer, Ms. McGrath. If I get the entry fee, I'm in."

* * * * *

Bruno sat next to Mary on a cement flower box in the plaza at the front of Oliver Kane's office building. She had approached him in the waiting room after exiting Kane's office shaking like she'd just come out of a frozen meat locker. He put his arm around her shoulder as she snuggled into his body.

If possible, Bruno felt worse than Mary. He was responsible for what she had gone through. He had pressured her into meeting with Kane. He had prepped her about what to say and how to say it. He had taught her how to command the room and convince Kane she was his last chance to climb out of the mess he was in. His first inclination was to mop the floor with Kane, but Mary grabbed his arm and convinced him Kane had not physically touched her. The last thing he needed was more incentive to eliminate the DUI Doctor forever after what happened to his fiancée.

"I'm so sorry, Mary. I was wrong in pushing you into meeting with Kane. You've gone through a lot of terrible things in your life. You can throw this encounter on that pile."

"Honestly, Bruno, it's just the opposite. I'm glad you made me do it." Mary took several deep breaths and gave him a synopsis of what transpired in Kane's office. "I had never met Oliver Kane in person. He has a commanding persona. If I didn't know anything about him and what a despicable person he really is, I would've been impressed. He had no problem that I would cheat for him. That sickened me. So I enjoyed making the creep squirm when I wouldn't let him have a say. At one point I even felt a little sorry for him - got over that real quick." Her words were coming faster with each sentence. "Still, I was scared out of my mind he'd do or say something I couldn't handle and that it would spoil the whole deal." She patted his knee. "You know what got me through it? Knowing you were in the waiting room if I needed help. I used almost every tactic you gave me. You were so right about him hitting on me. It was wise of you to have me bring my current Massachusetts driver's license. And that was good advice about not negotiating with him. When I put a hand in my purse, he thought I had a gun. It scared the crap out of him." She retrieved her cell phone. "Just as you suggested, my trigger finger was on your cell phone number. My gun was the can of pepper spray you gave me just in case."

"I couldn't be more proud of you, Mary. You took one for the team. You set the trap. Now we have to wait and see if the rat takes the bait." He squeezed her shoulder. "I don't have any medals or ribbons to give you. How about I reward your performance with a night out on the town?"

"Is that your lame way of asking me out on a date, Bruno?"

"I haven't had a lot of practice lately. Was it that bad?"

"No, it was kind of cute. Where can a girl get a glass of Grand Marnier around here?"

* * * * *

Kane picked up the phone as soon as Mary McGrath left his office. Was it too late for him to get a tournament seat? If not, would the money he requested through Big Tony still be available? His first call would determine whether a second call was necessary.

"Sid, this is Oliver Kane. Is there a seat available in the Hold 'Em tournament?"

"We still have one seat open. However, there's a player who's coming in some time today. First in with the money gets the seat. No exceptions."

"If I throw in a couple thou under the table, would you lock up the seat for me?"

"Let me put it to you this way, Mr. Kane. I will accept your bribe as soon as a rabbi becomes the Pope. In other words, no way. After all, it wouldn't be kosher."

"That son of a bitch," Kane grumbled, after hanging up and dialing a second number. "This is Oliver Kane. I need the quarter mil like we discussed the other day. I need it delivered to my office immediately. Will there be any problems?"

"So you're going to run with the big rollers, Ollie." Big Tony laughed. "You asked if there will be any problems. That depends."

"Depends on what?"

"The money will be delivered to your office." Big Tony stopped talking to take a puff of his cigar. "You'll have big problems if you don't return the money and the vig per our agreement. Capiche?"

Kane threw a fist in the air. The news felt like a shot of adrenaline. In two weeks his money trouble would be over if he got the cash to Sid Parker in time. He rose from his chair with vigor and moved to the window overlooking the front patio. He could envision "KANE TOWER" letters glittering on the outside of the building again . . .

"Huh." Mary McGrath was sitting with the unshaven man who had been sitting next to her in the waiting area. He had his arm around her.

Who is this guy? A boyfriend, bodyguard, mastermind behind the tournament plot, or all three? It didn't matter. Mary McGrath had brought him to his knees in his office. He was hell-bent on returning the favor.

CHAPTER TWENTY-FIVE

Oliver Kane's foot pounded down on an imaginary gas pedal from the cab's back seat. Each second that passed made the drive from his office to the country club ramp up his anxiety. He held his briefcase on his lap with both hands. If Rollie had been chauffeuring him, he'd be at the club by now or getting an earful from his boss.

"Can't you drive faster, driver?" Kane shouted. "I'm late and you're making me later."

"Listen, buddy, I've been driving a cab for over thirty years. I'm over the speed limit already. It's not worth it to me to drive at an unsafe speed and get into an accident."

"Would you be more motivated if I make it worth your while?"

"I'm listening." The cabbie made a sharp turn sending Kane sliding into the door.

"Would a greenback bill with Ben Franklin's face perk up your ears?"

"The C note would be my tip, right? It doesn't include the fare on the meter, right?"

"Sure." Kane gripped his case tighter. The cabbie was more interested in haggling than getting him to the club. "Now step on it, will ya?"

"If I get pulled over for speeding or reckless driving, that's on you too, right?"

"Absolutely. How's this: Officer, don't blame the cabbie. It was my fault entirely."

"Man, you're hugging that briefcase like its got a million bucks in it." The cabbie snorted out a laugh. "My old lady would like me to hold her that tight."

"I've got another tip for you. Quit your damn babble and just drive."

Kane gripped the case tighter. The driver would shit his britches if he knew how many hundreds were in the briefcase. What would happen if the other guy got the Hold 'Em seat? The DUI Doctor's whole world would collapse. He already owed millions. To make matters worse, he'd owe thousands of dollars more in mob loan interest.

The cab raced past a parked police car. Kane stomped his foot down on the floorboard. Being stopped by a cop was the last thing he needed. He pressed the briefcase to his chest and looked out the back window to see if the squad car was chasing after the cab. The cab turned the corner. His chances of getting the last tournament seat would be highly unlikely if a cop pulled the cab over to write out a ticket.

"Don't sweat the small stuff, buddy," the driver said, peering at him in the rearview mirror. "That Dunkin' Donut shop is one of their favorite hangouts."

The driver zipped through a stop sign without stopping. Tense breaths escaped from Kane's mouth. They were close to the club. Was the other potential player ahead or behind him?

WMC's granite sign appeared. The cab pulled up to the main entrance. Kane crumbled up Ben Franklin's face and hurled it at the cabbie. He pushed open the cab door and planted his shoes on the pavement while holding his briefcase.

"Hey," the cabbie yelled. "You still owe me for the cab fare."

"You've got a good case," Kane shouted back. "Call a lawyer."

Kane took a quick look north and south to see if another anxious person with a briefcase was rushing around. He sprinted into the club and headed toward the administrative offices. Several heads turned to observe a man in a suit dashing through the building carrying a briefcase. Sid Parker's office door was closed. Kane had no intention of offering a polite knock. He twisted the doorknob and entered the office.

Sid was standing behind the desk speaking into a small cell phone unlike any other Kane had seen - maybe one of those prepaid phones. It looked like Sid was talking into his palm. If a look could kill, Kane would be dead on the spot. He held up the briefcase and rubbed a thumb and forefinger together on his other hand to indicate what was inside. Sid turned his back on Kane, indicating he wasn't welcome.

"I'll call you back, babe," Sid said. "Someone just burst into my office without knocking. Don't worry, everything is still cool. Love you, too."

Sid placed the phone into the middle drawer of the desk and locked it. He dropped the key back in his pants pocket and eyed Kane. If there was a landline phone on the desktop, Kane couldn't find it among the paraphernalia. Sid grinned at him like the Cheshire cat. What was that about?

"You're too late, Mr. Kane," Sid said. "All the tournament seats are sold."

"What?" The briefcase dropped from Kane's hand. He lost his balance. The room was spinning. He grabbed for the desk, knocking several objects to the floor. With the aid of Mary McGrath's skill at manipulating a deck of cards, the tournament prize was his. It was his last hope. His legs gave out, sending him to the floor hyperventilating.

"It can't end like this," wheezed from his mouth.

Kane's vision blurred. He could make out a vague impression of Sid placing a hand on his protruding belly with vigorous laughter coming from his mouth. What a sadistic bastard. A fit of anger brought some life back to Kane. He looked around the office for a weapon. A lonely golf club was in a corner. If he could muster the strength to get the putter, Sid Parker was a dead man.

"I'm just screwing with you, Mr. Kane," Sid said, still chortling. "That's what you get for bursting into my office without even knocking, and being a total asshole to me and the weekly poker players. If you have a quarter of a million dollars in that briefcase, you get the last seat in the tournament. If you don't, get the hell out of my office."

Kane waited to get control of his breathing before attempting to stand. He lifted the briefcase and fell into a chair in front of the desk. What Sid did to him was beyond cruel, but at least his heart could take a shock and keep on ticking. It also told him Sid didn't know the tournament was rigged for him to win. The winner was responsible for paying Sid five percent and a tip. Why would Sid screw with him unless he thought Kane had little chance to win?

Kane's eyes bore their hate into the club manager. For a smart guy, Sid didn't know who he was dealing with. One way to get back at the prick with a masochistic sense of humor was for Kane to win the prize money and not pay the son of a bitch anything. None of the players signed any documents. Nor could they go to the police. They were playing for cash, leaving no paper trails. This arrangement was twelve wealthy men playing by gentlemen's rules. No one ever accused Oliver Kane of being a gentleman.

"Open the briefcase, Mr. Kane," Sid ordered.

Kane's demeanor kept shifting from euphoric-red to gloomy-blue. He had to remind himself he had a seat in the tournament and not to irritate Sid . . . at least until he was the winner. Then again, who was monitoring Sid? What if Sid changed his mind and gave the seat to the other guy? Who would know? Sid seemed to be an honest guy by turning down thousands under the table to secure the seat for Kane, but who was auditing Sid?

Kane opened the briefcase to show twenty-five packets of hundred-dollar bills. Each packet was ten thousand. He didn't take the time to count each packet. What if-

The phone rang somewhere from Sid's desk. He fished through several objects and lifted the receiver to his ear. His hand ran through what little hair he had left.

"I'm sorry, Mr. Brooks," Sid said. "I just sold the last seat. I know you came back early from England just to submit the entry fee. I promise you if a player drops out, you will be my first call." He stared at Kane. "I'm really sorry. I was rooting for you."

"Mr. Kane," Sid said, after disconnecting the call, "do you want to wait until the gentleman from Moore Safe Company arrives so you can witness your money being transferred into the safe? He's the only person who has the safe's combination number."

"You give me little choice but to wait."

Kane studied the safe. Someone was monitoring Sid after all. Was there some way to break into the safe? With all the unsavory people he knew, not one safecracker came to mind. If he could find someone, he wouldn't have to pay Mary McGrath her half-million bucks. Or shell out Sid's fee. Even better, Sid would probably take the blame.

"I have other business to tend to, Mr. Kane. I'd appreciate some privacy. Please wait in the lobby until the person from Moore Safe Company arrives."

"I'll be in the bar." Kane closed the briefcase and walked out the door holding it tight.

* * * * *

This time Bruno didn't have to wait across the street from his "office" in a doorway. Nor would Stanley be offering to spill his guts to put Kane out of business. A large knot pained his stomach. What did Stanley get for doing the right thing? A visit to the hospital.

Bruno led Mary into the pub and guided her to two barstools isolated at the far end of the bar, away from the other patrons. A low-level hum of background noise filled the room, with the exception of one loudmouth slurring his words. Bruno recognized many of the faces who had lost their souls to drinking daily.

"Is this one of your hangouts?" Mary craned her neck to take in the rest of the room.

"In a way," he said. "I have an agreement with the owner, who happens to be tending bar, to use his office to meet clients. In return, I give him tickets to the New England Patriots home games. He's a big football fan and I'm saving the expense of paying for an office every month." Bruno gestured to the owner with a hand. "He's under the impression I work for the CIA, and I've never told him otherwise."

"Isn't that dishonest?" she asked, shifting her view to the bartender. "Making someone think you are something that you aren't?"

"Not at all. I never told him I worked for the agency. Are you going to rat me out?"

"No way. If you do work for the CIA, you might have to kill me."

"On the contrary, Mary, you are always safe when you are with me."

"I know." Mary touched his hand. "I wish our relationship could be under different circumstances. Thank you again for urging me to play my role in the Kane scheme. As nervous as I was about being alone with him, I feel really good about myself right now, like I could do anything." She removed her hand. "Do you really work for the CIA?"

Bruno laughed.

The owner strolled over to stand in front of them. He ignored Bruno, grinned at Mary, and offered her his hand.

"Do you work with this man, miss?" the owner said, wiping the bar top with a wet towel.

"All I can say, sir, is we just came off a case." She kept a straight face. "My name is . . . you can just call me Mary. We're not here on business. I'd like a Grand Marnier please."

"My pleasure, ma'am. I must say you really pretty up the joint."

"Thank you. I'll take that as a compliment." She poked Bruno in the ribs with her elbow. "How come you never say nice things like that to me, agent ... I mean Bruno?"

"When you get to it," Bruno said to the owner, "I'd like a Grey Goose on the rocks."

Bruno's phone rang as the bartender put two cocktail napkins down in front of them.

"I don't know how, but you got your wish, Bruno," Sid Parker said across the cell towers. "Kane coughed up the entry fee. He's in the tournament. As promised, I will sign Mary up for dealer school."

"Thanks for the heads up, Sid." Bruno wanted to out-shout the drunken loudmouth.

"Bring two dice cups with the drinks," Bruno said to the owner. "Congratulations, Mary. You did it. Oliver Kane is in the tournament. Dealer school begins tomorrow. Let's start your education now. Have you ever played liar's dice poker?"

CHAPTER TWENTY-SIX

Oliver Kane visualized a ray of light at the end of his tunnel of debt. He'd spent three days on the phone offering insincere apologies along with fabricated excuses to the company's expecting payments from him. The volume of his voice ramped up after he shared optimism that his situation would soon be rectified once he received a settlement check from a case his law firm had been working on for two years - another blatant lie.

Kane rubbed his tender right ear. The oversized prize money presented a problem most people would love to have, but was still a challenge: how to launder that amount of cash without the tax man knocking on his door? Any cash deposit over ten-thousand is a red flag that a bank has to report. Some of his debts could be paid in cash, maybe at a discount since cash isn't traceable. But he was being crushed by a giant eight ball of maxed-out credit cards with brutal interest rates, as well as loans, overdue house mortgages, late office rent, and unpaid back taxes.

He was confident Mary McGrath could manipulate the cards his way so he'd win the tournament. After all, she had a vested interest in his winning, except . . . a sudden thought made him choke. What if his co-conspirator was double-or triple-dealing with other players? Maybe she wasn't as skilled as she boasted? If she contacted three or four others with the same deal she'd offered to him, the odds of her getting a slice of the pie grew substantially without her cheating at all. Maybe some of the other players offered her a better return. He had to get Mary McGrath alone in his office. He wanted her to demonstrate her sleight of hand with a deck of cards. Perhaps he could also get lucky with her performing other talents on his office couch.

Kane left his desk and went to the window. A fierce wind was affecting pedestrians and their garments. A man's hat flew off. Women were holding down dresses to prevent them from flying up. He wanted to leave the office for a walk to clear his head, but thought better of it. Rollie was no longer around to protect him. Too many people hated him, possibly even Mary McGrath. He couldn't get her out of his mind. Was she the real deal? She had all the right answers; now he wasn't sure. He needed a contingency plan.

A man heading towards the front entrance stopped in the patio and placed his briefcase on one of the cement planter boxes. He worked the tiny combination dials until the top of his case flipped open. It reminded Kane of how the Moore Safe representative worked the safe's combination for Sid to remove money from his briefcase and pack the bundles of cash with the other entry fees. He blew out an excited breath. It wouldn't be hard to break into Sid's office. The WMC didn't have security. How could he find someone to crack open the safe? After all, stealing money from the safe was no different than winning the tournament by cheating. He wouldn't know a safecracker from a saltine, but one of his contacts might have a connection. There were a lot of variables he hadn't worked out, but the concept thrilled him. Plan B could very well morph into Plan A.

He went to the Rolodex on his desk and fingered through the cards until he found the one he needed; the same card he'd used to rough up rat fink Stanley. As much as he wanted to give Sid Parker and those smug, wealthy poker players a piece of his mind after winning the tournament, breaking into the safe would have a better outcome since he wouldn't have to pay Sid or Mary McGrath. He'd love to be the fly on the wall when Sid walked into his office and found the safe door wide open and empty.

The phone buzzed. Most likely it was another irate person asking for payment. He glanced at the stack of invoices still needing his attention. How easy it was to mount up massive debt and a thousand times more difficult to pay it back.

"Mr. Kane," Vera said, "the owner of the building is on the line returning your call."

"This is Oliver Kane." He pressed the receiver to his left ear. "Thank you for returning my call. First and foremost, I apologize for being so late with rent payments. As much as it wasn't our fault, the bottom line is I'm still responsible. We invested well over a million dollars for a case that unexpectedly depleted our resources. But there's good news. I'm confident the case is finally about to be settled. We expect a large settlement within the next three weeks. You have been extremely patient and I thank you. All I'm asking is for a few weeks more of leeway."

"Mr. Kane, I highly doubt the excuse you offered is what put you so much in arrears. I've given you more than enough time to make up what you owe me, but you've ignored our letters until your phone call today. Frankly, I don't relish evicting a tenant, but you may be the exception."

"What if I make it up to you by adding five thousand in cash?"

"Let me get this straight. You owe me a substantial amount of money and you are dictating the terms? No deal."

"Three weeks. Just give me three weeks. I'll throw in my legal services as a kicker if you are ever in need of a lawyer."

"I have no need for your legal services, Mr. Kane. I don't drink or indulge in drugs. I've never even had a moving violation. You don't make the rules, but I'll offer you a non-negotiable proposal. Do not come back to me with a counter. I'm sending you an eviction notice effective today for the three months rent that you owe me. I'll give you twenty-one days to bring your account up to date, along with another three months worth of rent in cash. If I don't receive your payments by then you, your staff, and your belongings will be out in the street. I don't have to remind you how that outcome would look for you and your future if you don't pay me. Take heed, Mr. Kane."

"I guarantee you will receive your payments on time," Kane grunted out.

Kane slammed the receiver down to its base. The landlord never talked to him this way when his rent checks were on time. He'd never been friendly, but he was always cordial. The prick had him by the gonads; when you have nothing, you lose the power of negotiation. He plucked out the card from the Rolodex and dialed. The call was picked up on the fourth ring by the familiar voice of someone he had rescued from going to jail twice.

"I have another assignment for you," Kane said.

"Who gets it and when?" the voice asked.

Kane chortled after his former client got straight to the point. The assignment Kane had in mind would be disappointing.

"There's a safe that has something in it that I need to get. Do you know anyone who has the wherewithal to open it?"

"You mean a safecracker. I know someone. Not sure if he's in the joint. I can find out and call you back." He cleared his throat. "What's in the safe? What's my finder's fee?"

"Your finder's fee is half of what I gave you on your last assignment *if* I use the guy."

Kane hung up. His breathing was heavy with anticipation. Could he really orchestrate cracking open Sid's safe and get away with it? The prospect was growing more inviting by the second. He could pay off everyone he owed and have something left over. The phone buzzed again, breaking his daydream.

"Mr. Kane. There's a woman on the line who says she's your housekeeper. She's very upset. Some men are taking your car from the garage. She doesn't know what to do."

Kane took the call. "Open the Jag's glove compartment, take out Rollie's gun, bring it in the house, and put it on my desk in the den. Then tell them they can have the car."

Kane hung up. It didn't bother him they were repossessing the Jaguar. On the contrary, his wife wouldn't get it if she divorced him and now he had a gun.

* * * * *

Bruno watched Mary's hands carefully. She didn't complain when he asked her to demonstrate what she'd learned at dealer school after three days. He knew her fingers were achy and sore from the repetition of shuffling and dealing plastic cards, but she didn't have much time to become a professional dealer.

Mary flexed her fingers and gathered all the facedown cards into a pack to shuffle several times. She placed one card to the side as a discard, then dealt a card to six different ghost players. She repeated with another round to give each player a total of two cards.

Bruno reached across his small kitchen table and grabbed both of her hands. She didn't pull away. He questioned Mary by staring into her eyes. Her features creased together until she got the message and nodded.

"I did it again, huh?" She rolled her eyes. "I know. I have to learn to deal the cards low enough so players from any angle can't see them. I'm glad I only have to deal two cards to six players."

"You have come a long way in a short time, Mary." He released her hands. "If a player sees another player's hole cards it's a tremendous advantage, especially when they are playing Texas Hold 'Em for a three-million dollar prize. You also need to make sure you hold the deck in your palm tight before dealing so players can't see the top or bottom cards."

"How do you know all of this?" she asked.

"As part of a case, I went to dealer school. As a dealer, you rule the game. You make each player act accordingly. If they are having trouble deciding, have them call time. They must play in order. If they don't, take them to task. Players cannot take their cards off the table. There are players that will shoot angles. An angle is a fine line of cheating. A player will do it until the dealer or floor man tells him to stop. Don't worry, dealing will soon become second nature to you. Have they taught you how to stack the deck yet?"

"They'll actually show me how to cheat? Wait, you're pulling my chain aren't you?"

"Guilty," Bruno said. "Just wanted to see what you'd say."

One by one, he looked at all six ghost hands Mary had dealt out. If he were a player, only two of the hands would be playable. He gathered the cards and sent them back to her.

"Did you know that you have a tell, Mr. Santiago?"

"What is my tell, Miss McGrath?"

"Your handsome dark brown eyes sparkled at a couple of the hands you looked at." She grinned. "Sometimes you look at me the same way, which I certainly don't mind."

"Damn. I had no idea. Thanks for bringing that to my attention." He removed the deck of cards from her fingers. "It's almost time for me to get ready for the security job. Before I take off, I want you to learn a card trick."

"Why would I need to know a card trick?" she asked.

"Kane never asked you to demonstrate how you manipulate cards. If he does, this simple trick will impress him, especially if you word it the way I tell you and involve Kane."

"What if your trick doesn't impress him?"

"You always have me nearby. Promise."

"I'm going to hold you to that." Her blue eyes sparkled.

Chapter Twenty-Seven

A few ticks past midnight Bruno parked two blocks from WMC. He stepped out of his car wearing a navy-blue pea coat, gloves, and stocking cap to match the rest of his dark stake-out garb, just as he'd done on the previous nights of keeping watch on Sid's office.

Bruno faced a darkened house. The middle-class home was nicely kept up. If the homeowners were awake and peered out through their front window, they'd see an idling man wearing dark clothing. The sight of him standing next to an unfamiliar car by their front sidewalk would tempt them to call the police. Their neighbors might do the same. After a brief look in three other directions, Bruno dug both hands deep in the coat pockets and settled off at a fast walking pace.

Bruno took the security job seriously. It bothered him that Sid had been cavalier about safekeeping the prize money in the office safe. Sid had dismissed most of Bruno's suggestions, including a proposed surveillance camera focused on the safe. Granted, Sid wanted everything to appear low key so as not to create unneeded attention. Given, Sid's reticence to protect the money, Bruno didn't tell his childhood buddy about nightly visits to patrol the club's exterior.

Bruno recalled the mess on Sid's office desk. His friend wasn't about to change his ways or mindset. Rather than argue with the boss and lose, Bruno chose to go solo on his night assignments which thus far had been fruitless; a good thing. Perhaps Sid believed the safe was impregnable? Experience told Bruno there was always someone out there with the capacity to do the unimaginable. Sid didn't have the safe's combination numbers; a smart move on his part to cover his ass if something went astray. The Moore Safe Company representative was the only person who had the combination, but the rep could only be allowed in the office with Sid present. How did Sid know the safe rep was on the up and up? Three-million in cash was enough to lure Mother Teresa into a different habit.

The neighborhood looked different in the dead of night. A dog barked behind a gate giving his presence away. He moved his legs faster. The dog didn't stop barking until he was three houses away. The chilly evening and brisk walk were energizing. Normally he'd be sleeping at this hour. Stakeouts, day or night, were a necessary evil in some cases. Animals could be a hazard. Weather sometimes played havoc. Often there were no bathrooms available, which meant limiting his liquid intake for long periods of time. Nourishment consisted of munchies no nutritionist would recommend, and staying awake was a constant challenge.

He passed the club's granite entry sign. The club's parking lot was empty. Club activities shut down at 10:00 pm, with the exception of the weekly poker game. A janitorial service arrived at 4:00 am, two hours before the club reopened at 6:00 am. If anyone had aspirations to break into the club it would likely be between midnight and 4:00 am. Sid had told Bruno that the cleaning company and their employees were bonded and not allowed in Sid's locked office.

Bruno began to circle the outside of the building that had lighting attached to the eaves at ten foot intervals. The club's interior consisted of a multipurpose gym, lobby/information desk, event rooms, workout equipment area, storage, staff offices, and a restaurant/bar. Although the club had no alarm system, he checked all the doors and windows. Thus far, he'd found three windows slightly open, but they were structured to open only a few inches. No one could climb through that small of a space.

Bruno stopped moving to take in the natural light of a full moon. With all the discomforts, he enjoyed the peacefulness of early morning. Something brushed against his leg. He jumped away. By reflex, he pulled his revolver out and aimed the short barrel at the attacker's chest; but there was nothing to shoot. He lowered the weapon and looked down. The black and white cat wasn't impressed. He waved his hand as a silent warning for the cat to scoot. The feline rubbed against his other leg. He continued his security walk. The club probably had no problems with mice. The cat followed him.

Bruno holstered the gun and thought about Mary. She would have laughed herself crazy if she'd seen him jump up after being bumped by an affectionate kitty. He would have enjoyed witnessing her amusement even if it was at his expense. After a week of dealer school, Mary was now proficient with a deck of plastic cards in her hand and working the chips. If he didn't know otherwise, he'd have thought she was an experienced poker dealer. Each night she practiced dealing to him after dinner, then they played Texas Hold 'Em with chips. The stakes they played for were steep: the player who won all the chips would get to sleep in the bed. Mary had picked up the nuances of the game and played well. He was getting accustomed to slumbering on the couch.

If he had his way, he'd be sleeping in his bed with Mary beside him. Mary had indicated it wouldn't take much persuasion on his part to bring their courtship to another level, but he honored her request not to pressure her.

He could see the frustrated breath he blew out. They had settled on being platonic, and were living together as roommates. Everyday, they spoke to Rachel, Mrs. Green, and Virginia on the phone. Rachel whined that she missed him and couldn't wait for them to come home. The San Francisco female delegation had become his new family; just like it had for Mary, but it wasn't in the cards for him to live there.

Bruno drove Mary to dealer school daily and picked her up. They shopped for groceries and ate dinner together. Mary was a decent cook; but no one compared to Mrs. Green. They watched TV together. Took walks around the town together. After being alone for so long, he enjoyed spending every second of his time off with Mary, but understood she belonged with Rachel, Mrs. Green, and Virginia in a place where she thrived. In Boston, he had created a nice clientele base that had taken him years to establish. There had to be another way for them to be together, permanently.

Bruno shivered. It was getting colder by the minute. Standing in the shadows, he did a warmup dance from one foot to the other while flapping his arms across his chest. His nose ran like a spigot. He used his coat sleeve as a hanky. He felt the pull to call himself a dumbshit for taking on this solo task when he didn't have to. He could be sleeping under a warm quilt on the couch with his head on a soft down pillow while knowing Mary was in the other room.

His rounds came to a halt when he stood in front of Sid's office window. He could see snippets of illumination through cracks in the closed blinds, the same as every night. For some reason, Sid liked to leave his office lights on when he wasn't there. Maybe it was Sid's security tactic to make someone think his office was always occupied.

He thought he heard a female voice from the office. He pressed his ear close to the window, straining to hear the voice again. This wouldn't be the first time he heard a sound that wasn't really there. He came away with a chilled earlobe and no answers.

He started to walk away when a loud noise came from the office. It sounded as if something heavy fell to the floor. The sound was loud enough to make the cat scamper off. Bruno tried to peek through one of the tiny cracks in the blinds and saw nothing. He wasn't sure about hearing a woman's voice, but he knew the other sound was coming from the office.

Bruno stared at the window and considered his options. Breaking into the club would be a bad move on his part. The building had three entrance/exit doors located like a triangle. The person inside had only three ways to escape. The best opportunity to leave would be between twelve and four in the morning before the cleaners arrived. Bruno figured the person inside Sid's office wouldn't try to leave through the main entrance. Bruno hurried to station himself between the two back doors.

He waited an hour for the back door to open. Maybe he guessed wrong about which door the intruder would use to exit the building. He decided to check out the front door. A half hour later he reverted to standing between the back doors. At 3:00 am, he opted to move between the two back doors like a soldier on guard duty.

He lost count of how many times he'd gone back and forth when the door behind him opened. He turned and dashed to that entrance. It was ten minutes to four. The door was closed. He could see two people walking ahead of him, about fifty feet away. He followed a woman and a man carrying a salesman's sample case as they sauntered away holding hands. The man slipped his arm around the woman's shoulder to keep her warm. The woman was almost as tall as the man. She cuddled into him while they giggled to each other like teenagers. They had no idea someone was trailing them. Bruno wanted to keep it that way. His nose was still running. Sniffing or any other sounds would give him away. The couple wouldn't have been able to identify him in the darkness, but they would have known someone was watching them. He held back until he could barely see their images.

Bruno scurried behind a bush three blocks from the club. He saw the couple approach their cars parked away from street-lights. The man stowed the case into his back hatch. They hugged and kissed before leaving in their respective vehicles.

Bruno stepped back onto the sidewalk. He had been too far away to see their faces, but that didn't matter now. The street-lights down the block allowed him to recognize one of the cars speeding away.

"I'll be damned." Bruno ran a sleeve under his nose and headed back to the club. He wanted to see if Sid left the light on in his office. "I'll be damned."

CHAPTER TWENTY-EIGHT

The Camaro idled to a simmer while parked in its allotted apartment space. Bruno placed both hands on the steering wheel and yawned from lack of sleep. He closed his stinging eyes. His patience was down a few quarts as he waited for Mary to appear. She was never this late for the morning ride to dealer school.

His eyelid's crept open. He usually caught a few Z's on the couch after making sure Sid Parker's office was secure during the early morning hours, but he couldn't get his mind off what he'd witnessed. His foot pounced on the gas pedal, revving the engine, and sending clouds of exhaust fumes into the air. What was taking Mary so long?

His tall, blonde neighbor strolled by the Camaro and smiled. She was wearing an overcoat that most likely covered a short dress revealing sculptured legs. Bruno responded with a polite wave and pseudo grin. She had blatantly flirted with him for months after she moved in. He didn't respond in kind. Her smile turned upside down when Mary sprinted into the parking area and jumped into the Camaro's passenger seat.

Mary was modeling her new dealer's uniform for the first time: black slacks, white tuxedo-like blouse buttoned to the top, green vest, and a crossover bowtie. The rookie dealers were being tested today by volunteer Hold 'Em players willing to partake in a tournament-like setting. Their reward was a free lunch at a nearby restaurant. When a bell rang out, the dealing would stop and players would grade the dealer at their table. Then the dealers would rotate to different tables. If Mary was nervous about the upcoming evaluations she was hiding it well.

"Sorry I'm late." She was out of breath. "I was about out the door when Virginia called."

"It's like 5:30 in the morning in California."

"It's normal for Virginia to be in the office at that hour. I would do the same if it wasn't for Rachel. Virginia has been unbelievable about me starting work a few hours later so I can get Rachel off to school. She's not only my boss and mentor; she's my best friend and a terrific aunt to my daughter."

Bruno watched Mary attach her seatbelt. By calling so early, Virginia must have had a good news for her.

"Virginia wanted to remind me of an important date." Mary giggled. "A year ago today, I walked into Proffitt Advertising to interview for a job. I was so scared she wouldn't like me, I almost wet myself. Rachel waited in the lobby. Virginia sent some colored pens and paper to keep Rachel occupied. The interview lasted over two hours. I was exhausted when it was over. Virginia reminded me of Mo. I remember thinking she wouldn't hire me, but I really wanted to work and learn from this woman. She finally leaned forward and said, 'by the way, your Bear Moon Wine presentation was a big hit with our client after we tweaked it. I see why Mo sent you to me. You're inexperienced, but extremely talented. The position is yours, Mary, if you want it.' I cried, Bruno. Then Virginia took us out to lunch. After we got back to the office, she called Mrs. Green about a place for Rachel and me to get situated."

Bruno nodded. Virginia's early morning call solidified why, much to his chagrin, Mary should return to San Francisco.

"She also wanted to recount her call to Oliver Kane disguised as Marilyn Harrison the movie producer. It's just too funny. We laughed like crazy all over again."

Bruno nodded. He would have liked listening to Virginia duping Kane as movie bigwig.

"You're quiet this morning," Mary said. "Actually, you seem like you're somewhere else. Is something wrong? Are you feeling okay?" She placed the back of her hand on Bruno's forehead. "I can stay home and take care of you."

"That's sweet of you. Thank you. I'm a little fuzzy-headed from lack of sleep."

She lowered her hand to his cheek. "You're not running a fever, but I can tell something is bothering you, Bruno. You're not one to complain. Is your arm hurting? Did I do something to upset you? Please tell me."

She was right. In a short period of time they had gotten closer than he thought he would ever get to a woman again.

"Yeah, something is bothering me, Mary." He removed her hand from his cheek. "Last night, besides almost shooting a cat, I saw something that wasn't meant for my eyes and it was damn disturbing."

"You can't just stop there," she said. "What did you see?"

"Two people were inside Sid Parker's office after midnight; a man and a woman. I couldn't identify them in the dark when they left the club, but I have no doubt they're involved in a tryst. I followed them to their cars parked behind each other and recognized one of the vehicles. It was Sid's blue Caravan. Now I know why Sid didn't want camera surveillance in his office."

"Sid has a mistress? You said you couldn't see their faces. Maybe he was with his wife? Or maybe it was another blue Caravan?"

"I recognized the dent in back. Sid and I have been friends since childhood. Hell, I was an usher in Sid's wedding. His wife Beverly is barely five feet tall. The woman last night was almost Sid's height. Beverly is a real sweetheart and a great mother. They have three kids. She's just as much of a friend to me as Sid is."

"What are you going to do, Bruno?"

"Good question. If I say anything to him before the Hold 'Em tournament he will know about my early morning security. I have a feeling he'd fire both of us, which would ruin our scheme for Kane. There's probably more to this. I aim to find out what's going on, but I won't go to Beverly and rat Sid out. Perhaps after the tournament I can get Sid to fess up and save his marriage." Bruno looked at his watch. "It's getting late. I better get you to school before they give you demerits."

"You really look sleepy," she said. "How about I drive myself in the Camaro to the class so you can get some shuteye?"

"Nice try, Laura Lead-foot. Remember, I've experienced your driving before." He threw the gear shift into drive. "I'll take you to your class. When I pick you up, can I take you out to dinner to celebrate your one-year anniversary. Deal?"

"Deal."

* * * * *

Oliver Kane paced back and forth in his office with the door open. It was a mistake to allow his next appointment to come here, but he feared leaving the building to meet somewhere else without Rollie's protection. What does a safecracker look like? He didn't expect a man in a suit with spit-shined shoes and manicured fingernails to show up. Nor did he picture a foul-smelling derelict in ragged clothes to appear.

"Mr. Kane, uh . . . a Mr. Jones is here," Vera said, after buzzing him. "I don't have him on the calendar. He says he has an appointment with you."

"Send Mr. Jones in and hold all of my calls."

Mr. Jones entered through the open doorway. Kane closed the door and returned to his chair behind the desk. He made no attempt to shake the professional thief's hand. Jones grabbed a seat without being directed. He was in his late thirties or early forties; over six- feet tall and thin, with an acne-scarred-face, and dirty blond hair. His eyes shifted to different areas of the office, and then focused on Kane.

"I'm assuming Jones is not your given name?" Kane asked.

"Nice call. Let's do away with the pleasantries. What's the job?"

"Are you a cop, Mr. Jones? Obviously you know the reason why I'm asking you."

"Do I look like a cop?"

"You didn't answer my question."

"I'm not a cop. Nor have I ever been in law enforcement and I don't give to the Policeman's Ball." Jones placed a hand on the desk. "Are we being recorded?"

"No. Think about it. I requested your services to commit a crime. Both of our hands are dirty. You're here to convince me you can pull off what I want done."

"And you have to convince me that what you're asking me to do is worth my while."

"I need a standing metal safe opened and all the contents delivered to me," Kane said.

"I don't do banks."

"The safe is in an office. You will have to break into the building. I'm assuming you are capable of doing that and disarming an alarm system if there is one?"

"I'm capable of almost anything. What would I be delivering to you?"

"That's not important now," Kane said. "We have to be on the same page or this won't work for either of us."

"Wrong. If it's hazardous chemicals, drugs, weapons, or bodies, I'm not in."

"None of the above." Kane picked up his letter opener. How could he trust an admitted crook? "The product is paper. A lot of paper. That's all you need to know."

"Wrong. If you want the use of my services, unless I know everything, it's a no-go?"

Kane ran a finger along the edge of the letter opener. He couldn't tell if Jones was packing a gun, but the man before him was not a warm and fuzzy person. Would he be this ornery if Rollie was sitting in the room? At least Rollie's revolver was available in the desk's top drawer. This wasn't the way he anticipated their meeting. Bonding with Jones had been only on his terms. What if Jones emptied the safe and walked away with three-million in cash? Unless he could turn this negotiation around quickly, stealing the tournament money from Sid Parker's safe was just a fantasy, not likely to be a reality.

"What is your fee to break into an office and crack open a safe, Mr. Jones?"

"That depends on what's in the safe."

"If I said there is three-million dollars worth of jewels in the safe, what would you say?"

"You told me paper was in the safe. Which is it? I don't fence jewels, by the way. Too messy. My fee is two hundred thousand in cash."

"That's unacceptable."

"I don't know what I'm supposed to deliver to you and you're negotiating my fee," Jones said. "Let's get real, man. Play it straight with me before we haggle over my cut."

"There are thirty-thousand hundred-dollar bills in the safe. All counterfeit." Kane watched Jones blink twice. "I have a source who will take all the bills for a percentage; basically pennies on the dollar. That's why two-hundred-thousand is out of the question."

"Fifty thou. I'll do it for fifty-thousand."

Kane winced like he was in pain. This was priceless. He wouldn't have to pay Sid or Mary McGrath. Furthermore, as the tournament winner, he'd scream the loudest about being cheated out of three-million in cash and Sid Parker would take the blame. Priceless.

"You'll do it for twenty-five thousand?" Kane responded. "Otherwise, there's no deal."

"The bills must be counterfeit. I'll do it for thirty grand. I want to case the building first. If it smells right, I'll break-in tomorrow night."

"Twenty-five and I'm going with you."

"I work alone."

"Not this time." Kane said with authority. "I don't drive. Pick me up here at midnight."

"You better be on the level, Kane." Jones rose to his feet and left the office.

"Nice doing business with you, Mr. Jones."

CHAPTER TWENTY-NINE

Bruno timed his strides to the rhythm of a song in his head on the way to his patrol of Sid's office. A cloud covering the moon meant less illumination than the other nights. The tournament was in three days, giving him two more nights of stakeout. His legs bounced into a trot to crank up body heat. At the end of his run he was standing outside of Sid's office, out of breath, sweaty, and warm.

Snippets of light snuck through the blinds; same story - different day. Bruno leaned closer to the window, but couldn't hear or see what was happening inside the office. Last night, he'd followed Sid and his playmate to their cars parked at another location. What else was going on inside that room other than Sid likely scoring a little nookie? He doubted they were filching the money from the safe. The Moore Safe Company rep was the only person who had the combination. What if the rep was Sid's mistress?

Sid wasn't much of an athlete, but mentally he could outperform almost everyone. He'd always been pudgy, but recently he had put on weight and shed a good portion of his hair. Did his wife Beverly find her husband unappealing enough to compel him to sneak some time with a mistress? Or was it the other way around? Maybe Beverly could shed some light on what was going on?"

Bruno's lips curled into a smile. His attempt to take down Oliver Kane had almost become an afterthought. Often in bad situations there is some good that comes out of it. In spite of the pain and misery inflicted by The DUI Doctor, it was Kane who brought Mary to him. If their sting proved to be the demise of Oliver Kane, it would also send Mary back to San Francisco a continent away from Boston. Losing Wendy to an unnecessary death had sent him into the depths of depression. Bruno had no doubt Mary going back to California would have the same effect on him.

Yesterday was Mary's last dealer's class. She was a certificated dealer. When Bruno picked her up at the school, he found her beaming. Only one other student had a higher evaluation rating . . . by a mere point. Mary reminded him what her life had been like a year ago. She was convinced Rachel would be better off without her as a mother. A dying Morgan Proffitt had stopped Mary from committing suicide by persuading her to take a different path – a path that brought her to Virginia, Mrs. Green, and a private detective.

Bruno brought Mary to one of his favorite restaurants for an intimate dinner to celebrate her one-year anniversary at Proffitt Advertising and being a prize student. After their meal, they toasted with Grand Marnier at the bar and walked hand-in-hand back to the Camaro like a loving couple enjoying an evening out.

A chill overtook Bruno's warm thoughts. He headed towards the door that Sid and his lover had exited several nights in a row. If they followed the same routine, he had three more hours to wait. He leaned against the wall and kept a sharp eye out for the black and white cat that made him jump the other night. A pair of headlights shined on the entry road to the club. The vehicle stopped, but didn't venture in. Maybe the driver was lost. What looked like a pickup truck backed up and went the way it came.

Seventeen minutes later the club door opened. Bruno sprang from the wall and moved closer. Sid and his companion exited the building several hours earlier than usual. After the door closed, they performed a high five; as if rejoicing in an accomplishment. Sid continued to carry a salesman's sample bag. Had Sid brought something into the club or was he taking something out? Perhaps it was both?

Bruno began to follow them. He expected to find their cars parked behind each other. The couple veered to the left; a different direction from last night. Sid put his free arm around her. Bruno shook his head. That arm should be around his wife Beverly.

Movement from the right caught Bruno's attention. He stopped and backpedaled away from two figures in dark clothing who were heading towards the club. The cleaning people wouldn't come this early dressed like break-in artists wearing black gloves. They chose the door opposite the one Sid and friend exited. One of the men, the shortest one, seemed to be the guide who knew the layout of the club.

Bruno was close enough to hear their voices, but couldn't detect what was being said. The taller man leaned forward to examine the door while holding a pen light between his teeth. He placed what looked like a black leather bag down on the cement walkway. He reached inside to remove a lock pick set from the bag and selected a tool to his liking.

The black and white cat rubbed between the smaller man's ankles making him leap in the air and holler. He dropped a flashlight and a small narrow box he'd been carrying and tried kicking the cat, but his shoe whiffed by a few inches. The taller man turned, removed the pen light from his mouth, and shouted to the smaller man to "shut up." The scolded partner picked up what he'd dropped and didn't respond back.

In less than five seconds the lock was picked, and they were inside the club. Whoever was working the lock pick was damn good. Bruno pulled his gun. If they were stealing anything he wanted to catch them with the goods.

Bruno hustled around the building to stand outside of Sid's office. Sid always turned the light off when they were leaving. He couldn't see light coming through the blinds. Why would anyone break into a country club, unless they knew there was something valuable to steal? The dues to the WMC would amount to a great deal of money, but members paid with checks or credit cards. The fitness equipment was worth multiple-thousands of dollars, but it would take more than two men and many trucks to swipe the heavy equipment. The only asset of value worth stealing was three-million in cash secured in a safe. The only way to get the money would be to know the combination or be a safecracker.

* * * * *

Oliver Kane's flashlight led Jones to Sid's office. Jones was wearing all black including his running shoes. Kane looked down at his Dior black Oxfords and shook his head. Running shoes would have been more practical. Kane held the light on the lock for Jones to work his magic. In a matter of seconds, the door flew open. They entered the unlit office. Kane worked the flashlight around the room, stopped for a second on the cluttered desk, and then he directed the beam at a large metal safe against the wall.

"Man that guy's desk looks like it threw up." Jones said, while removing his right glove.

"The desk isn't important," Kane said. "Crack open the damn safe so we can pack up what's inside and get the hell outta here."

"Will you shut up?" Jones placed the bag on the floor. "I told you before I manipulate by myself. Having a Nervous Nellie with me is why I work alone."

Kane moved closer to the safe and centered the light's ray on the dial. He tried to control the shake of his hand. If he was caught in here at this hour by the police, the embarrassment alone would be worse than going to prison and doing hard labor.

Jones kneeled on one knee and rubbed his fingers against his thumb. He leaned his ear a fraction of an inch to the safe and turned the dial until he received the answer he was looking for. He reached into his black bag and pulled out a stethoscope. With earplugs inserted, he placed the diaphragm on the dial and began turning slowly until he heard something that made his head nod. He twisted the dial in the opposite direction and stopped with another nod. Sweat dripped down his cheeks. He continued the process until both hands removed the earplugs and placed the stethoscope back into the black bag. He blew out a breath, wiped his face with a jacket sleeve, and rose to his feet. Kane's pounding heart felt like it was lodged in his throat. All he'd done was aim the flashlight on the safe's dial, yet he was sweating as much as Jones. He placed the flashlight under his arm. His gloves made it difficult to remove a heavy-duty black trash bag from the box he'd been carrying. Lack of forethought made him shake his head. How many plastic bags would it take to carry three-hundred packets worth ten thousand dollars each? How many packets would the plastic bags hold? Would he be strong enough to carry the bags?

"Hold the light on the handle," Jones said in an irritated

tone. "I hope you're a better lawyer than you are a bag man. I can't believe I allowed you to come along. Twenty-five- thousand smackers probably swayed my decision."

Jones yanked open the safe's door. For a second time, Kane peeked at three-million dollars in cash. The packets were stacked neatly in rows except for one on top. Jones removed that packet and ran his thumb down the side.

"Green has always been my favorite color," Jones bellowed, studying the packet.

"Each bundle of counterfeit hundreds amounts to ten-thousand. It would have been easier if they were fake thousand-dollar bills."

"Have you ever seen a thousand-dollar bill in person, dude? Most people haven't. Grover Cleveland's mug is on it. Jones slapped the packet into his gloved hand. "The buzz around this town is that Oliver Kane is a cold-hearted bastard who would do anything to get his own way. I believe that. You fucking lied to me. The C-notes aren't counterfeit. They're very real. Why are they here?"

Kane had trouble swallowing. Jones was sharper than he'd thought. It felt like they had been in here too long. Jones was pissed off that he lied.

"In a couple of nights there's going to be a rich-man's Texas Hold 'Em tournament here. Each entry puts up two-hundred and fifty-thousand dollars. Winner takes all. I'm one of the players. I had to scrounge up the entry fee. This is the general manager's office. He's running the tournament."

"And you obviously aren't a good enough player to be the winner. Why take a chance when you can just steal the prize. Your lie is going to cost you, big time. I'm taking five-hundred-thousand and I'm in no mood for a cross examination. Throw me a bag."

"Listen, Jones. We made a binding deal. I've got the twenty-five-thousand we agreed on in my pocket."

"How binding is a deal that includes breaking into a building and cracking open a safe?" Jones laughed and pulled a gun from his leather bag. "Not that I need this for a wuss like you."

He snatched the plastic bag from Kane's hand. "I've done my part. I'm taking fifty packets and leaving you on your own."

Kane leaped back in a panic. Lightheadedness threw his balance off, making him knock objects off Sid's desk. Jones wasn't going to back down. Rollie's bulky form flashed in his head. Rollie would have mopped the floor with this punk. No one was here to protect him; only himself.

"Please," Kane pleaded. "I should have told you the truth. Look, I didn't know if I could trust you. I didn't know if you could actually open the safe. I've got twenty-five thousand in my pocket that I promised you. Take that money and then we can negotiate the rest. Please, put the gun away. I know we can resolve this issue. Please . . ."

Chapter Thirty

Bruno pulled his gun from the holster on his belt. He'd heard frantic shouting followed by a gunshot inside Sid's office. He pounded on the window with his knuckles and yelled "police," then shifted to the side to avoid a potential bullet. He waited for another response. Was it possible they cracked open the safe. Did one of them get greedy and shoot the other? Were they still in the room or . . .

Bruno sprinted to the door the burglars had entered to confront them. He'd rather hold the culprits at gunpoint and call the police instead of exchanging bullets. Sid would strongly disapprove. The Hold 'Em tournament would be canceled along with their mission to eliminate Oliver Kane, but it would be the right thing to do.

Bruno turned the corner. The side door was closed and locked. The sound of the main entrance door being slammed echoed back to him.

"Damn. I picked the wrong door." Bruno raced to where the noise had come from.

By the time he arrived at the front door he heard a pair of hard-soled shoes beating down on the pavement towards the road. He aimed the barrel of his gun at the fleeing runner, then pulled his finger away from the trigger. It would be too dangerous to fire blindly in the dark. The other thief was most likely injured or lying dead in Sid's office. He punched a button on his cell phone. The call was answered after one ring.

"It's never good news if someone calls at this hour," Sid said. "What's going on, Bruno?"

"You better get your ass down to the club ASAP, Sid. There's been a break-in and it's possible someone was shot."

"Shot! How the hell would you even know there's a break-in, let alone a shooting?"

"This week I've been doing surveillance around the club's perimeter at night."

"What the hell prompted you to do surveillance without my say-so?" Sid demanded.

"Three-million dollars in cash stashed in your office safe. I was just doing my job as head of security."

"Who else have you called?"

"You're my first call. Without a key I can't get into the club unless I break something."

"I'll be there in ten minutes. Whatever you do, Bruno, don't call the police."

Sid disconnected the call before Bruno could say he'd be waiting at the front door. Bruno had ten minutes to figure out what he'd say to Sid. In the meantime, he checked the other side door and found it locked, but there were droplets of blood on the pavement. He removed a flashlight from his pocket and followed the trail into shrubbery that bordered the club.

Sid's blue Caravan screeched to a halt in front of the country club in eight minutes. He flew from the driver's seat, leaving the door open and ran to Bruno. Sid had always been a cool customer under pressure, but his dead-serious features showed his alarm.

"I'm totally pissed you provided a stakeout without telling me, Bruno," Sid barked. "What the hell happened?"

"For starters, I'm well-aware you've been in your office these nights with another woman. Do you want to talk about it?"

Sid's head rocked back. "It's personal and none of your business, Bruno."

"If I didn't know you and Beverly, I wouldn't give a damn, but Beverly also happens to be a close friend. I don't want her to get hurt."

"How did they get in?" Sid asked, changing the subject.

"There were two of them. It was too dark to see their faces. The taller one picked the side door lock and probably picked your office lock. I'm thinking the guy with the lock pick might have had the skill to crack open the safe in your office."

"This is a fucking disaster. Are they still in the club?" Sid jammed a key into the front door lock, then nodded at Bruno to go in first.

"No, they ran when I pounded on the window and yelled 'police.'" Bruno led the way into the club. "I heard a shot while standing outside your office window. One of the perpetrators most likely shot the other. I believe the perp with the gun escaped through the front door. I heard him running. The other perp was wounded and fled through a side door leaving a trail of blood on the pavement."

The door to Sid's office was ajar. Bruno pushed a hand back to stop Sid from entering. He turned on the lights. The safe's door was wide open showcasing neat green bundles of hundred-dollar bills. Blood was smeared on the floor in front of the safe.

"Be careful not to step in the blood, Sid." Bruno zeroed in on the money. "You may have lucked out. It doesn't look like they took anything."

"Each stack of hundreds amounts to ten-thousand," Sid said. "As you can see, everything is perfectly in line. I purposely left one bundle of hundreds cockeyed on top. If it was straightened out or gone then I'd know someone had messed with it."

"So you're saying they got away with ten grand?" Bruno's eye caught something on the desk. He removed the .357 shell casing. "How do you want to play this, Sid?"

"I don't want the police involved." Sid counted all the straight rows twice and closed the safe door. "I will replace the ten-thousand out of my pocket." He held up a hand. "Hey, thank you for the security, Bruno. It was a good call on your part to provide surveillance. Fortunately, there are no dead bodies to report and I will take care of the money. Therefore, no need to contact the cops."

Who were the two robbers and how did they learn about the three-million in Sid's office safe? Sid was more than happy to supplement the ten thousand-dollars since he would get close to two-hundred thousand from the winner of the tournament. Just as important, if the police didn't get involved, their Oliver Kane scheme was still in play.

"I'll go along with being quiet unless we or the police find an injured or dead body. From now on, I will make all the security calls." Bruno drilled his index finger into Sid's soft chest. "Before your janitorial service arrives at 4:00 am, get a bucket and mop and wipe clean the blood trail that goes all way into the bushes. I'll follow the trail from there."

* * * * *

A stabbing pain in Oliver Kane's abdomen made him stop running. It took over a minute for him to regain some semblance of normal breathing. He was dripping with sweat, yet shivering out of control. How far away had he run from the club? If the police were after him for killing Jones with Rollie's gun, he needed to get home as fast as possible. He couldn't call a cab since he left his cell phone, money clip, and wallet behind on purpose.

Kane slipped off his oxfords thinking these boots weren't made for running. His house was several miles away. He removed the revolver from his coat pocket and stared at the menacing weapon. He almost dropped it into a clump of bushes, but thought better of it. There had to be a more efficient way to dispose of the evidence. He had never fired a gun before. Nor had he killed someone by his own hand. Ordering someone to be terminated was different. Hordes of people had accused him of committing murder based on his prowess in the courtroom. No jury would ever convict him, not even as an accessory.

Firing one bullet changed him tonight. He was responsible for Jones' death even if it was self defense. Jones had aimed a gun at him with a finger on the trigger. What was he supposed to do? Let Jones shoot him? He'd reached into his coat pocket saying he would give Jones twenty-five-thousand dollars he'd promised for the job of cracking open the safe. The only thing of value he had in his coat pocket was Rollie's gun. He didn't remember pulling the trigger. The bullet hit Jones, sending him down to the floor like a fallen tree with his head bleeding. Sudden pounding on the window from the police made him panic and flee from the office without the money or anything else.

Kane bent down to slip his shoes back on. He closed his eyes to rewind the whole scene in his head. Who knocked on the window and yelled "police?" Did the club have security? If so, what did the guy see or hear besides a gunshot? The blinds were closed and the overhead lights were off. He doubted the guy outside heard any verbal exchange or saw him pull the trigger.

Kane moved to stand under a streetlight. What evidence did he leave? He was wearing gloves. He removed his shoes again and studied them to see if there was any blood. They seemed clean. He examined his black slacks, turtleneck, and sports jacket for splatter. His naked eye couldn't see any trace of blood, but crime experts had other methods of picking up evidence. Once home, he would remove every stitch he was wearing, place it in a plastic bag along with Rollie's gun, and throw it all into the bay.

He slipped on his shoes feeling more secure about not leaving any evidence except . . .

"Besides grabbing the money from the safe, I should've frisked Jones. He might have had a wallet or a cell phone on him, or a slip of paper with my address. What about his red truck? The police would eventually make that connection after finding his keys." Kane stood up and turned to go back to the club. "What the hell am I thinking? A cop is already there. There's nothing I can do about it now."

Kane threw his hand into the air. What else did he leave: a flashlight and plastic bags? He had wiped them clean of prints before they left his office. Maybe he could skate from being implicated in the murder or break-in?

He hurried his pace to get as far away from the club as possible. He was dressed nice enough to make a roaming cop think twice about stopping him, except he was wearing all black. He hadn't heard any police sirens yet. Maybe the guy standing outside and banging on the window was just a low-paid security hire?

Kane began to run, but his feet barked back at him. He walked as fast as his hooves would allow. If he was stopped by the law, he'd state his real name and tell the officer he often went for a walk in the middle of the night to clear his mind about an upcoming case in court. Since he'd walked further than usual, he'd ask the officer for a ride home.

Kane shivered. He was back to Plan A and counting on Mary McGrath's ability to cheat for him to win. He hadn't heard from her, but she'd been right. They needed each other. What if he put some last-minute pressure on her? That thought moved his legs faster. Tomorrow he'd call Mary and find out just how much she needed him.

Chapter Thirty-One

The Moore Safe Company greeter escorted Bruno to their conference room. She assumed he was a potential customer and spouted the merits of each safe they passed. He had been told Walter Moore was the person who handled the WMC account. She left Bruno in the spacious room as a young man entered.

"I'm Walter Moore, Mr. Santiago. I'm told you work at WMC with Sid Parker. What can I do for you?"

"Call me Bruno." His head pivoted to different sections of the conference room. "I'm head of security for the club. Were you expecting others to join us?"

"I use the conference room to meet people when it's available," Moore said. "I barely fit into my office. With another person in there, it's like standing room only."

"With the last name of Moore, I assumed you were the owner of the company."

"I get that a lot." Moore chuckled. "My uncle Charlie owns the company. He hired me as an account executive after I graduated from college. WMC is my first client."

"No offense, Walter, but it's difficult for me to understand how someone straight out of college was given the responsibility of being the only person to know the combination to a safe holding enough money to start a bank."

"To be honest," Moore said, "no one was more surprised than me. I was told Sid Parker had requested a point person whose status in the company would keep the assignment hush-hush. Since I'm *low* man on the company totem pole, I was awarded the job."

"Are you privy to how much money is in the safe?" Bruno asked.

"I haven't added it up, but it has to be quite a lot."

"How many other Moore Company employees have access to the combination?"

"That's a good question," Moore said. "I have no idea."

"What happens if you're run over by a bus, God forbid?"

"I never thought about that, Bruno. I'm sure the company must have a back-up combination plan in their files for each safe we sell or lease." Moore's eyes squinted in confusion. "Why are you asking? Is something missing?"

"If you're correct, I'm concerned anyone in your company can get WMC's combination, including Uncle Charlie who is also on the club's board of directors."

"Everyone in the company is bonded, even my Uncle Charlie."

"Bonding protects companies against the risk an employee will steal or damage company property or the company's clients' property. But that wouldn't stop an employee from acquiring a combination to steal." Bruno studied Walter's eyes. "Do you know if Sid Parker has access to the combination to the safe that's in his office?"

"I don't see how Mr. Parker or any other employee could get the combination. The whole point of my involvement is for his protection. He's never asked me for the combination. I don't even know what event the money is for. I open the safe, Sid places the packs of money inside, precisely the way he likes, and I close the door and make sure it's secure. All the packs seem to be the same size and line up accordingly. Am I in any kind of trouble?"

Bruno's questions were unnerving Moore. The owner's nephew unbuttoned the top button of his white shirt collar and loosened his tie. When queried, even someone who is totally innocent, thinks he may have done something wrong.

"Does your firm have access to a safecracker?" Bruno asked.

"A safecracker?" Walter scratched his head, messing his hair. "That's a good question. I have no idea."

"Do you know how many hundreds are in a bundle?"

"Honest, Bruno, I never counted. I wish you'd tell me why you're here asking me these questions."

"Could Sid Parker have gotten the safe's combination without you telling him?"

"I don't see how."

"How many times did you go to the club to open the safe?"

Moore looked down at the linoleum. "I don't know for sure. Maybe nine or ten times."

"Where was Sid standing when you worked the safe's dial?"

"I have no idea. I was too preoccupied with dialing the correct numbers."

"If you were standing behind someone working the dial, could you have gotten the whole combination?"

"I never thought about that," Moore said. "If the person was turning the dial fast, I don't think I could have made out the combination."

"Since you went back to the club nine or ten times, could you have made out some of the numbers to eventually retain all of them in their proper order?"

"That's a possibility." Walter's eyes widened. "Holy shit, have I just hung myself?"

"Not in the least, Walter. You've been a big help."

* * * * *

Bruno hurried up the walkway, but something on Sid Parker's lawn made him stop. He picked up the plastic bat and ball, smiled, and thought about Rachel. They had numerous conversations on the phone since he and her mother came to Boston.

The front door opened. Beverly Parker came out to greet Bruno with a hug. Her puffy, red eyes expressed how she was doing. Beverly still had the same petite figure and short brunette hairstyle from the first time they met. She was like a sister to him, but both knew this wasn't a social call. She led him inside to the living room.

"You want to know what's going on with Sid." Her voice was shaky. "Wish I could tell you, Bruno. He's a different person than the man I married. Different from the boy you grew up with. He's irritable with the kids. Barely talks to me. He goes out at night and doesn't come home until dawn. All he seems to care about is that damn poker tournament. He said you were working security for him."

"I'm not going to lie to you Bev, I've noticed the change," he said. "Can you recall how long ago it started?"

"Maybe a month or two before he found out the tournament was going to happen." She cradled her face into her hands. "It has to be another woman. I don't know what to do."

Bruno put a brotherly arm around Beverly. He could answer some of her questions, but the answers needed to come from Sid. There was more to what was going on with Sid than having a woman on the side. Maybe Beverly could lead him to that answer.

"I want to help you and Sid as best I can without getting in the middle," Bruno said. "What does he do when he comes home in the early morning?"

He sleeps for a few hours, takes a shower, works in the garage for a while, and then goes back to the club."

"Do you know what he's doing in the garage?"

"Not a clue," she said. "If you take a look at our garage, you'll see it's hard to move around, let alone work. He doesn't want me or the kids in there; says it's too dangerous."

"Do you mind if I take a look in there if I promise not to get hurt?"

"If you think it will help, but you may be taking your life in your own hands." She led him into the kitchen, opened the side door to the garage, and turned on the light. "As you can see, it's a total mess. We haven't been able to put a car in there for years. What are you looking for, Bruno?"

"I'll know it when I find it."

"Feel free to move or uncover anything you want." She crossed her arms from the cold.

Beverly followed him to the workbench that was piled with tools, along with metal, glass, and plastic canisters. Cobwebs ran in different directions. He opened the drawers underneath and found nothing exciting. Away from the workbench, he lifted or moved things. All the paraphernalia reminded him of Sid's office desk – disorderly and chaotic. Furniture, sports equipment, clothes, tools, toys, magazines, rug remnants . . . the garage needed a sale or to be blown up.

Bruno lifted a green tarp from a lawnmower that looked like it had seen its better days. He removed paint-stained overalls covering a filing cabinet. He pushed the overalls aside and opened all six drawers finding old tax returns and other papers. He concluded that the Parker garage was a perfect place to hide something from someone who didn't know what that something was.

Bruno turned and stumbled on a toy doll, causing him to bump his shin into something hard underneath an old drape. He bent down to rub the sore area on his leg. To his right, he saw another drape of the same material rolled up neat on a shelf. He lifted the drape and discovered a hope chest that might be found in a girl's bedroom. It was secured by paddle lock.

"Do you know what's in this chest, Bev?"

"That was my hope chest as a young girl. I used to keep all my private things in there, including a diary. I forgot we had it."

"Do you have the key to the lock?" Bruno asked.

"No. I used to have the original key, but I have no idea where it is."

"It looks like this lock was put there by Sid." He went to the workbench and returned with a bolt cutter. "Do I have your permission to cut the lock off?"

"Under normal circumstances I'd say no. Sid doesn't like us messing with his stuff. But there's nothing normal about this garage or our lives. You have my blessings."

Bruno cut both shanks, threw the broken lock onto the cement floor, and lifted the top. A child's yellow blanket covered what was inside. Bruno threw the blanket on another pile. He waved for Beverly to have a look-see at her hope chest filled with blocks of green hundred dollar bills.

"I doubt this was part of your bridal dowry, Bev. We now know why Sid spends so much time in this garage and his office at night."

"Oh my God, what has Sid done?" Beverly cried out.

Bruno's cell phone rang. He held up a hand that said "hold that thought."

"Bruno, Oliver Kane just called me." The words rushed out of Mary's mouth. "He's nervous about my ability to make him the winner of the tournament. He wants me to come to his office immediately to convince him I can manipulate the cards the way I promised without the other players knowing I'm cheating for him. He said he was leaning towards another alternative. If I don't show and prove to him I'm a card mechanic, the deal is off."

"Mary, don't go. I'll pick you up and *we* will convince Kane."

"My cab is here, Bruno. I can do this. I handled Kane before, I can do it again."

Mary disconnected the call.

CHAPTER THIRTY-TWO

Oliver Kane plopped down in his desk chair. His eyes closed. They say desperate people do desperate things. He must have been out-of-his-mind in despair to concoct the scheme to break into Sid Parker's office safe. This morning he threw away every piece of clothing he had on last night into the bay, along with Rollie's gun. Although there was no mention about what happened inside Sid's office on the radio or TV, he was sure the bullet he'd fired killed the man who referred to himself as Jones. Was it a good decision to get rid of the weapon? If the police traced Jones' murder back to him the gun would be incriminating evidence. But, without a weapon or Rollie, he felt defenseless.

He twisted the chair around to pull a bottle of Pepto-Bismol, his favorite stomach calmer, from the credenza. The pain in his gut was more acute and constant. He ignored the directions on the bottle and slugged down three large gulps. Why was pulling the trigger and killing someone affecting him so differently than hiring someone to be murdered?

The phone buzzed, jolting him back to present time.

"Mr. Kane," Vera said. "Mary McGrath is here to see you. She's not on the calendar."

"Is she alone, Vera?"

"Yes, Mr. Kane."

"Send Ms. McGrath to my office." He cleared his throat. "You can take the rest of the day off." The silence on the other end was deafening. "Make sure you're on time tomorrow morning."

He exchanged the Pepto-Bismol bottle for a vial of Clive Christian cologne. He poured ten bucks worth of "smell good" into his palms and slapped it on both cheeks. His stomach made an eerie noise, followed by a sharp pain. Nothing would stop him from passing up his last chance to nail Mary McGrath on his office sofa.

Mary took three steps into the office and stopped in her tracks. She wrinkled her nose and blinked several times.

"Whoa," she uttered. "I've never been in a whorehouse before, but I imagine the aroma would be something similar."

Kane lifted his shoulders and grinned. Mary made sure to leave the door open when she entered. If possible, she looked even sexier in tight jeans. She stood ten feet away from his desk while holding the straps to her leather purse. Kane rose from his chair and headed to the door.

"I left the door open on purpose, Mr. Kane."

"And I'm going to close the door on purpose, Ms. McGrath." He shut the door and locked it. "Our conversation is confidential, and I want to keep it that way."

She wedged a hand into her purse like their first encounter. He had no doubt that she was harboring a gun in the bag. Would she shoot him if he made a move on her?

"The poker tournament is in a couple of days," Kane said. "I want you to assure me that nothing will go wrong. You were verbally convincing about being a card mechanic. Now I want you to prove it to me."

"Prove it to you how, Mr. Kane?" Her hand dug deeper in her purse.

Kane's eyes never left her purse. He guessed the gun would be smaller in size - maybe even a Derringer. Was a Derringer powerful enough to kill someone? Why did he throw Rollie's revolver in the bay?

"I've never seen you in action with a deck of cards in your hands, Ms. McGrath. You need to prove to me that you are what you say you are."

"A little late for that, isn't it?" Mary said with a quick laugh. "Are your nerves getting to you, Mr. Kane? We both know I hold all the cards here, no pun intended. I shouldn't have to prove anything to you. If you win the three-million, I get half a million. If you don't win, I get nothing but measly dealer's pay and a tip." She scowled at him. "I'm going to be really clear here. If I sense you are going to renege on our deal, I can guarantee you won't win the prize. In addition, if you don't hand over my half a mil to the person who will be your ride home, you're a dead man."

"You've made your point. I'd appreciate you showing me a sample of your card skills."

"Do you have a deck of cards?" she asked.

"No, " he said, with a quizzical expression . "Why would I?"

Mary took a seat in front of the desk and removed a pack of Kem Playing Cards from her purse. She rested the bag on the other chair. Her right hand pushed the pack across the desktop to Kane. He gazed at the cards, confused.

"I want you to remove the cards from their case. Pick out all four aces, kings, queens, and jacks from the deck and hand them to me." She waited until Kane completed the assignment. "I'm now holding in my hand sixteen cards: four aces and twelve face cards. Next, I want you to put the four of spades face up in the middle of the desktop and place the remaining cards back into the case." Again she waited until he finished what she asked him to do. "Now, Mr. Kane, I want you to shift your ogling eyes from my chest and focus on my hands."

"A difficult task, but I will do my best."

"This isn't a stunt, Mr. Kane. I'm testing your ability to concentrate at all times. You have to be able to recognize when I will be dealing you a winning hand. Understood?"

"Understood," he said in a serious tone. "But how will I know?"

"When I hold the deck, it is always in my left hand. My right hand distributes the cards. I will give you the indicator later."

"I'm very impressed, Ms. McGrath."

"The four of spades represents a barn with four rooms. I'm going to place an ace face up near each corner of the barn. Then I'm going to do the same with the kings, queens, and jacks. As you can see, Mr. Kane, each of the barn rooms is holding an ace, a king, a queen, and a jack." She turned over each four-card stack and created a sixteen card pile.

"Now, Mr. Kane, I want you to cut the sixteen cards as many times as you want."

Kane cut the cards five times, paused for a moment, and cut the cards three more times.

"If you're convinced the cards are properly mixed up after cutting the deck eight times, please slide the stack of concealed sixteen cards to me."

Mary placed the concealed cards in her left hand. With her right hand, her fingers deftly distributed the cards one at a time into each barn room until each stack contained four concealed cards.

"You're a gambling man, Mr. Kane. I will bet a half of a million dollars that I can tell you where the respective cards are in the barn rooms. Will you take that bet?"

"You seem too confident," he said. "No bet. My guess is an ace, a king, a queen, and a jack is in each barn room."

"You'd be wrong, Mr. Kane. Turn over the four cards in each barn room."

Kane turned over the first stack. It didn't reveal an ace, king, queen, and jack as he predicted. Instead, it held all four aces. The other rooms contained all four kings, all four queens, and all four jacks.

"How the hell did you do that?" Kane stood up and moved to the front of the desk.

"It doesn't matter how I did it. What matters is I can manipulate cards that will win the Hold 'Em tournament for you." She began to gather the cards. "I hope I erased your doubts about my abilities."

"You bet you have, Ms. McGrath."

Kane handcuffed her hands with his hand. She struggled to free a hand to reach for her purse. The bag fell from the chair. He forced her down to the floor.

* * * * *

Bruno gunned the Camaro through a stop sign that was followed by a symphony of angry horns. Kane Tower on High Street wasn't far away. He gripped the steering wheel as if it was Oliver Kane's neck. His car weaved in and out of heavy downtown traffic to gain a few car lengths.

His foot stomped on the brake pedal. Traffic ahead was at a standstill. It was happening to him again. He'd promised to protect his fiancée, Wendy, and failed. And now Mary was in peril and he was stuck in a jungle of metal. He aimed the Camaro into on-coming traffic. His hand pounded on the horn. Cars avoided him by inches as if he was a speeding emergency ambulance. A lane opened up ahead. He slammed the accelerator to the floor, squeezing through the hole as if it was an express lane.

A man in a suit darted into the street. Bruno swerved close to the sidewalk to miss him. He was out of breath. Only one more block to Kane Tower. He skidded through a right-hand turn and sent the Camaro over the curb and onto the front plaza of Kane Tower. He jumped out of his car praying this time the outcome would be different.

Chapter Thirty-Three

Oliver Kane groaned in pain after Mary McGrath kneed him in the groin. He had to move his groping hands from Mary to defend himself from another attack. She'd proved she was a master card manipulator and now a fighter to be reckoned with. It made him want her all the more.

Mary tried to crawl away from him to reach her purse lying on the floor. Kane grabbed her ankle to prevent her from pursuing a weapon. He pulled Mary towards him while her fingers fumbled inside the bag. Suddenly she aimed a metal canister at him with a forefinger on the trigger. He stopped pulling on her leg.

"Mace!" he shouted in surprise, while still holding onto her leg. "A can of mace is the weapon you were carrying in your purse to protect you. I thought for sure you had a gun. Do you think mace will stop me from having you?"

"Damn right mace will stop you. Let go of my leg or I'll spray the entire can at you."

"Okay. Okay." He released her leg and threw his hands in the air. "My apologies. I'm so attracted to you it made me crazy. I'm sorry."

"Kane, if you ever touch me again I will —"

Kane jumped on top of Mary, knocking the can of mace from her hand. He had her pinned She was out of breath. He may have knocked the wind out of her, but she still continued to struggle.

The office door flew off its hinges and landed onto the floor with a bang. Kane moved off Mary's body when he saw a tall man with whiskers enter the room by stepping on the fallen door. The man threw him a threatening look. Kane searched for the can of mace only to find it in Mary's hand. Before he could defend himself, she blasted streams into his face. He covered his eyes, screaming he was blinded. The tall man picked him up with two hands and hoisted him across the desk and into the credenza. He crumpled to the floor staring at fuzzy images of pink Pepto-Bismol and expensive cologne that wouldn't take away any of the pain and humiliation he was experiencing.

* * * * *

Bruno lifted Mary to her feet. She threw her arms around him. He walked her through Kane Law while Kane shrieked in the background. They stopped in front of the elevator. Bruno pressed the down button and looked up at the light above the metal doors.

"If I told you I'm really, really sorry that I came here without you," she said, with tears in her eyes, "will you still love me?"

"You've got some nerve asking me that question after scaring the hell outta me by coming here alone." His hands caressed her cheeks. "I don't recall saying I loved you."

"You don't have to, Bruno." She stood on her tiptoes and kissed him.

The elevator door opened after a ding, breaking up their moment of pent-up passion. They entered the elevator, arm and arm.

"I read on the mace can that anyone who gets sprayed will experience intense burning sensations on their skin and eyes," she said. "Also their eyes will become irritated and swollen. Do you think Oliver Kane will be able to play in the Hold 'Em tournament?"

"Usually the effects aren't long-lasting. If Kane flushes his eyes out with water or milk and applies soap to his skin, the burning and stinging will eventually disappear." Bruno gave her hand a slight squeeze. "Kane has no choice but to play in the tournament even if they have to roll him in on a gurney."

"That card trick you taught me sold Kane on my dealing skills." She kissed him again. "Someday will you explain how that trick really works? I don't have a clue."

"If I give you the secret to how the trick works," he said, "do I get the bed tonight?"

"If you enlighten me with that answer, you can have the bed tonight with me in it."

They were in another embrace when the elevator door opened to the building's lobby. Two suits with briefcases in hands waited for them to release their clinch. Bruno held Mary tight as he hurried out of the elevator.

"Where are we going?" she asked.

"My car is double parked on the front plaza." He pulled Mary through the front door and saw his car was where he left it. "We are heading to Sid Parker's office. I'll give you three-million guesses to predict what I discovered in Sid's garage."

* * * * *

Bruno and Mary found Sid Parker in the club bar. Bruno tapped him on the shoulder to get his attention. If The Boston Strangler had been standing behind Sid, his expression would have been the same. He downed what was left in the shot glass and slid off the barstool. They followed him to his office without saying a word.

"A little early to be drinking, especially for someone who doesn't drink," Bruno said.

"I know why you're here," Sid mumbled. "Beverly called me. I'm up shit creek in a leaky canoe with no paddle."

"What turned you, Sid?" Bruno asked.

"You don't know what it's like to be around these filthy-rich club members on a daily basis. I told you before that the club was originally named the Wealthy Man's Club before being renamed the WMC. Don't get me wrong, Bruno. They pay me well enough, but that barely covers a house payment, two cars, private school tuitions, braces, three kids, and a wife who spends money like water."

"There's a lot more to it, Sid. What was the plan? Steal most of the three-million prize, then go to some other country with your floozy? Does she have a name?"

"It doesn't matter, Bruno."

"I wouldn't have asked if it didn't." Bruno raised his tone. "Either you start talking or I'll hand you over to the police instead of saving your dumbshit ass. Time is of the essence. What's it going to be?"

"There's not enough time to correct what I've done." Sid wiped his eyes with his hand.

"If you put the money back in place, you've committed no crime. We can help you if you let us. What we can't do is save your marriage. You're the only one who can do that."

Sid was close to a breakdown. His cheeks were red. He was reacting like a person who'd been caught with both hands in a three-million dollar cookie jar.

"Her name is Sandra Belle Ryan, a waitress here," Sid said.

"My guess is Sandra Belle Ryan has a number of aliases and a lengthy rap sheet. After you hooked-up with her, who suggested the money scam?" Bruno pushed a palm out to Sid. "Sandra planted that seed, didn't she? I bet if you tell Sandra the scheme to abscond with the money got aborted, she'd have nothing to do with you."

"You'd win that bet, Bruno," Sid said in a low tone. "I spoke to Sandra after Beverly got a hold of me. She called me every name in the book before quitting."

Sid put his face into his hands and sobbed. Mary took him by the arm and led him to his chair behind the desk. Her enlarged eyes shifted to Bruno, telling him silently to lighten up on Sid. He answered her by shaking his head.

"You acquired the safe's combination by standing behind Walter Moore each time he came to your office, didn't you?" Bruno said. "Then you siphoned the majority of hundreds from the safe to the hope chest in your garage. How much is in the chest?"

"Two-million-four-hundred-thousand." Sid's voice could barely be heard.

"Where is the missing six-hundred-thousand?" Mary asked.

"There are three-hundred packets in the safe," Sid said. "We put ten one-hundred dollar bills on the top and ten on the bottom of each packet, and filled the middle with eighty one-dollar bills. I had to sell our life insurance policies to replace the hundreds with twenty-four thousand one-dollar bills.

"That's kind of ingenious," Mary said, nodding to Bruno.

"Sid is also extremely dumb to think he could have gotten away with this scam." Bruno's stare bored into his childhood buddy. "What's it going to be, Sid? Mary, Beverly and I, are willing to help you fix the disaster you created, if you agree to a few conditions."

"I'll agree to anything to get me out of this mess. It doesn't matter what the terms are."

"First, you will give your fee for running the tournament to the pregnant wife of an Oliver Kane employee who is still in the hospital from getting beaten up by Kane's thug. Bruno put his arm around Mary. "The other condition is that you'll agree to see a marriage counselor with Beverly."

"I doubt Beverly will be willing."

"You may be surprised," Bruno said. "We need to get the hope chest out of your garage and bring it back to your office."

They walked to the parking lot. Bruno was helping Mary into the passenger seat and closed the door when his cell phone chimed. He picked up, said hello, and barely uttered another word.

"This is unbelievable. It's like a dream come true. I can't thank you enough, Virginia."

He went around the Camaro and slid into the driver's seat with a smile.

"Whatever the call was about, you seem very pleased," Mary said.

"Virginia had great news."

"Well, spill it. What did she say?"

"The answer to our prayers," Bruno said. "Frank Prescott, the San Francisco Police detective, called Virginia looking for me. Prescott is retiring soon and wants to start a private investigator service. Apparently I impressed him. He wants to talk to me about joining him." Bruno took Mary's hand into his. "If it works out, we can be together."

Mary was quiet after hearing the amazing news, confusing Bruno. Didn't she want him there? Finally, she looked up at the car's ceiling teary-eyed.

"My guardian angel Mo gave me the precious gift of something to live for," Mary said. "He gave me a second gift by sending me to Virginia and Mrs. Green. Although Mo failed to take down Kane, it led you to save us from Larry and Rollie and paved the way for me to meet you. It's a beautiful wonder that a man like Morgan Proffitt can make such a positive difference in so many people's lives. And it's sad that a horrible man like Oliver Kane can continue to wreak havoc in people's lives. Despite that, I believe Mo is smiling down at us, Bruno. Whether the mission to take Kane down works or not, a wonderful life together awaits us."

"No matter what," Bruno assured her, "no matter what happens, we will have that new life together."

CHAPTER THIRTY-FOUR

Bruno could smell the tension in the crowded poker room. Adrenaline buzzed through his body. Game day always excited him. He was waiting for something unexpected to happen, be it positive or negative. He knew from experience that it is the law . . . the law of unintended consequences.

This day, for Sid Parker, was a different story. His face was etched with deep lines from exhaustion and guilt. Bruno, Mary, and Beverly had worked vigorously around the clock alongside Sid to replace the one-dollar bills with hundred-dollar bills in the safe's packets before the players arrived. The odds of rescuing Sid and Beverly's marriage were a toss-up at best, but at least Sid wouldn't go to jail and the tournament would be played.

Earlier, Bruno had checked with each ex-cop stationed outside the club's entry doors before returning to the poker room. There were no other activities going on at the club.

Bruno made sure the holstered gun on his belt was visible. He stood in front of a metal cart that held three-million in cash. Most of the twelve players and one male dealer were seated at their tables. Mary was conversing with Sid near the back wall. A player interrupted them by yelling out a question. Sid left Mary to provide an answer. Oliver Kane swooped in to confront her.

"I tried calling you numerous times," Kane said, in a low tone. "You need to tell me what the signal is."

"I'm sorry, sir," Bruno said, after squeezing Kane's shoulder hard from behind. "Talking to a dealer in private is forbidden. Tournament rules. Please take your seat."

"You can't do this to me. How will I know when she's manipulating my winning hands?"

"My thumb moves to the right on the deck," Mary whispered, before heading to her table.

"By the way, sir," Bruno said, "your eyes are abnormally red. Could it be contagious pink eye?"

"You know damn well what's wrong with my eyes," Kane grunted out.

* * * * *

Oliver Kane took his seat with five other players. Mary shuffled the cards without looking at him. All the players on both tables had two-hundred and fifty-thousand- dollars worth of colored chips in front of them. The progressive ante started at ten-thousand.

Mary held the deck in her left hand with her thumb on the left side. She dealt two cards down to each player. Kane looked at his cards: an ace and a king of diamonds. No sane Hold 'Em player would fold that hand. Normally he would have raised, but he just called the ten-thousand bet. His hand didn't improve after she exposed the three-card flop.

Nor did it get better when Mary revealed the turn card. He detected a slight smirk at the corner of her lips after he folded. Was she screwing with him?

Mary's thumb switched to the right side of the deck on the next hand. His hole cards were a seven and a ten. Kane wasn't sure what to do. Mary declared other players were waiting. Kane folded, even though she'd given him the signal. The last card Mary exposed would have given Kane an inside straight and the best hand. His stomach made an ugly sound that caught most of the other players' attention.

Kane left his seat to quench an irritating thirst. His hands shook in anger as he secured bottled water. He wasn't sure who he was pissed off at the most. Was Mary really a card mechanic? If she couldn't manipulate the cards, he still had a chance to win, but how would he know for sure?

He moved back to his seat in a daze. For the next three hands Mary's thumb stayed in its normal position and he folded. He could have won one of the hands. Did that mean she wasn't cheating? A player from the other table rose from his seat, threw his hands up in the air, and left the room. There were ten more players to beat.

Kane's next hand was two tens. Was that an omen from two previous games he had played? He raised the bet, praying two tens would be exposed like before. Mary turned over a deuce, seven, and nine, all in different suits. His tens were top pair. He bet fifty thousand. One player called. The turn card was a three. Kane bet another fifty thousand. The other player folded. Mary pushed the chips to him. Maybe he didn't need her to manipulate the cards in his favor after all.

Another player from the other table dropped out. Nine players were left to defeat. His heart thumped out positive beats. The antes had risen to twenty thousand. He had never played in a tournament before. The play was different; a lot more reckless. Big Tony from the mob would probably do well in this type of game.

His win had put him back to even. Mary's thumb moved to the right corner on the deck. Was that sign real or not? Sweat formed on his forehead and neck. He studied her fingers, but felt more confused than ever.

Mary dealt him a pair of twos. Not a good hand, but her thumb said to play. He folded, but watched intently what cards she turned up in the middle. There was heavy betting from three players. On the turn card she placed an ace down. Two players put all their chips in. The last card she exposed was a deuce. He would have had three deuces and a humongous win. He felt sick to his stomach. Mary didn't show any emotion. The two players who had gone all in were out of the tournament. Only seven players remained.

Two hands later, another player was out. Mary moved her thumb to the right. He looked at his cards and was surprised to see a king and queen. He came out betting a hundred- and-twenty-thousand. There were two callers. A queen came up on the flop. Kane pushed all his chips in. One player dropped out. Kane had an urge to put a hand over his heart. The turn card didn't pair the exposed cards. The river card was a jack. Kane turned over his king and queen. The other player had a queen, but couldn't beat the king kicker. Kane had more chips than anyone on the table.

Sid interrupted play. They were down to six players. The players from Mary's table had to move to the other game. Mary left to stand next to Bruno. The other dealer remained in his chair. Kane shook his head at Mary. She had said she would be his dealer for the whole tournament. Sid waved Kane over to the other table. The last thing he wanted to do was move from his current table and hot seat, but he couldn't complain since it might let on the fix was in. Reluctantly, he took a seat at the other table.

The male dealer was faster than Mary. The game moved quicker. He held the deck in his right hand and dealt with his left hand, the opposite of Mary. Kane was uncomfortable sitting at a different table, different seat, and playing at a different tempo. He overheard Mary say she was getting some fresh air outside.

Kane kept folding, but the antes were eating up a good portion of his chips. One player at the table had more chips than he did. At this point, the measure of a good or bad player came down to luck rather than skill. He had been on a lucky roll for a while now. Would his good fortune last long enough for him to win the tournament?

Another player lost all his chips. Kane was one of five players left. The player with the most chips was a WMC board member. He made a power play by raising four-hundred-thousand to the three players who were still in the pot. Kane looked at his hole cards and found two aces. It was a now or never. Kane pushed all of his chips into the pot. So did three other players. The board member was he only player with leftover chips. The player who won this hand would most likely win the tournament.

Some of the players who were out of the tournament had stuck around to see who would win the three-million dollar prize. The room became as silent as a library. The dealer commingled all the chips out of the way away for the community five cards he was about to expose. Kane's mouth opened to suck in as much air as he could get.

The dealer slowly turned over the three-card flop: jack, four, eight, all different suits. One of the players turned over his cards since there was no more betting; a jack and an eight. Kane had the best hand going in, but he was now losing to someone with two-pair. The dealer waited several seconds, sending Kane's heartbeat into overdrive. The turn card was an ace of spades.

"I've got three of a kind," Kane roared, turning over his two aces. "Wow! I'm on a roll, boys."

Kane put his hands together and chewed on a forefinger knuckle. His heart was banging out of control in his chest. The dealer announced he would turn over the river card. The dealer exposed a ten of spades.

"There is a Hold 'Em God." Kane jumped up and down and glared at Bruno. "I'm back in a big way. All that cash is mine."

"No, sir," the dealer said. "The gentleman with the five-spade flush in seat one takes the pot and is the grand prize winner."

"No. That can't be," Kane screamed. "I'm supposed to win."

Kane pointed at Bruno. His other hand held the table to stay upright. Bruno darted at Kane to break up any trouble. Kane grabbed a fistful of chips from the middle of the table and hurled them at Bruno, hitting him in the face. Sid ran at Kane and received a fist to his nose for his efforts. Blood splattered as Sid hit the floor. Kane tipped over the table spilling chips and cards, then ran from the room. He could hear footsteps pounding behind him. The guard outside was surprised when Kane pushed open the front door and fled. Kane ran towards the entrance road. Big Tony and several of his cronies were blocking his way. They formed a human wall.

"Let's take a ride, Ollie," Big Tony announced.

"Big Tony, you know me. I'll pay you back."

"Unless you have the cabbage on you right now, Ollie, you're shit out of luck."

Kane turned and ran in the opposite direction. Bruno was coming after him to his left. Kane saw Mary on the walkway. He sprinted to her. She stood her ground with her fists clenched. If he was going down, so was she. He had fallen for their sting, the same way Morgan Proffitt had gotten to him.

The sound of tires burning, and an engine's roar made Kane halt his momentum. A speeding red pickup truck was zeroing in on him. Kane couldn't see the driver's face in the dark, but he knew who it was: Jones, the man he thought he had shot dead.

* * * * *

Jones never slowed down, sending several mob members diving out of the way from his speeding truck. Bruno held Mary and led her away from Kane's mangled dead body lying in the road.

"I despised Oliver Kane," Mary said, "for what he did to me, your fiancée, Katie Proffitt, and so many other innocent people, but I wouldn't have wanted anyone, including Kane, to die such a horrible death."

"Kane got what he deserved. If the guy in the red truck didn't get him, the mob would have made him disappear." Bruno took hold of both of her hands. "It's over, Mary. We are both free. Let's go home."

CHAPTER THIRTY-FIVE

Bruno stood in front of the window and took in the neighbor-hood's busy activity. It wasn't a scenic view like the Golden Gate Bridge, but the small office was perfect for a startup private investigator agency located off the beaten path of downtown San Francisco. Frank Prescott walked into the space and joined Bruno.

"What do you think, Santiago?" Prescott asked.

"Between your contacts and Virginia's help, we've got enough of a caseload to afford it. In Boston I worked out of my apartment on a folding table. It's a step up and I like it."

"I like it, too."

They shook hands as partners do.

"I bet Mrs. Green will be happy to have you working some-where other than her den," Prescott said, with a smile.

"Are you kidding, she loves me. And it's mutual. I've become part of their family."

"It's beyond me how an ugly guy from Boston could snag a fox like Mary."

"She loves me, too. And that is also very mutual. It's Proffitt Karma." Bruno looked at his watch. "I have to pick up Rachel's birthday present. Don't be late for her barbeque birthday party. We're having a Wiffle ball homerun hitting contest before a feast of hamburgers and hotdogs, Rachel's favorite."

"I haven't played Wiffle ball since I was a kid. I'm look-ing forward to your family get- together. What are you getting Rachel for her birthday?"

"Something she's always wanted."

* * * * *

Bruno noticed Mrs. Green carrying a plate of hamburgers and hot dogs for him to barbeque. The white-hot coals were ready.

He would throw one more pitch. Frank Prescott gave a catcher's target like the pitcher was going to fire him a fastball.

The batter pounded the paper bag home plate with the Wiffle bat. Bruno lobbed an underhand pitch to her. The batter squinted at the white plastic ball with holes. She swung with all her might and connected. Virginia watched the ball sail over her head and over the fence. Mary let out a yell, ran straight to Bruno from home plate, jumped into his arms, and kissed him.

"My talented daughter Rachel taught me how to hit home runs just like Baby Ruth," Mary said, still in Bruno's arms.

"It's Babe Ruth, Mom." Rachel was sitting on a swing holding Bruno's birthday present in her arms: a Golden Retriever puppy. "Mrs. Green, is there kissing in baseball?"

"Rachel dear, I believe when the batter and the pitcher love each other, kissing is permissible. Thank you."

ACKNOWLEDGEMENTS

**A Special Thank You goes to Joyce Hyland, Debby Rose,
Joanne Davis & Martha Clark Scala
for reading *After Proffitt* before it was ripe.**

I would like to thank Debbie Aldred, Fred Aldred, Ava Archibald, Bill Archibald, Bob Archibald, Julie Archibald, Nancy Archibald, Frank Baldwin (*Author of Balling the Jack & Jake Mimi*), Alyn Beals, Scott Benner (Mayor of Bennerville), Robert Berry (Soundtek Studios), Barrie Burnham, Barbara Butera, Frank Butera, Dennis Cacace, Sharyl Carter, Shiela Cockshott, Carroll Collins III, Al Connell, Georgia Cornelliusen, Diana Crosetti, Brian A. Davis (Host of Damn Good Movie Memories – The Podcast), Darryl Davis, Joanne Davis, Barbara Drotar (Author of *Searching For Sophia*), Allison Evens, Gin Geraldi, Joni Gimnicher, Steve Gimnicher, Mary Garon, Barbara Hembey, Bill Hembey, Laurel Anne Hill (Author of *Heroes Arise & The Engine Woman's Light)*, Shaun Holly, Gary Hoffman, Renee Hoffman, Jen Ingalls, E.J. Jones, Mark Jones, Connie Kendall (Owner of Windsock, the best bar in Prescott Arizona), Natalie Korman (copy editor), Julie Kosmides, Naty Kwan, Garret Lee, Jana McBurney-Lin (Author of *My Half of the Sky & Blossoms & Bayonets)*, Jennifer Lindsey, Kathy Love, Dr. Mike Ludovico, Serena Ludovico, Laura Lujan, Jacqueline Machado, Alicia Mazzoni, Sharen McConnell, Lorraine McGrath, Tracy McNamrara, Amanda McTigue (Author of *Going to Solace*), Carole Medica, Tom Medica, Princess Kristina Merlina, Kristol Miles, Sue Murray, Dr. David Nichols, Jasmine Partida, Beverly Paterson, Alicia Robertson (Robertson Publishing unsurpassed), Ken Rolandelli, Lora Rollendelli, Howard Rose, Mike Rose, Leslie Rose, Elaine Silver (Story Editor extraordinaire), Scott Smith (Author of *The Ruins & A Simple plan*), Dr. Kalpanu Srinivasan, Steve Stahl, Dr. Lisa Stiller, Dylan Stratinsky, Kelli Jo Stratinsky, Scott Taylor, Catherine Teitelbaum, Gail Tesi, Joanne Thooresell, Marlena Willoughby, Linda Williams

www.ingramcontent.com/pod-product-compliance
Lightning Source LLC
Chambersburg PA
CBHW020445270626
47155CB00022B/1512